CW00671096

THE AVALANCHE

To you
with love and thanks
for your encouragement

THE AVALANCHE

Belinda Seaward

Constable · London

First published in Great Britain 1996
by Constable and Company Limited
3 The Lanchesters, 162 Fulham Palace Road
London W6 9ER
Copyright © Belinda Seaward 1996
The right of Belinda Seaward to be identified as author
of this work has been asserted by her
in accordance with the Copyright, Designs and Patents Act 1988
ISBN 0 09 476120 5
Set in Linotron Palatino 10pt by
CentraCet Ltd, Cambridge
Printed and bound in Great Britain by
Hartnolls Ltd, Bodmin

A CIP catalogue record for this book
is available from the British Library

For my brother Stefan, whose courage inspires

Time present and time past
Are both perhaps present in time future,
And time future contained in time past.

T. S. Eliot

Sleep laboratory studies suggest that violence in sleep is a physiological phenomenon which cannot be readily understood in psychological terms. R. J. Broughton (1968) found that it was impossible to demonstrate potentially causal psychological activity in these disorders and suggests that they may arise in a 'psychological void'.

Christopher Howard and P. T. D'Orban,
Psychological Medicine 1987, 17

Recurring

This region is as clear as the beginning of time. The dazzling peaks have no discernible end, merging with the sky which is not sky but space. There may be forests and lakes, continents and civilisations buried here, but the snow reveals nothing except itself. Last night's fall is still visible, a shower of lighter, purer powder which will soon cave in and join the history of the heavy depths. A blue crystal glacier beckons like a truth. This is where they are heading. She has never seen a glacier before.

She leads. He follows her flaming red hair which glows against the white. She is faster than he is, light as the water crystals flecked in her hair. The ice beads melted against his face when he kissed her. He can still feel that kiss now, a small burning, a match spitting into the numbing cold. He quickens his pace, but she forges even further ahead and he wonders if she's experiencing euphoria.

After an age in which he feels he has travelled a whole continent of ice, she bends down to adjust her boot. He catches up with her and steadies her and they rock together. She gazes at him wildly and he has to resist pulling her down to the snow. He wants to have her here. He wants to begin with her here and end with her here. He wants to see her red hair staining the snow and the warm light in her eyes. He feels like the first man in time. She is the first woman and together up here in this elemental ice kingdom they will make history. But he knows exposure would mean certain death. They continue.

Together now, they talk of the past. She is missing their child, she tells him, and to distract her he takes her photograph. He hands over the camera for her to do the same. He wants to make a record of this. She laughs. But there is no echo, no confirmation, no reminder. It is as if her laughter is contained in a cloud. The muffled sound both fills him with joy and disturbs him. He won't tell her, but he feels as if they are on the edge of something magnificently terrible.

They have been walking now for five hours, but neither feels tired. The glacier keeps them going and their wonder at wandering into the abstract. He has climbed mountains before, but never with her. She is part of this discovery and he feels a gravitational love. His fear lifts.

They cross a plateau, a frozen Atlantic which leads nowhere and everywhere. The snow is so soft it folds in on their tracks, sifting down slowly like the sand in the egg timer he gave her once. Now he remembers that she has given this timer to their child to help him sleep. In another age their son is watching golden grains of sand falling through glass while his parents are enjoying the time of their lives. But he does not believe this is wrong. They will bring the boy here when the time is right.

He checks his watch. Two more hours have passed, but they do not appear to be any closer to the glacier. Its glittering blue lips seem further away than ever and he wonders if he has miscalculated. It is so difficult to judge space in this region.

He suggests they take a break. A dry wind starts to blow, sending the powder snow into flurries around her. Now he is worried about frostbite. They move closer to a peak and slide down against the ice walls. They are both exhausted and he finds brandy and glucose to revive them. He wants to kiss her again, but notices that her mouth is sore. She flinches at the first sip of brandy and her lips turn red and start to bleed. She says nothing, her eyes fixed on the shimmering glacier. He wants to tell her that they could turn back and head for the valley, but there is such a longing in her that he can't.

After another hour of walking they reach the end of the plateau. Now he sees that they must climb down a sheer face and back up another to reach the glacier. Now he sees why it appeared to float in space. She descends quickly and is out of his sight when the first strong gusts of wind blow. He calls her name: 'Theresa!' There is a darkening and a growing heaviness which is making him feel uneasy, but she does not hear him. He begins climbing down after her. The snow crumbles like soft cake and he starts to slide. He digs the heel of his climbing boot in hard to slow himself down and feels the first flutterings of panic somewhere deep inside the layers of extremity clothing. She is nowhere to be seen. All is whiteness. Blankness.

The silence is broken by the wind, which builds up to a soft, hoarse roar. He continues sliding. Swathes of snow and ice ripple and shudder under him and then effortlessly glide away like boats released from their moorings. The wind whips his face in icy blasts, forcing his eyes closed. His snow glasses have been torn off and he slips further into the void and shouts her name again. Still nothing. Then there is a splitting and hail begins to fall in a crazy torrent. The wind accelerates, whipping the hail into a storm of nails, knocking him off his feet. As he falls, he feels a sweet urge to surrender to sleep, but the thought of her drives him on. He slides down on his back, cradling his head in his hands, and finds her with his feet. She has fallen awkwardly and she is sobbing. He sinks down into the deep snow and holds her, trying to warm her as the tempest rages about them, but her confidence has gone. He tries to distract her. 'Look, the glacier – we're almost there!' But it has vanished in the turmoil. The region is churning up into something unrecognisable.

— 1 —

My piano teacher once asked me what I would do if I had three minutes left to live. Old Sergei was fond of questions like this. He liked to tease me with riddles about time and the nature of the universe. It gave him immense pleasure to sit and watch me try to make sense of his mysterious ideas. I would like to say that I enjoyed working them out, but I'm afraid I was too stupid. I was a good candidate for tricks and illusions because I never questioned my master. Back then I was simply too much in awe of him. I never knew what he'd conjure up next.

I took the three-minute question literally. I was far too naive to consider the gravity of a man's last act. At the time I had just won a music competition. There was my silver trophy on the table, reflecting my sixteen-year-old winner's face. That was all I knew. It summed up my life so far.

'My trophy,' I said. 'I'd leave it behind. I'd put it in a field or something.'

Sergei laughed. 'Whose trophy? It does not have your name on it.'

'Well, I'd have it engraved . . .'

'Three minutes, think, there would not be enough time.'

I remember I felt angry then and looked for something to make my mark. In my shirt pocket, I found the fountain pen Sergei had given me after the music competition. I pulled off the pen's heavy nib case and wrote my name on the kitchen table. I felt fierce and a little afraid as I pressed down hard, making the ink bleed into the wood.

'There,' I said triumphantly. 'I'd leave the trophy right here on the table next to my name. Now show me what you would do.'

Sergei raised his hand and for one awful moment I thought he

[13]

was going to hit me. In Russia, he'd told me, people hit each other all the time, even in the conservatoires. I closed my eyes, anticipating a stinging slap, and then counted to three. I was going to count the whole three minutes but that would have been unbearable so I counted a long three and took a deep breath before I opened my eyes.

There was the sound of a slap but it was not directed at me. Sergei had slammed his hand down into the pie dish which still contained the remains of our supper. The sight of his big white fingers splayed in the dish with gravy from the beef and leek pie oozing all over his knuckles and nails made me cry out.

Sergei had left a hand print. It was a brutal, primitive gesture which jolted me to my stomach. I read my name on the table: ANDREW SCHIDMAIZIG. I had thought it looked bold when I scratched it into the wood, but against Sergei's raw paw print my name seemed like nothing but squiggles. A score of meaningless musical notes.

Now the time has come to write my name again. I'm using the same fountain pen, which is comforting and reminds me of that sixteen-year-old time when I knew nothing save my own burning reflection.

I am thirty-six years old. I still know nothing. But now my reflection chills me. As you may have guessed, my three minutes are up.

What do I have to say? What can I say? In a way my life has already been summed up. I was put on trial for what I did. I was acquitted and pronounced sane. The trial was hysterically reported in the press by tabloid journalists who wrote about me as if I were the star of some fiendish film. They condensed my life into ghoulish paragraphs. They used me to shock and I was frightened of myself when I saw what they'd written. The newspapers wanted more and I was offered huge sums of money for my story, but I refused and told them to leave me alone. My story was best left untold. I did not want to live through my history again.

Now my time is up, it does not matter.

I came here last night and slept on the beach. It was too dark and too dangerous to start making my way up the cliff, so I slept huddled against an old fishing boat, waiting for morning. The light woke me. Gold and coral pink, it stroked me awake, crept softly through my stiff old coat and warmed my bones. The sea was calm and milky pink, breaking along the shore in silky waves of crushed opal. I went down to the edge and skimmed a pebble. It bounced on the water four times. In spite of myself, I laughed.

I started walking up the beach. I thought I might see the coloured fishing boats – there were some humped shapes in the distance – but as I drew closer I saw they were not the bright craft I had sailed across the stones and known by name. *Rosie*, *Sifida*, *Marylou* and *Bella* had gone. These boats were painted a dull military green and had numbers instead of names. They had also been rolled over on to their bellies. Presumably to stop children clambering into them.

The gulls welcomed me back with nervy cries, swooping low as I made my way up the beach. The weight of my heavy brown overcoat with big cream sweater underneath made the going slow and I began to sweat. It was perhaps a mile to the other end, a mile which years before I would have taken in a shifting sprint, but now I shambled like an old man.

The wind whipped up fine stones which stung my eyes and for protection I moved closer to the cliff. I stopped. The great red face was not how I remembered. It had always seemed to me like a magnificent cathedral with soaring spires, flutes, arches and ledges where cormorants perched like the statues of saints. Now the clay spires were rough and crumbling and the whole façade was sagging. Near the top there were blackened areas where molten skeletons of gorse clung and bald patches where trees and bushes had been wrenched out by the wind. The cliff seemed thinner. In some places the earth was violet. A wooden sign attested the cliff's state of exhaustion. It was painted with crude black letters and the sign writer had not bothered to touch up the drips. It read: DANGER FALLING ROCK.

I continued walking, keeping my eyes on the cliff, trying to find a piece I recognised: the grassy ledge where I used to lie for hours looking out over the glittering arc of sea, my head swirling with childish dreams. One was to take her on a cruise, to India or somewhere else hot and spicy. Darwin appealed, although I had no idea where it was, and Mauritius. I liked the word

[15]

'Mauritius'. It sounded like a secret. 'I'm going to marry you in Mauritius!' I used to sing. I can't remember how old I was, perhaps six or seven. But I do remember what she said: 'You'll marry someone much cleverer than me.'

Or the cave. I couldn't see the cave either. She had refused to come with us the day we found it. She was busy working on a new picture and so Tim and I had gone alone. We'd hauled ourselves up to the mouth on a rope, nervous of what we might find. We believed we were the first to discover the cave and we had the idea that we would carve our names in the red rock, or perhaps write them in blood, sealing our new vocation as explorers. But DANIEL H, FRANK, MARGARET and LEEDS UNITED had got there before us. There were even some fake cave drawings, including a mammoth which Tim said looked more like an Alsatian dog. He carved TIMOTHY PHILLIPS near the dog's jaws. I was too disappointed to make a mark.

Tim was my best friend and I was in awe of his looks. He had springy black hair, dark Spanish-looking eyes and caramel skin, smooth as a bar of dark sand. When Tim had a scab, even that looked good. He wore his injuries proudly like tattoos. Mine were prone to infection.

I coveted Tim's beauty because it was so dark. Darker and more glossy than even the Belgian chocolate cake we found in an old copy of *Woman's Realm*, saved to be drooled over on wet afternoons when we grew tired of Monopoly. My hair was red, strawberry blond, she said, and my skin bubbled up in small watery blisters in the sun. In the evenings it throbbed and burned and she dabbed camomile on to soothe it. I always got the blisters worst on the hands, which was bad. My grandmother didn't like to see anything wrong with my hands.

Once she made me cover my hands with white cotton socks, which made Tim shriek with laughter. 'Namby pamby handy Andy!' he'd shouted as I felt my way across the rocks with my swaddled hands. They felt thick and numb inside the cotton, not like hands at all, more like stumps. 'Flid! Flid!' Tim shouted, mocking me by curling his own strong fingers into grotesque claws. 'You look like a Flid.'

'What's a Flid?'

'You know, you've seen them. They've got no hands. They do everything with their elbows.'

[16]

'How do they eat?'

'Someone feeds them, stupid. They're like babies.'

'That's sad.'

'It's sad that you're so stupid.'

Timothy Phillips. I wonder what he did with his looks? I imagine him in a foreign bar dressed in something white and sleeveless to show off his tanned, muscled forearms, his black hair sleek as satin – he'd be the type to use brilliantine – twirling a cocktail as he smiles that smile. The smile he made when killing things.

Tim enjoyed snaring rabbits. We went looking for them at dusk and found them twitching in the wires he'd set up, eyes huge and beautiful with fear. Tim smiled that smile when he brought a rock crashing down on a rabbit's head, splintering the bones like fine china. The awful cracking disturbed me. It made me remember the times I had knocked china off the dresser at home when I wandered in my sleep. I always hid the pieces in a drawer, but my grandmother threw them away when she found them. Like the rabbits, the china was smashed beyond repair.

Tim helped me cut the cliff path. But he wouldn't let me use the machete and I had to stand and watch while he savagely chopped at the greenery, whooping like a Red Indian, the muscles in his arms twitching under the smooth skin. I remember afterwards touching the newly amputated branches with my fingers and feeling the sap as sticky as blood.

Tim let me use the spade to cut steps in the red earth. I worked slowly, careful not to disturb the huge black beetles which scuttled around like toy Daimler cars. Tim watched impatiently, leaning against one of his brutalised bushes, smoking a cigarette, pursing his lips like a fish as he blew blue smoke rings in the air. Tim was an expert smoker. Then he told me: 'I won't be coming next year.' He held the cigarette between two fingers, close to the burning end, and flicked his ash nonchalantly. 'My parents are taking me to Sicily.'

I was sick with jealously. Sicily was not Mauritius, but it was far away. I wanted to go far away, but foreign holidays were dreams for us. My grandmother couldn't afford them. Coming down here just fifty miles away cost her all her savings. She put money away every week in the holiday jar which sat on top of the dresser. Once I stole some of the money to buy a box of paints. But I was too guilty to use them and they stayed neat and fat in their white tubes, lozenges of pure shame under my bed.

The secret path – we were convinced no one else knew about it – meant we could reach the hut from the beach instead of through the wood. I preferred it this way. The dark wood worried me. There were too many shadows, black bogs and dead trees spilling their brains of fungi. The larger trees were wreathed in thick ivy, transforming the branches into hammerheads or immense glossy wings. From a distance they appeared like prehistoric predators, silent and watchful over the twitching wood. The birds always sounded terrified here.

Tim told me a hermit lived in the wood in one of the old donkey sheds. The area had once been cultivated by bulb growers who used donkeys to carry the flowers in heavy swinging baskets up the cliff. We never saw the hermit but one day we found the hut. It was fenced in by coils of bleached brambles which snapped easily under the blows from Tim's machete. The windows of the hut loomed as he cleared away the undergrowth. The broken glass, scumbled with thick grey webs, seemed to snarl at us. Near the doorway, we found a skeleton of a crow which Tim said the hermit must have eaten. Imagining this macabre meal made my heart race with fear.

It took me a long time to find the path again. The erosion had changed everything. Trees and bushes had slipped into new places or disappeared altogether and so many rocks and boulders had fallen I thought the path had gone too. But then I saw it: the horse's head. One ear was missing but the fine nose was still intact and the curved cheek. The path started at a pink sanded gap under the horse's mouth.

The steps had worn away but the path was still passable. Using my elbows, I tore through the brambles, relieved that I was not carrying much. I had just a small shoulder bag containing a sleeping bag, a few clothes, my notebooks and some tins of food. I put the strap across my chest to secure the bag and climbed, hauling myself up the steep parts by grabbing clumps of thick fern. The gritty red soil grazed my knees and gorse pricked my face. The light dancing through the green dazzled me into dizziness and my eyes were streaming when I reached the top.

[18]

The hut was in a sorry state. The dark timber walls were bleached white from years of storms and rusted sheets of corrugated iron shuttered the two windows. The garden had grown wild. Tropical succulents smelling faintly of camphor formed a dense thicket around the verandah, which was snarled with hibiscus and passion flower. The dwarf palms were almost full-grown and the strange orange berry flowers my grandmother had called corned-beef plants ringed the hut, glowing through the green like Chinese lanterns.

Plant juice soaked into my trousers as I waded my way through to the verandah. It felt spongy when I stepped on it and the padlock left red rust stains on my hand. The door was stiff and I had to give it a few good shoves with my shoulder to open it. Inside there was a strong animal smell, badger or fox, I couldn't tell, and puddles of greenish water on the floor. In one corner there was a bundle of dried grass that looked like a nest. I walked over and kicked it. The nest exploded in a shower of silky dust.

The hut was sparsely furnished. There was a large wooden bed, the white counterpane now blue with mould and dotted with rabbit droppings, a scuffed table with two chairs, a sawn-off part of a tree my grandmother had used as a footstool, a small Primus stove and a sink surrounded by a faded green velvet curtain. We had washed there. There was no toilet. That was at the bottom of the garden beyond the vegetable patch.

I used a dead beech branch to sweep the floor and pulled handfuls of leaves from a rhododendron bush outside and used them to wipe down the table and rub some of the salt from the windows. The water supply still worked and I filled a saucepan to boil water for tea. I lit a cigarette and surveyed my hiding place.

The pictures were still there. I had expected them to be missing. On the train down from London, I had imagined that tourists had broken into the hut and taken them or, worse, defaced them in some way. But they were all there. About a dozen of them, tacked low on the walls. A spider had made its home in one picture, inside a small cockle shell which served as a football for a little twig boy.

The twig boy appeared in most of my grandmother's pictures.

She had made them to amuse me in the mornings when I was too exhausted to play on the beach. The twig boy was never exhausted but that was because he never slept. He didn't suffer dark dreams; he played on a beach of dried berries under an orange-peel sun, flew aeroplanes of silver paper and sailed feathery boats of pampas grass. He was alone, like me he had no brother, but he was free from fear. What I wanted most in the world was to be like him.

My grandmother had made butterflies and insects for me too from strands of wool, coloured scraps of material and glass beads. She pinned them on to cards and I gave them names. There was Nelson, a magnificent red admiral, a yellow polka-dot ladybird I called Julie after a girl with yellow plaits I liked at school, a virescent dragonfly called Vincent and a huge ghostly white moth my grandmother named Gabriel. She pinned Gabriel over the head of the wooden bed. She said he was a guardian angel who would protect me from the dark.

I left the hut and went outside to take down the sheets of corrugated iron. They came away easily from the soft wood. I dragged the sheets under a tree and went to look over the edge. Rain was beginning to come in from the sea and soft bundles of lilac mist scudded at the base of the cliff, providing a trampoline for the gulls which dived in and out with muffled cries. I peered over further and saw the path corkscrewing round like a small green grass snake against the belly of the cliff. The sea hissed. From this height the sound was soothing. What had she said? 'It's the mermaids whispering the sea creatures to sleep.' Feeling suddenly weak, I sank down on to the soft grass.

It is dark and hot and I'm in a cave. I must get out. I'm shouting to be let out, but no one comes. I'm worried about the birds. They are flapping around the entrance to the cave and their shrieks echo horribly. One bird breaks away from the flock and comes swooping towards me. Its eyes are red, as if a fire is burning inside its head, and I cover my face with my arms, then I smell burning feathers and I know the rest of the flock has turned. They are coming for me. Their wings brush my face and I see the golden glow of their smouldering beaks as they flap around me, whipping up a shower of sparks around my hair. One bird flies in closer, its mouth open in a squawk, revealing the molten tongue like a deadly strip of lava. It comes in, flapping black and red, black

[20]

and red and gold and black. Smoke as thick as blood, the burning, I can feel the burning . . .

A coolness as I am pulled to safety. Something chill yet soft is on my brow. 'It's all right, there's nothing there,' she says.

I drink glass after glass of water, but I still feel hot. 'Let's move the bed,' she says.

We drag it to the window. I am laughing nervously, feeling guilty again.

She climbs in beside me. I can hear the sea. 'Sssssssshhhhh.'

She starts to tell me a story about mermaids and fish.

— 2 —

My psychiatrist told me this was not a dream. The birds were not part of a nightmare. I was not hallucinating. It was 'a night terror', Dr Chase says.

I do not understand. It is the first time I've heard the term. We are sitting in his consulting room, a blindingly bright place in Highgrove Hospital. I am in shock and Dr Chase is being professionally kind.

'Night terrors are fairly common in childhood but most people grow out of them,' he says.

I try to speak but my mouth feels dry and gritty as if I have swallowed sand. Dr Chase offers me some coffee. I watch him get up from his chair and walk over to a glass percolator bubbling away like an alchemical experiment on the top of a corner bookshelf.

My eyes are streaming. I wish he would pull the blinds. The light is making my head ache. There is too much glass in here. The windows are huge, clear rectangles such as you might find in a modern church. Sunlight streams through, illuminating more glass – the glass of my doctor's fine spectacles, the clear crystal paperweight on his desk, the glass light shades and the glass frames on the wall. These contain Dr Chase's professional certificates and invitations to conferences. I read them. I see that he has been to Sydney and Stockholm. There are many from the

United States. One invites him to a conference in San Francisco called 'Sane or insane? New thinking on somnambulistic automatism'. I wonder why he keeps these invitations when they are out of date.

Dr Chase pours my coffee carefully into a tiny cup. He has a poise, a lightness of movement like a dancer and soft, graceful features which make him appear more than a little effeminate. He has tried to counteract this by growing a moustache, but the golden dusting of hair on his slender top lip looks like a forgery.

His clothes are careful too – immaculate pale-green suit and honey-coloured suede shoes which squeak as he walks. There is a yellow rosebud in his lapel. The faint scent makes me want to weep.

Dr Chase takes his time pouring the coffee. Things are moving slowly. He is giving me time to adjust to being here. I am a voluntary patient, or client, as he prefers to call me. I have been wondering about the legal term. Will I become a *patient* after the trial? Or an *inmate*?

I am here because Dr Chase needs to collect evidence for my defence. He has asked me to start by telling him about my earliest dreams and memories. 'Tell me everything, even the smallest details,' he said. 'I need to draw a map of who you are and what made you.'

He comes back with my coffee and places it on a small glass table between us. We are sitting in identical blue chairs cushioned like airline seats. They also recline and Dr Chase has already asked if I would prefer to lie back. I declined. Right now I need to stay upright.

I sip my coffee. It is a little muddy, but the perfume is good and I breathe in the oaky aroma deeply. I have never smelled coffee like this before. But I am finding that now I am more sensitive to such small things.

'Is it all right?' Dr Chase asks. 'I usually make it too strong, people complain.' He gives a small grimace which makes the moustache squirm like a startled caterpillar.

'It's fine,' I say. 'Thank you.' We are being polite, cautious with one another as if we are guests at a party, forced to make conversation by a host who is not coming back to rescue us.

There is a small tape recorder on the table. Dr Chase clicks it on. The slight hissing noise reminds me of the sea again.

[22]

'You see, in nightmares we rarely call out,' he says. 'We may think we scream, but most of the time it is part of the dream. In a classic night terror the screams are real and very frightening for anyone who hears them.'

'My grandmother told me I was screaming that I was dying.'

'Do you remember that you were?'

'No, but when I woke my throat was sore. That made me believe it was real. I thought I was choking on the smoke from the birds.'

'Did you experience this dream again?'

'No.'

I sip some more coffee. The throbbing in my head seems to be getting worse. It's also affecting my eyesight. I try to focus on the doctor's yellow rosebud, but it has become a blur.

His hand comes out and covers mine. It's tiny, no bigger than a child's hand, pale and smooth. My own hands are unusually large, knotted with bulging veins and ending in big splayed fingers covered with coarse red hair. Strong hands that once created art. Musical hands. The hands of a pianist I once knew.

I bunch my hand up into a fist and pull it away from the doctor's. I cannot bear to look at my hands now. They are monstrous to me.

Dr Chase leans forward and looks into my eyes. 'We can stop here if you wish.'

'No, no, I've got to get through this, I want to understand,' I say.

He smiles faintly. 'Take your time.'

I fumble for words, trying to force my mind into some sort of order, but I am finding this so difficult. I'm still in a dream, still in the process of waking up numbed and confused. Still trying to understand. Still trying to stop the screaming inside.

I run my hands through my hair. It feels cold and greasy and I'm suddenly aware of how terrible I must look. I haven't changed. I'm still wearing my performing suit. It feels stiff around me and smells of stale wine and cigarettes and something else. A perfume, something like hyacinths, which is both familiar and strange. They offered me hospital clothes, but I refused. I wanted to stay the way I was. I think this means I'm trying to deny it all, trying to push things back to where they were, where I was before, before . . .

[23]

'Here, take this.' Dr Chase is pushing something soft into my hand. It is a white tissue. I rub my eyes with it.

'I'm sorry,' I say.

'That's all right. Don't worry about crying. You're still in severe shock.'

I gulp down the rest of my coffee and look around the room, trying to find something that will help me stay in control. Dr Chase's desk is in the centre of the room. It is a large desk made of dark, almost black, polished wood. I focus on its solidity. It is one of the neatest desks I have ever seen, functional and low-rise with just one slim stack of white filing trays. There is little paperwork in the trays, nothing spilling over the sides as on my chaotic desk at home. No pens dribbling ink, no doodle pads. The doctor's pens are arranged in graduated grey tubes and sit near a grey telephone. Red lights flash but so far it has remained silent. Dr Chase has asked for us not to be disturbed.

The uncluttered desk makes me feel calmer. I need order right now. I need to count things and organise things. If I could play (God, will I ever play again?) I would choose Beethoven. One of the sonatas, perhaps Number 8. *Pathétique.* Something – anything – to quieten the mad intermezzo in my head.

I turn away from the desk and back to Dr Chase, who is lounging in his chair, one finger pressed vertically against his nose.

'The night terror,' I say. 'What causes it?'

He frowns. 'We still don't know. It's not something that can be easily explained; I mean, from a psychological point of view. Unfortunately sleep disorders don't seem to follow any sort of identifiable pattern. Rather like sleep itself.'

He removes his finger from his nose and studies it intently as if he might find the answer to the sleep mystery there, in the map whorls of his fingerprint.

'How is a night terror different from a nightmare?' I ask.

But I don't want to know. I feel crazy asking questions like this, like a good student. I don't want to find out, but I have to grasp hold of something, some detail, some little thing to fix me here. I wonder if this is how it feels to be told you have cancer or some other terrible disease. Sympathy or concern is unbearable so you ask for information instead.

'I don't want to confuse you with too much science at this

stage, but the night terror takes place in a different phase of sleep. What we call non-REM sleep. REM, you may already know, means rapid eye movement. For dreams to occur there must be REM. The frightening images of the night terror such as your burning birds are not dreams but delusions.'

I lean forward and put my head in my hands. I am in pain, but it is a strange sensation, not hard or stabbing, not the pain of sickness or injury, somehow deeper and darker. I feel as if a great hole has been carved into the centre of my being.

'Have they given you tranquillisers?' Dr Chase asks.

'Yes.'

'Are they helping at all?'

I look at him hopelessly.

He switches off the cassette recorder and rewinds the tape, which makes a thin whine like a mosquito.

'I think we've done enough for today. I'll request some stronger sedatives for you. Now you should just rest.'

We both get up awkwardly. I am easily a foot taller than he is, but I feel diminished. Dr Chase reaches up and touches my shoulder. Then, as if he has just become aware of my strange dress, he says: 'I'll see about organising something else for you to wear. Is there anything you want from – '

'No,' I interrupt quickly. 'A nurse offered me some hospital clothes, I'll take those for now.'

He steers me out to the corridor, pressing his small hand lightly on my back. I feel like a child.

I can't remember exactly how long I've been here. Is it days or weeks? It must be days. They wouldn't have let weeks go by without making sure I changed my clothes. I am looking at myself now in the mirror in my private bathroom. I look insane. My long red hair is not just dirty but tangled and matted like a tramp's. It smells like a tramp's hair too. Vomit, whisky and cigarettes.

I was once vain about my hair. It set me apart from the rest and I kept it in good condition as it grew almost down to my waist. I liked the sensation it caused on stage and critics always mentioned it in reviews. It made them edgy, though. One critic went as far as to wonder if it were not really a wig and another described it as a 'cynical prop'. At first I was surprised at the reactions, then I became amused. I said in interviews that it helped the flow.

Anyway, fetishes were not unique on the concert circuit. A pianist I knew well used to spend a long time before a performance manicuring his nails. We'd often joke about our pecularities over a few pints in the bar. He said it was a primitive male ritual. If we'd had peacock feathers we would have displayed them before we sat down.

I now have a beard. It is rough and quite thick and the curls taste salty in my mouth. I should shave it off, but I don't trust myself to hold a razor still. I stare at my face. There are deep red lines running down each side of my nose that I do not remember seeing before. My skin has a bluish tinge and is flaking around my lips and corners of my eyes. My eyes are red and look drunk sore, the eyelids yellowish pouches which ache. Everything aches: my buttocks, my chest, my back. I feel gnawed at.

I was never fat, gaunt I suppose in a way, but now I look ill. My arms are thin; they already look like hospital arms. But my legs feel heavier, somehow weighed down, as if I am being forced to walk under water.

When I was young I used to play a game with the mirror. By clenching my fists and squeezing my eyes partly shut, I could make myself into different people. It was quite scary, the images I could summon up. I could turn myself into a hydra, a wizard or a ghostly spirit. Looking at myself now, I am scared.

I should take a bath. It would feel pleasant to slide into warm water, but I would be trying to comfort myself. This makes me uneasy. I don't deserve to be comforted.

The hospital has other ideas. Here they have been doing everything they can to comfort me. I have been given a light, south-facing room which looks out over the lawn where I can see magpies hopping about with little diagonal movements like chess pieces. There are rose bushes and willow trees and a fountain, but it has been turned off for water saving and the birds now come to wash their wings in dust.

My room is quite large and painted a soft green. There is a muted watercolour on the wall in the style of Monet, which I've been told is the work of a former patient, H something, I can't read the rest of the signature scrawl. I wonder whether this was

H's room or his painting has been saved to adorn the best. I have stayed in intercontinental hotel rooms worse than this.

There is a big black television and video and a stereo system, complete with CD player. No music, but I do not want to hear music. I have twisted the dial to one of the London commercial stations. On Radio Three, there is a danger that one of my own recordings might be played and I need no reminders.

I am paying for this.

I don't have to be here. I am not committed. I am just unable to be anywhere else. I could not cope with being at home, alone with the madness, so the police contacted Dr Chase, who came to collect me in his own car, a blue Jaguar. Unbelievably, we talked cars all the way here. I used to have a passion for them. I collected old ones and fast ones and every weekend when I wasn't performing I would select one (I had five) and take it for a spin, down to Salisbury Plain or across the city to Brighton. Often I got stopped for speeding but I could usually get away with an autograph. I kept a stash of cassettes in my cars for fines too. Speed and music were always synonymous.

I am not allowed to leave the country, that is one of my bail conditions. But there is nowhere I want to go. I can't become a fugitive from myself.

There have been letters and flowers from sympathisers. In my room right now there is one huge bowl of pink roses, a tall vase of irises, a jug of yellow daisies and several baskets of mixed flowers. I have spent a long time studying these flowers, looking at each floret and petal, comparing leaves and stems, types of pollen, shades and tones of colour; anything to stop me thinking about why they have been sent.

I read only one letter. It was from a woman who described herself as my most faithful fan. She said that she had been to every single one of my concerts and that I should draw strength from art. 'Your music will lift you from this terrible experience,' she wrote. She also said she was sorry and that she cried when she read the newspapers. I threw her letter away and then all the others too. There were perhaps fifty or sixty, but I could not bear to be touched.

Now there's a soft knock at the door. A slight pause before it opens, in case I'm naked, I suppose, and then a nurse comes in. I have not seen her before and she looks embarrassed. I can see a red flush around her ears and cheekbones. She looks young, vulnerable, innocent and wary – but perhaps all women will look this way to me now – as she indicates the sedatives clattering like small orange dice in the bottom of a plastic cup. I swallow them down without water.

'Is there anything else you need?' she says. Her voice is soft, Irish, comforting, but God, I don't want that.

'No.'

She walks away slowly, leaving me in darkness again.

— 3 —

It feels odd to be here without my grandmother. This hut is so infused with her, I'm finding it impossible not to wait for her. I have been sleeping lightly (peacefully, even) and waking up early, not quite believing that she won't be coming in with hot, damp bread from the village bakery, singing softly in her country voice, reaching around, putting things away in a whirl of bare arms.

Her skin was as smooth as driftwood and she smelled of yeast and freshly mown grass. 'Morning, sunshine,' she'd say, tickling me under the chin with a buttercup. 'Yes, he loves butter, but he loves this too.'

A glass of dark-gold, fresh apple juice would appear by my side. A flute of sunlight, tasting of honey. I'd down it in one and leap out of the bed, slipping past her as she tried to push me towards the sink.

We didn't plan anything. She was not like that: her approach was mellifluous. She liked to slowly peel off the layers of each day, as if unwrapping something precious, never hurrying, never revealing too much as she went about things in her calm, clear way. Living with her was a delicious tease. If I asked her about 'tomorrow', she always said: 'Wait and see.'

Our time here was decided by the sun and the rain and the wind and the waves. In the mornings we would climb the path down to the sea. I waited for her at the bottom, jigging up and down on the stones in a singing agony of impatience, anxious that she had not caught her cardigan on sea holly or hawthorn. She walked so slowly down the path, stopping to inspect new flowers and insects, making drawings in the black hardback notepad she always carried with her. Some days I was convinced that she deliberately took her time coming down the path to torture me. But I tried not to call out to her. There was something about her that checked me, a quiet sadness that I recognised but could not explain.

She always looked startled when she reached the beach and the white light made her appear older, highlighting the map of tiny veins and broken capillaries on the brow of her cheeks. I would feel protective and less in a hurry then and ask her to show me what she'd drawn.

She revealed the contents of her notebook shyly: the fine pencil whispers of silver weed, cloudberries and lucerne (she taught me all the names) were more secrets. New layers. And I would feel guilty at being a goblin again.

'Rush, rush, you want to gobble up your time, you little goblin. The sea will always wait for you.'

The waiting sea. The wait-and-see sea. Deliciously cold, glacial green jelly sea. It took my breath away as I dived in headfirst like a proper boy. She would wait at the edge for me, warming the towel against her body until I came out, crab-walking on the shifting small stones, talking nonsense through my teeth which chattered like pennies in a moneybox. My skin would be on fire, itching crimson as if I'd been boiled. Then she would dry me, rough on my back and buttocks, tender on my face, ears and the creases in the back of my knees, rough again with a twisted nub of towel between every one of my toes.

On wet days we would stay up here in the hut, listening to the rain play Chopin on the tin roof. She would work on a picture and I'd sit at the table handing her feathers, tiny stones, glass beads and pieces of silver paper from my fruit sweets. Sometimes I'd pretend that she was a surgeon performing a life-saving operation and these bits of paper and beads became cold silver instruments which the great doctor accepted wordlessly. I never really knew if she liked me helping or not. She was so absorbed in her work that my efforts seemed clumsy and intrusive. I often dropped things and spilled things, but she ignored me and calmly worked on. There were many things I wanted to ask her, but her silence put me off.

The roof concerto would quieten to an occasional percussion splash and we would go out to find a new steaming tropical garden. The trees would be gleaming as if they'd been dipped in silver wash and the glittering grass oozed truculent slugs which clung to my sand shoes. The worms would come out too, wriggling like tiny terracotta penises as they tested the new, warm air.

My grandmother was at her happiest in the garden. She worked for hours without a break, tugging at the bindweed and tending to her rhododendrons and hibiscus. The white of her hair became brilliant under the sun and her face would glow as if the heat had steam-ironed out all the creases. She seemed quicker in the garden and bolder as she raked and pulled, the muscles rippling across her broad back, shifting the material of her dress around her shoulders to reveal a white strap mark in the shape of a cross.

Later, when the sun became hotter, she would take down the straps and work bare-breasted. I took her breasts inside my mind, although this made me feel nervous and strange. I couldn't help it, they were so extraordinary, like pale, heavy lemons dipped in dark chocolate. The skin was scored with silvery ridges which remained like the trails of a snail when the lemons turned purply-brown under the sun.

In the afternoons I left her alone. She wanted to sleep then. She never did this at home and I knew it was important to her. 'Off you go, monster. I need my rest, you kept me awake again last night with your kicking.'

I worried about this. I never remembered lashing out at her and I felt sorry and ashamed.

'Do I hurt you?'

'Nooo, don't be daft!'

I usually went to the fishing boats. The old men there had dark-brown faces, broken teeth and bloodstained hands. They smelled of diesel oil, tobacco and fish. They were shy and said little, answering my stream of questions with an 'Ar'.

'How many do you catch a day?'

'Ar, depends.'

'What's the best fish?'

'Ar, he's all right.'

One of the men gave me a small mackerel to hold. It was still alive and felt stiff and surprisingly heavy. I stroked its green rainbow back and peered into the gills, which throbbed like a small heart. There was a tiny pearl of blood by the open mouth.

'Can I throw him back?'

'Ar.'

When the men went for tea in their pink and white stone cottages, I followed them. I was interested to see how they lived. I couldn't imagine a fisherman in a house. It didn't seem right. Their feet were too big, for a start. But I didn't discover much. I could never see inside the cottages. The doorways and halls were too dark for my sun-streaming eyes.

I never saw children. For a long time I thought the village simply didn't have any. It made sense to me that old people needed somewhere quiet of their own by the sea. Somewhere without playgrounds and maddening footballs and bicycles. Somewhere still and old. I thought there were lots of childless, ball-silenced villages like this all over England.

The villagers were kind. The women always called hello to me from the doors of their cottages where they sat reading or knitting. They put up blinds of multicoloured plastic ribbons which made a soft flipping sound in the breeze. Flip, flap, splap, flip, flip, the blinds went. Like tiny dying fish.

Sometimes I would go to the sweet shop. It had a yellow canvas sun blind and sold pyramids of creamy tooth-melting fudge, spongy pink shrimps, walking-stick rock and pebble sweets. It was dark inside and smelled sweet and old and dusty. The shop assistant was young with a big smile and she let me spend a long time choosing. But I always bought the same – a quarter of pebbles, which made a wonderful musical sound when she poured them out of the jar. I took my white package of pebbles back to the stones to compare. The likeness never failed to amaze me.

Tim didn't like pebble sweets or rock or paper boats. He thought the coloured blinds were 'tacky', a word I didn't understand, and he said the fishermen smelled and were 'illitrait', another word I didn't understand. 'Ar, ar, ar . . . they're so stupid, they don't say anything else.'

I said nothing. Tim often made me go silent and I wouldn't know why.

[31]

To make me talk he suggested setting fire to *Marylou*.

'They'll never guess it was us.'

'They will. They know things,' I said.

'What things?'

'Just things.'

Another silence.

When Tim came we shared the wooden bed under the window while my grandmother slept on a camp bed. I was restless and Tim complained. 'You make funny noises.'

'Do I, what like?'

'You talk funny, all jumbled up. And you shout.'

'What do I say?'

Tim threw back his handsome head and cupped his hands. 'Help meeeeeeeeeeee!' We were on top of the cliff and the sound echoed back. 'And you go like this – ' He started pushing up with his hands as if he were trying to climb out of a deep hole. 'Then you thump me.'

'What else do I do?'

'You get really sweaty, all slippery and horrible. It's awful sleeping with you.'

Silence again. I was wondering if she was telling the truth when she said I didn't hurt her.

We fought only once. Tim beat me, but I didn't care. We were down on the beach and he'd found a dead seagull. He was kicking at it, sending the flies buzzing angrily around the stones.

'Let's open it up.' He pulled out his Swiss army knife from the pocket of his shorts. 'I've been dying to try this.'

I looked at the knife glinting dangerously in the sun. 'No.'

'Oh, come on, you're so boring. It's dead.' He kicked the bird again and there was a soft thud, then a small crack.

'No, leave it,' I said.

Tim raised the knife and grinned at me. 'Try and stop me.'

I ran towards him and grabbed at his legs. He fell on the stones and then lay on his back and started kicking at me.

'This will pay you back for all the times you've kicked me,' he screamed, lashing out at my face with his feet. 'You say you're asleep, but I think you're lying. It's the only way you can beat me.'

I put up my arms to protect my face but he carried on kicking. He was hysterical and I was afraid.

[32]

'Tim, stop it!' I shouted.

He twisted himself up and threw himself at me, wrestling me to the ground. I banged my back on the stones. We rolled around and he punched me hard on my shoulder and chest. I was finding it difficult to breathe. Then I saw Tim take the knife and move it in slow motion down to my face.

'Say you won't kick me again.' His eyes were hard like the rarest black pebbles. The flashing knife was almost blinding me.

'I can't help it.' I was crying now. 'I'm ... don't know ... I'm asleep.'

Tim dropped the knife. He turned away from me and stared out to sea. When he turned back, I saw that I'd scratched him down one cheek. I felt glad. My back throbbed from where he'd thrown me on the stones.

'My mum said I shouldn't be unkind to you,' he said. His voice was soft, almost a whisper. 'She said that you were sad.'

Sad? I didn't understand. I didn't feel sad. I felt, until he'd gone for me like that, perfectly, gloriously happy.

'What does she mean?' I asked.

Tim hunched himself up and wrapped his slender arms around his knees. 'I suppose it's because you don't have a mum and dad, only her – ' He jerked his head up towards the cliff. 'And you're poor, not like us.'

I stared at the dead bird on the beach. The flies were buzzing around the dried beak and there was a strong, fishy, rotten smell.

'I like it here,' was all I could think of to say.

Tim started digging a hole in the shingle with the knife. 'What's it like?'

'What?'

'Not having a mum and dad.'

I stared at the sea. The tide was coming in quickly now, hissing over the stones. I threw a pebble and watched it bounce on the glassy green surface three times before it sank.

'I don't know. I don't remember them.'

'That's weird,' Tim said and threw a stone. His bounced four times.

My parents were killed in Italy. I was two years old, too young for the mountain trip they made to celebrate the publication of my father's book. It was a book about birds. My father was an ornithologist and he travelled all over the world studying his birds. He was a big, shambling man with dark, curly hair and crinkly eyes framed by square glasses. He looked serious but at the same time bemused, as if he could not quite believe his own seriousness. He had big red hands and feet which looked huge in his ski boots, like buckets for horse feed. I saw all this in a photograph of him taken on that last trip. One of the mountain rescuers sent my father's camera to England. It was all they found.

My mother was smiling at my father in the picture. She looked like a young girl on her first trip abroad. Her eyes were bright with excitement and there was something reckless about the way her red hair tumbled around her shoulders which were framed by a white fur collar. My father had taken off his ski gloves to hold her for the picture, which must have been taken with a self-timer since they had travelled through the Alps alone. My father never used guides.

My grandmother had put the photograph in a silver frame. It sat on top of the piano at her house in Somerset. I didn't feel sad when I looked at it. I had no memory of my mother and father so there was nothing to be sad about. I felt excited. They looked so free and brave and exotic with their ski poles and rucksacks and fur-trimmed clothes, just like the real explorers in my *Book of Knowledge*. I was proud to have parents like them. They sought adventure and lived the way they pleased. They were romantic and strong and different. They were a little boy's dream. I didn't know anyone else with parents like that.

Tim's mother was beautiful, but her beauty was hard work. She spent hours in the bathroom, Tim said, putting on her make-up and doing her hair. Sometimes she spoke softly to me and ruffled my red hair. 'Rufous', she called it. I didn't know what this meant and I was too shy to ask. She frightened me: she could change so quickly. One minute she'd be soft and singsong, teasing the boys; the next quick and brittle, clattering across the kitchen tiles in her high heels, a prickly chemical smell about her of nail varnish and hair lacquer. 'Get out of my sight now and go and play.'

My mother wouldn't have been like that, I decided. She would tell me fantastic stories of her trips with my father while she made funny cakes. She would laugh and sing and open all the windows, unlike Tim's mother who kept the curtains drawn all

[34]

day. My mother wouldn't have wasted time in the bathroom. She was so beautiful she didn't need to. My mother would have made Tim's mother spit with envy. And all the other mothers who waited outside our school at four o'clock, looking sour and tired in their long cardigans and sloppy sandals. My mother with her slim ski legs and long red hair. My mother with her laugh and her stories. My mother. I would say the words over and over to myself, like a prayer.

My grandmother told me I would haul myself up on the piano stool and stare at the photograph for hours, leaning over the keys with my chin cupped in my hands, talking softly to myself. Sometimes, though, she got worried and put the television on to try to distract me. But the cartoons and puppets and games could not hold my attention for long. I always went back to the piano. And after a while I started to play. My grandmother told me I was three years old when I began improvising on the theme tune from *The Magic Roundabout*.

She told me my mother had played. 'But she had to give it up when your dad started travelling. He was always off somewhere after the birds. She wouldn't stay behind, she liked a bit of adventure, that girl. I thought it was a shame, she was so good. She might have gone professional if it hadn't been for the birds.'

There was a copy of my father's book in our bookshelf. *The Last Flight: a study of the disappearing birds of the world*. It had a golden eagle on the cover and a photograph of my father, red-faced and squinting, climbing gear draped around him like armour. His name was a vapour trail in the sky, Donald Schidmaizig, the tail of the *g* curled in a glamorous arc of flight.

I spent hours poring over the book, learning the names of the birds in Latin, lost in my father's adventures. He had been to South America and the Middle East and Canada. He was, like his subject, migratory. But his wanderings were not idle. His flights were based on the Roman principle that the study of birds was auspicious. The flights and songs of birds held secrets of the future and even the outcome of important events could be discovered by cutting open the birds to examine their organs. I remember reading this in a state of high excitement. The birds can tell us things! But my tender ten-year-old heart knew that already.

I learned many other things from the book, things I was never told at school. From my father I discovered that flightless elephant birds, nine feet tall, had roamed the earth seven hundred years ago. I shared his near-delirious joy at finding an egg, perfectly preserved, in a stream in Madagascar. It was huge, six times the size of an ostrich egg, and held two gallons of yolk and albumen. I learned that cities had gobbled up the whooping crane and that the Australian cassowary could run up to thirty miles an hour and swim across jungle rivers. I learned that my father took tinned rice pudding with him when he travelled. Ambrosia. 'The first taste of the delicious thick, nutty cream from a cold spoon at the end of a hard day's climbing is worth the extra weight in the rucksack,' he wrote. I felt his despair when he lost his notebook in Norway and laughed when he described feasting on a goat in the Yemen. 'I was honoured with the tongue, barely cooked, lilac in colour and pocked with what looked like crusty sores. They smiled encouragingly as I picked it up. What could I do except hold my own?'

In Egypt, my father studied the legend of the sacred ibis. The ancient Egyptians believed this bird was the god Thoth, the scribe who recorded the stories of every human being. My father wove into his study stories of the Egyptians he met; the fellahin who sailed the Nile on graceful white boats with sails as pure as the wings of swans, the Arab jockeys and the alfalfa farmers. In Luxor he drank sweet red tea with a papyrus salesman who knew *Macbeth* by heart.

There were other marginal wonders. A passage on cloud formation, a description of pissing in an ice hole, a page or two on the formation of glaciers, anecdotes about frostbite, windburn, dysentery, sunstroke and love. From Papua New Guinea, he described sighting a Count Raggi's red-plumed bird of paradise which reminded him of my mother's hair.

The book of birds was my book of life. But how could I tell Tim this? He didn't like reading books. Well, I never saw him with one. He preferred magazines. Especially women's magazines. Between the glossy, fragrant pages he found something he liked: food and sex. Tim got funny over adverts for body cream.

'Cor, look at that!' We were lying on the beach a few days after our fight. Tim was flicking through a magazine while we warmed our bellies on the stones after a swim.

'What?'

[36]

'That leg. It's so nice and smooth. Like coffee ice cream. I could lick it.'

'Eeergh.'

'You're stupid. You don't know anything. I've done it.'

'Done what?'

'*It*, stupid! I did it last year. She was only our age, but she knew what to do because she watched her big sister and her boyfriend one night. She was supposed to be in bed.'

'Watched them do what?'

'I could show you if you like.' Tim moved closer to me and suddenly shoved his tongue in my mouth. It felt horrible, thick and rough and greasy.

'Get off!' I spat the taste of him, bitter with a hint of soapy sweetness, out on the stones.

'What did you do that for?'

'You wanted to know what it felt like. I could show you more.'

'Leeeuurgh! No.'

'I bet you don't know what a hard-on is.'

'I do.'

'What is it then?' Tim said nastily and turned over another page. I was saved from his challenge by an advert for a Wonderbra.

'Phwaaaar, cor, pah, ummmm.'

'You're disgusting.'

'You're queer.'

That night Tim went to sleep as soon as we climbed into the wooden bed. He slept with his back curled away from me, sniffing and snuffling like a baby pig. His back twitched when I poked him with a finger. I tried again harder. He grunted, but still didn't turn round. I pressed my finger into him again and watched as the white indent filled up. Two more indents and he angrily turned round.

'Cut it out, loser!'

I was silent and stiff with pain. I'd only wanted to ask him what a hard-on was.

Tim slept and I listened to the crickets outside. Their shrill whistle almost drowned the sound of the sea. I strained hard. I always had to hear the sea before I could sleep. I was superstitious about it. Then it came; the deep bass voice, boom, boom, ssssssssssh. It silenced the fluted insect chorus flat. Now I could hear my grandmother breathing deeply like a soft echo of the sea and the timbers of the hut creaking in the wind. I relaxed and settled down to sleep.

Tim's scream shook me awake. I was standing over him. He was on the floor, sobbing and clutching his pillow, which he'd made into a ball under him. My grandmother was kneeling beside him, stroking his head.

'It's all right, Tim, it's only a dream.'

'It's not me,' he shouted. 'It's *him*! He kicked me out.'

My grandmother gently sat me down. I felt confused and I could not speak. She held me in her arms and allowed me to sob.

Tim got up from the floor and I noticed the scab on his face was picked. A thin line of blood glittered in the moonlight. An image drifted into my mind of a small boat bobbing on the waves. Inside the boat was a boy and he was tearing at his face which seemed to be covered with limpet shells. He was asking me to cut them off with a knife. 'I'm sorry,' I said, 'I didn't mean it. You asked me to do it.'

Tim screwed up his face and looked as if he wanted to cry again, then he turned to my grandmother. 'I don't want to stay in this bed any more. Can I sleep over there?'

'All right,' my grandmother said.

We watched in silence as Tim climbed into the camp bed.

— 4 —

The tape recorder stops and Dr Chase slips in another microcassette. I wonder how many of these it is going to take before he has enough evidence. Dozens, hundreds? How much of my life does he want?

'You're doing very well,' he says. He looks fresh and bright this morning and there is a new rosebud, a dazzling pink one, pinned to his suit. For a moment, I despise him for his jauntiness – he is too uncomfortably excited by all this.

[38]

'Was this dream the same?' I ask. 'I mean, I didn't feel so much terror myself. It was more *his* terror frightening me.'

Dr Chase gets up and slowly paces around his office. He stops at the window and clasps his hands behind his back. I watch as he laces his fingers together, interlocking them in an intricate puzzle, and feel even more irritated.

'There was sleepwalking. You found yourself out of bed when you woke up. Again you were having vivid delusions,' he says slowly, working his thumbs in a circle. 'I would say it's the same phenomenon, the same Stage Four sleep phase.'

'But was it a night terror?'

Dr Chase stops playing with his hands. I feel relieved. 'There are degrees of terror, Andrew. You felt anxious, you were worried when you had the knife?'

'Yes.'

He returns to his chair and sits down, giving a slight sigh.

'What's important is that you were suffering from a sleep disorder, in your case from a very early age. Your defence will need to show this quite clearly.'

Although it is warm in the room I feel a sudden chill. I wish I had something else to wear instead of this thin hospital uniform.

The embarrassed nurse brought the clothes to my room this morning with breakfast, which again I couldn't eat. She tried to coax me. 'Not even a piece of toast, Mr Schidmaizig?'

I told her my mouth felt too dry. I just wanted coffee. Lots of it.

She made a face and told me that the tranquillisers were to blame. 'Dehydration, unfortunately it's a common side effect.'

She whisked away the breakfast and left me with the clothes: a pair of baggy white cotton pants and a thin, long-sleeved white T-shirt, embroidered with the hospital logo in blue. The logo was a tiny open door.

I fingered the clean white cloth and decided I ought to have a shower. I smelled gamy, of hot blood and old feathers. I smelled hunted.

The water shocked me. I deliberately turned it on colder than usual and stood with my legs splayed like an animal. The jet needles of water raining down on my head felt good. Sharp white knives. I bit my lip and picked up the hospital soap. It too was embossed with a tiny open door.

The nurse came back. 'I'm going to change the sheets now!' Her voice was singsong.

I turned the jet higher, raised my arms and felt the cold knives scrape down my back.

'I'll take the suit, Mr Schidmaizig!'

I twisted off the jet quickly, wrenching my fingers. 'What did you say?'

'I'll take the suit. We can dry-clean it for you.'

'No!'

I grabbed a towel and ran out, slipping on the wet tiles. I'd forgotten to pull the shower curtain.

'Leave it.'

The nurse dropped my performing suit as if it had burned her. 'I'm sorry,' she said very quietly.

At the door she hesitated as if she wanted to say something, but I ignored her, so she left, closing the door quite firmly behind her. When I was sure she had gone, I changed into my new clothes. She had brought size X-large, but the pants and top were too small. The elasticated bottoms felt tight around my ankles and the sleeves of the T-shirt ended a good three inches above my wrists. I went to the mirror. I looked ridiculous, a caricature of a mental patient.

The performing suit lay on the bed, a stiff, black skin. A skin I had now shed. I picked it up. It was not enough simply to shed it. Now I wanted it dead. I wanted to cut it up into tiny pieces and bury it somewhere. The suit was history now. I padded around my room in my white pants with the suit crumpled in my arms like an exhausted dance partner, looking for something to destroy it with. There was nothing, of course. All the cupboards and drawers were empty and someone – the nurse perhaps – had removed my razor from the bathroom. I crushed the suit into a black ball and shoved it in the waste bin. The nurse would think I was mad after making such a fuss about it, but then she would be used to that.

'Are you all right?' Dr Chase asks.

'Yes, fine, carry on.'

'I'd like to talk about your relationship with your grandmother.'

The dryness suddenly creeps back into my mouth again. I look around for some coffee, water, anything.

'Are you sure you're all right?' Dr Chase says. His brow is creased with concern. I realise I'm holding things up.

'Just thirsty, that's all. The drugs . . .'

'I'll get you some water.'

He goes over to a small water filter and pours me a glass. I drink it gratefully.

'We were very close,' I say, painfully aware of the crack in my voice.

'Yes, it seems so. It also seems that she was very understanding about the night terrors. It's common for parents or guardians to be frightened – or concerned enough to seek medical help.'

I feel defensive. 'It wasn't that bad. She didn't think there was any need.'

Dr Chase nods and smiles. I see that his teeth are slightly protruding. He nods again. I realise that he is not being antagonistic. He just wants me to talk.

'I knew early on that things were difficult with money and everything,' I say. 'But I respected her. I didn't want to cause trouble. My friends were all trying to become estranged from their parents, you know the usual childhood battles, I suppose you'd call it assertion of personality or something, but it wasn't like that for us. I enjoyed being with her. She wasn't an educated woman but she taught me a lot.'

Dr Chase smiles. 'You were fortunate.' Then the smile fades as he realises how inappropriate this comment must seem to me. He changes direction. 'What makes you angry, Andrew?'

I am confused. 'Well, I . . .'

'Real anger, Andrew. What makes you want to fight?'

I wonder why he's asking me this. There are many things that make me so angry I could lash out. I believe it's all part of being a performer, the frustrated fury at not being able do anything else and never being able to do the work as well as you think you can. I always played sublimely in my mind, but when it came down to it, I think I tried too hard. In a strange way, I used the piano as an instrument to channel my fury at not being a better player. At the same time the piano *was* my fury. Maybe this had something to do with the violence of the instrument – you strike a piano, not pluck or blow or suck or stroke with a bow. With the piano it's all in the hitting and every pianist is both creator and abuser. But I think it might be dangerous to say this.

Art makes me angry, shall I tell Dr Chase this? No, think of something else, think of your fights. Berlin, the oboeist? No, I was drunk and so was he, and that was about art again. Or what he saw as my lack of it. He said I played with my penis. What was it? 'Your playing is too sexy, Andrew, you ram it down their throats, you should learn moderation', or some such crap. I called him a purist prick before punching him on the nose.

Causes? Politics? Was I angry about the state of the economy, the recession, the men in grey suits, the disappearing rainforests, the birds – I'd almost forgotten about them – starving children, the homeless? I feel frantic now. Chemical pollution? War? Music critics? Cruelty? Injustice? The hole in the ozone layer? What can I say? Now I'm angry at my inability to find an answer.

I realise why. Everything I once felt angry about now makes me feel foolish. All of it seems petty and futile, like sitting in a traffic jam fuming at not being able to move. Then feeling ludicrous at pulling away with all the other ludicrous drivers in the world. Now I'd welcome an insignificant anger like that. It would be glorious to blow my top, get into a frenzy over something trivial. A queue, an abusive shopkeeper, something minor and everyday. Something normal. Was it Nietzsche who said: 'I am not a man, I am dynamite'? I can't remember, all I know is I have this one big unspoken anger fizzing away inside me, waiting to explode. I can't calm it down. Right now I can't even fight it because I don't understand it. But it's there, I can feel it, a sort of black pressure somewhere deep in my skull.

'Evil,' I tell Dr Chase, 'I'm angry about evil.'

He watches me closely and my palms begin to sweat. The dryness has come back and I reach for the water glass, but find it empty. Without saying anything he gets up to pour me another.

Back in my room I lie down on the bed for a while. I don't know if this is a good idea, all this talk. Dr Chase should simply section me and have done with it. I should be left in a white room alone with my blackness. Talking means nothing. Talking brings out the badness, the blackness, and all I want is the light. The light. I would do anything to return to the light.

[42]

I stare at the watercolour. H has used the colours of a bruise, deep thundery mauves, soft pink greys and veiny lilacs. Trees, clouds and shadows are blended into one billowing purplish mass around a ribbon of clear water, a centre of calm, which draws the eye. Once I might have described this painting as dreamlike. Now I know better.

I am seeing everything in shades of darkness. I must go to the window and find the light. There – it's a brilliant day. I hadn't noticed until now. Dr Chase pulled the blinds this morning.

I would like to smell grass and fresh air, but the window has been sealed shut. Frustrated, I bang my head against the glass. I should have guessed: open doors, closed windows. This is a psychiatric hospital, after all. But it isn't called that. Highgrove has some other name: the London Academy of Mental Health, I think. I know it's important and new and I believe I once heard someone describe it as a 'psychiatric university'. I must remember to ask Dr Chase about this.

The hospital, or academy, is in a leafy green dip of north London called the Vale of Health. People walk their dogs near here and children play in the fields. Kites fly and there are swallows and sometimes geese in the sky. A safe place to go mad.

But the hospital building is too modern and threatening to appear safe. From the outside, it looks mixed up, a crazy architect's wet dream. A compact low-rise octagon, it has windows of bulletproof amber glass, arches and escape routes. Masses of pipes, tubes and cylinders snake over the exterior like a giant vascular system.

I remarked on its strangeness the day I arrived in Dr Chase's Jag.

'Yes, it is a bit extraterrestrial,' he said. 'One for Prince Charles's hit list. It's known among the doctors as the Brain.'

The sound of my own laughter had surprised me.

I wish this window would open. I need to breathe something besides my own air-conditioned breath. I suppose I could go outside. I am not locked in. I could go to the garden and sit on one of the benches. I could smell the roses. I could read poetry or music or sit with my eyes closed in the sun. I could die.

The garden is empty. But for all I know, the entire hospital could be empty. I have not met a single other patient. Not that I want to. It would confirm things about myself. Things I cannot accept.

I could walk out of here. I could go to a bar. But what about my wild beard and hair and too-small hospital clothes? The barman would notice the open-door logo and call the police. I could not protest.

'I'm a concert pianist.'

'Yeah, and I'm fucking Beethoven.'

But I need a drink. I need a bottle of whisky. These damn sedatives are no good. The effects wear off by the afternoon. I need to be drugged all the time. They can't expect me to just be here with myself. Don't they realise what I'm going through?

These horror echoes, they keep coming and going. I've slipped into a void and I'm frightened, not of dying, but of remaining suspended like this, clinging to the ledge of normality, feeling nothing not even pain now. If I could make it real, maybe it would be different. Like the time I came close to death in Ireland. I don't remember coming off the road. I woke to find the Lotus caved in around me like an awful metal tomb. Then came a farrago of strange noises, off-key wails, flashing lights, a smear of red on the windscreen, the tape still playing Prokofiev. A smell of burning from the cutting gear. I must remember that I survived. I survived that.

— 5 —

I am running out of tinned food. I ate the last of the Ambrosia creamed rice this morning for breakfast and now it is too late to go out. And too wild. A storm is blowing. The wind is shaking and rattling the hut's wooden walls and the rain has gone into an orchestral frenzy on the roof. I sit in the midst of all this creaking wood and drumming tin, wrapped in a damp blanket. A lone sailor on an old ship.

The utensils I put on the floor a short while ago are now close to overflowing. I watch a small wave lap over the side of a milk saucepan and splash on to the wooden floor.

''Tis no use crying over spilt milk, my love.' Who said that? The lightning flashes are playing tricks on my mind.

Here comes another, bathing the hut in a white light like that thrown by an old-fashioned camera flash. We are sitting at the table playing cards, and everything – the table, the moth-fizzing lamp, the pictures, the velvet curtain – looks frozen in time as if the lightning is illuminating images from the past.

Thunder. 'It's God throwing out his piano.' I hear her say this so clearly it raises every single hair on my arms.

She's here. She's standing before me, shrouded in white, holding out her arms and smiling. Her white hair is a shimmering corona and she appears to be trapped in a moonbeam. She looks young and unafraid. A ghost or a trick?

A delusion. I can summon them up at will now.

Another crash. 'His violin case', but the voice is fading. It must be my own inventing hers again.

I was frightened of storms. The gradual build-up of thick pressure in my head, the glimmerings behind the eyes, then all the falling and crashing, creaking and crushing, it was unbearably close to the terror I knew in my dreams.

I believed that the hut might collapse into a pile of logs, flattening us underneath, cracking our bones, compressing us into beetles. But my grandmother said the hut would never fall down because an engineer had built it.

The engineer was my grandfather. He was Austrian, that much I knew, because my grandmother often had to explain the source of our unusual name. In Somerset, among the Rayners, the Martins and the Summers, Schidmaizig stuck out like a flamboyant hat in a drab congregation. It didn't really belong but it was too interesting to be left alone. 'Shedmaarzeg,' the man on the bakery van called it. 'Where's he from then?' When I said 'Austria', he laughed and gave me an extra doughnut. I didn't understand the country approach to strangeness – the combination of intense curiosity, mockery and sympathy reserved for all things foreign – but I secretly enjoyed the attention.

I never met my grandfather. I knew that something had happened soon after the mountain accident that killed my parents, but precisely what I was never sure. My grandmother said that after the accident, my grandfather 'went away'. She never spoke about him and she kept no reminders or mementos of him at home. I came to the romantic conclusion that he had died of grief.

I did not miss having a man around. There was Sergei, my piano teacher. He was not exactly a father substitute, but he kept me in check.

When I was fourteen, Sergei entered me for the Young Musician of the Year Contest. I practised hard. I thought I was in with a good chance, but Sergei was not impresssed. He berated me every night, picking holes in my timing, my style: 'Too fast, Andrei.' (He always Russified my name.) 'You are not in a race.' My position: 'Don't fall over the piano, you look like rubbish and the judges will think you are rubbish.'

He even wanted me to change my diet.

'No fat, tell your grandmother to cut it off the meat. You need to be lean, hungry for it.'

'I'm not an athlete, Sergei!'

'Wrong,' he said, slamming the Rachmaninov score down. 'You are! You are preparing for a marathon.'

'But you said I was not in a race.'

I earned a stinging slap on the ear for this.

Although I swore at him under my breath and vowed that one day I'd play so brilliantly he would never hit me again, I adored Sergei. He looked incredibly old – I secretly thought he must be at least a hundred – but he was probably nearer sixty. He was quite grotesque with his bald, speckled head, which made me think of my father's elephant-bird egg, slanted murky green eyes and flat, Eskimoid face covered in great warts. The warts fascinated me: they were like faces on a face. They had their own hair, eyes and even teeth. When Sergei got angry they turned bright red.

My grandmother told me Sergei had spent time in a labour camp. But this meant nothing to me. Sergei rarely spoke about his past life and I was too ignorant to ask. Sometimes, though, when I played Prokofiev or Rachmaninov well, he would become uncomfortably emotional. His oriental eyes would moisten and he would graciously excuse himself.

'I must use the bathroom . . . cool my hands.'

His playing was seraphic. I have never heard anyone work a piano like Sergei and I could have listened to him for hours, but he never let me. I would flounder dully on a piece, and he would stand behind me, cracking his warty hands until it became too much. Then he would edge me off the stool with his backside and, without saying anything, start to demonstrate how the piece could be lifted. His playing was so clear, so fine and sharp and yet so completely rounded, it was almost impossible to believe that such a rapturous confection could come out of something so ugly. But if I said anything, made a comment on his playing, he would become angry and roughly shove me back on the stool. 'It's in you, boy,' he would say. 'Find it.'

Sergei lived in a tiny cottage behind Wells Cathedral. The cathedral music school had given him the cottage in return for his services as a part-time piano and composition tutor. By this time, I was attending the cathedral school, but I never had Sergei for lessons. He thought it was good for me to experiment with other tutors.

'You must learn all you can, good and bad,' he said.

'But I must learn which is which, Sergei!'

'When you know what is bad you will have learned something.'

But I only dabbled with my school tutors during the day, and they were kind and not so blunt about my faults. They indulged me and taught me nothing. It was only with Sergei that I felt I made music.

Once he arranged for me to play on the cathedral organ, a thrilling, almost supernatural experience, and I have never forgotten the sight of him pacing up and down the aisle like a nervous bridegroom while I sat up in the honey-stone eaves playing Bach as if my life depended on it. When I came down he paid me what I believe was a compliment, the first and last I ever extracted from him: 'Andrei, you are no angel. You are a demon.'

A glossy black Steinway dominated Sergei's cottage. He'd had to get rid of most of the furniture in order to squeeze it in. The sofa was out in the strip garden at the back. I could see it through the window, sitting in an overgrown cabbage patch, still wearing its lace antimacassar, like an outraged monarch turfed unceremoniously from the throne.

This left room for two hard-backed chairs, a bookcase filled with Russian texts of Dostoevsky, Tolstoy and Turgenev and a small suitcase Sergei used as a table. On top was a painted *matryoshka* doll, the only splash of colour in the room. I liked to disembowel the *matryoshka*, which was really six dolls tucked inside each other. The smallest one was no bigger than a pea.

Walking normally was impossible in Sergei's cottage. Doll steps were required, mostly to avoid the piles of newspapers. They were everywhere, brown and crisp and dating back to the 1940s and 1950s. When I asked him why he had them, he said that he needed to submerge himself in history to prove to himself that there was history.

This made no sense to me. I loathed history at school, lessons about the dead, dates, facts I immediately forgot: why should I care what happened three hundred or even thirty years ago? History lessons made me feel suffocated and dull. I couldn't think why anyone would want it cluttering up their living room.

Sergei believed history was a 'right'. He asked me how I would feel if someone stole my time.

'What do you mean?'

'Your time, say someone took away a very precious time from you.'

'Like now?' It was our last lesson before the young musician contest and I thought I was being clever, making him think that I thought my time with him was precious to flatter him a little. I don't think many people flattered Sergei.

'Yes, like now, when you are so hot with yourself because you think you are going to win this competition. You dream every night of being the new Young Musician of the Year. Then someone comes in and bundles up this time and takes it away.'

'Well, I'd want it back, of course. I'd do anything I could to find it.' Then I paused, feeling puzzled. 'But I might not win, I could have been wasting my time. I wouldn't care then. I don't think that's a good example.'

'No, Andrei. It is the most good example!'

'But I can't miss what I haven't had yet. That's crazy!' My voice shot up an octave.

Sergei raised an imaginary baton, indicating that I was out of line.

'Andrei, you must understand you have a choice. If someone steals your time, you have no choice. Your precious time no longer exists. It has been murdered, better to forget it. What do you do? You allow it to be buried, you have no choice, that vanished with your time.'

I said nothing. It was too confusing. I could hear Sergei's big brown clock ticking away on the mantelpiece. Why all this talk of time? What did he mean by it?

'I don't see what all this has to do with history,' I said, jerking my head towards the pile of newspapers.

'Every human being has a right to his own history. If they steal your time, they steal your history. It is the same,' he said.

'They – ?' I started, but he wouldn't let me finish.

'We must move on, time for you to work!'

That night we worked late on my competition pieces. I had chosen Rachmaninov's Sonata Number 1 in D minor and Tchaikovsky's Grand Sonata in G minor. I was technically better with the Tchaikovsky, but I knew that if I was going to win, the Rachmaninov would do it for me. Rachmaninov made me feel shivery and afraid. There was so much movement, so much soaring and falling off, so much energy. Ending a Rachmaninov piece, I would feel exhausted but at the same time exhilarated. There was nothing I could compare it with except perhaps the feelings I experienced during my urgent (and now increasingly frequent) times behind the locked door of the bathroom.

It was very late when I got home. I'd been practising so hard I'd forgotten to eat, so I went into the kitchen and carved a huge slice of bread which I smeared with gooseberry jam. I ate the bread leaning against the Aga, listening to its sleepy sucks and gurgles as it warmed my back. The Aga was the great throbbing heart of the house and my grandmother never let it go out. It stayed lit throughout the summer and when it became too hot she simply opened the windows.

The kitchen was my favourite place. It smelled of bread, cinnamon, dusty apples and earth and was an extension of my grandmother's greenhouse and sick-plant nursery. People brought their plants here to be cured. My grandmother could coax life back into the meanest crop of stalks and was known locally as the 'plant doctor'. She spent hours mixing feeding solutions and medications from herbs and crystals. She fed her plants with the same pipette she used for tending to injured fledglings, which people also brought in boxes. I didn't think any of this was at all strange, but the boys at school said she was a witch.

Her sorcery kept her busy. Trays of seedlings covered the wide kitchen windowsill and all around the floor and on every shelf were pots waiting to be filled or their contents transferred to larger ones stacked up in the corner near the Aga in a brick-coloured pile. There were baskets of bulbs and sheaves of dried flowers and grasses dyed peacock blue and burnt orange which my grandmother sold along with her pictures and insects in the marketplace on Saturday mornings.

Recently she had set up a contraption something like a distillery on a low table under the window. It consisted of several glass jars, a small methylated-spirits burner and lengths of orange rubber tubing. She called it her 'petal extractor' and said she was trying to make perfume and flower waters to sell as another sideline.

Through the kitchen window I could see the old apple tree. The winter had stripped it bare of fruit and leaves, but it was still magnificent. The gleaming white trunk was thicker than two men standing side by side and the great silvery arms were muscled and gnarled from years of fighting the wind.

It was windy outside now and the tree was swaying and groaning at the challenge. I shivered. The sky was crow black and I could feel the vibrations of a storm. I bent my back towards the hugging warmth of the Aga and laughed nervously, telling myself not to be so stupid. It was only a storm. I poured myself a glass of milk and went up to bed.

The wind noise is terrific, a long-drawn-out howling and yowling. A dog left chained too long. It whips up everything: rocks and stones and apples. They come cracking at my window like gunshot. An icy finger of fear rakes my scalp. Crack. Crack. The window is going to smash. Now a moaning. Where's the door? Here, but I can't open it: the wood is soft green velvet, a drowning cloth. Now clattering stones. Now tapping bones. It's getting closer. I can see it. It extends a lean bone arm. I must stop it. She won't be able to escape. Her bones are too old. She'll fall down the stairs. Bone on glass. A glitter shower of mica and ice, freezing and stinging. Wind whipping through a black hole. A stinging. A wet blinding red stinging. Pins and needles multiplied a million times . . .

'Don't move, just stay there. I'll fetch some water.'

'What's . . .? Oh, my God!' There was glass all over the floor. 'What have I done?'

'I think you smashed the window. Don't move, keep your arm up.' My grandmother's face was tight and white.

Something hot trickled slowly down my arm.

'Oh no, oh no, oh no!' I became hysterical.

'I'm going to call an ambulance. It's all right, it doesn't look too deep.'

I started to choke.

She grabbed me by the shoulders and shook me. 'Breathe, breathe, breathe.' She sounded angry.

I inhaled slowly and lifted my hand higher. Blood dripped on to my knees. I clung to her, smelling the musky, powdery smell of her dressing gown.

'Keep it up, that's it, love, just hold it there.' Her eyes were darting around looking for something. She went over to my bed, pulled free a white pillowcase and then came back and wrapped it around my wrist.

'I'll go down and telephone. Just keep it up.'

I watched a red butterfly stain appear on the pillowcase and tried to stop myself feeling sick. Fractured parts of her conversation drifted up. I heard the words 'accident' and 'son', no, she must have said 'grandson'.

She came back up the stairs, breathing hard and carrying a mug. 'Drink this.'

'What is it?'

'Camomile tea.'

I sipped it. It was stronger than I expected and warmer.

'I put some brandy in it.' She stroked my face. 'Oh, Andrew . . .'

Then she had to go downstairs again because the ambulance people were banging on the door.

The hospital was very quiet. There seemed to be only one other emergency, a woman in the throes of labour. She was being wheeled towards us at speed on a trolley pushed by two young men in short grey coats. They shouted at us to get out of the

[51]

way. We flattened ourselves against the wall in a narrow corridor and the trolley hissed past, bearing its twitching mound of sheets which concealed a shape not immediately recognisable as human. Only the woman's hair was visible, hanging over the edge of the trolley in a stiff dark coil. She was not screaming, just making a low groaning sound, which somehow was worse.

We found the waiting room. A thin man with greasy yellow hair was sitting on the edge of his seat, smoking. He looked pleased to see us.

'Not long now,' he said.

My grandmother smiled at him.

'I thought she was going to have it in the van,' the man said. 'Never drove so fast in all my life, didn't think she had it in her.'

My grandmother laughed and carried on talking with the man. It was Somerset talk; vans, gardens, storms and sickness. But there was nothing complaining about it. It was a way of passing the time. This way of talking was ever present: the low warm buzz of it filled the shops, the post office, the market, the dentist's surgery and now the hospital. I found it boring at times, but I did not want to escape from it. I needed the reassurance of something familiar. Especially now.

I stared down at my hand. The pillowcase had been whisked away by a nurse and replaced with a spongy pad of white cotton.

'How does it feel?' my grandmother asked.

I shook my head. 'It's all right,' I felt nothing except a faint echo of the pins-and-needles sensation from before. 'It just stings a bit.'

The nurse came in again. She had thick white legs and looked older than my grandmother.

'I'm afraid you'll have to wait. There's only one doctor on duty and he's going to be busy for some time.' She said this in a whisper so the man with the yellow hair wouldn't hear.

I looked over at him. He was chewing at his fingers, tearing at the skin with his front teeth as if he were eating chicken wings.

The nurse walked away and I slumped back in the waiting-room chair. It was made of orange plastic and bolted to the next one, where my grandmother sat stiff in her green wollen coat.

'Why?' I said it quietly, but there was a part of me that wanted to shout it out loud. I wanted to jump up and unleash a howling 'why' down the corridor, as if to dislodge the terrible force, the

[52]

force that was whipping through my dreams and turning them wild.

'I don't really know, my love.'

Her voice had lost the edge I'd heard earlier. In the ambulance she'd been silent and rigid and her face had looked hard in the brutal blue light. We had not spoken a word all the way.

'Were you angry with me?' I said.

'No, I . . .' She hesitated, choosing her words carefully. '*It* makes me angry, not you.'

'That I have such bad dreams?'

'Yes,' she said very quietly. 'It's terrible for you.'

'Did you ever . . .?' I asked.

'No, but this is not the time or place.'

She stopped. Her face was rising and falling through a range of emotions.

'There was someone . . .'

I gripped her arm. She looked over at the yellow-haired man; she was worried that he would hear. She shook her head.

'Tell me,' I said.

— 6 —

'You missed the competition?'

'Yes.'

'How long was it before you played again?'

'Two months. I'd severed a tendon. I had to have physiotherapy.'

'The hospital knew how you'd been injured?'

'I told the physiotherapist that I'd cut my hand fighting.'

'Why didn't your grandmother tell anyone about your bad dreams?'

'She was frightened.'

'She told you about your grandfather?'

'Yes.'

'Were you frightened?'

'Yes. I knew – well, I sort of knew then that it was never going to end.'

'Why?'

'Because it was in my blood.'

'Ok, we'll stop here. Relax. I'll pour some coffee.'

Another cassette. Another day. Dr Chase is in a hurry. I wonder why. Are we getting closer to the trial? He hasn't said. In fact, he's hardly said anything at all today. It's all been questions and answers, the yes and no of my life.

He comes back with the coffee, smiles professionally and selects another cassette from a drawer in the desk. Now he frowns as the telephone rings. He picks it up. I hear the tinny voice of a woman. His secretary? I don't know. Perhaps his wife.

'No,' he says and frowns again. 'I'll let you know.' He puts down the telephone and makes a face. 'The newspapers,' he says.

'What do they want?' I ask.

'Your story,' he says and, seeing my stricken face, adds: 'Don't worry, I'm not going to say anything.' He frowns. 'Where were we?' Then he answers himself by turning on the cassette machine.

'Tell me about your grandfather.'

I lean back in the chair and close my eyes. Now I'm back in the hospital, but this time I'm lying on a bed under a green sheet with my arm outstretched for the doctor who is stitching my wound with what looks like black fishing line. The nurse pats my arm as everything explodes in white sparks of pain.

'Don't worry, it'll soon be over,' she says. 'You're being very brave.' She sounds Scottish, but I'm not sure. Everything seems strange and foreign now.

The nurse walks over to the other side of the room to fetch something, cotton wool or another cold silver probe, I don't know. I've never been in a hospital before. The nurse has a big fleshy bum which swings from side to side like a cow's udder, and soft breasts. I watch her as she fiddles about near the sink. The doctor calls her back and she drops something in the sink. Forceps, he asks her for the forceps. There is another piece of glass buried in my arm.

I close my eyes again. I let myself go back there. My grandmother is breathing heavily as she begins to tell me.

'It started when he changed jobs. He'd been working on a reservoir project and he liked that. He used to fish at lunchtimes and he would bring his catch home, lovely rainbow trout. He liked them grilled, plain, no butter or anything. He preferred things to be simple.

'Then the company moved on to a big motorway project. They made him site manager. There was more money, but I could tell he wasn't happy. He looked so tired all the time, really worn out; his eyes would be red and sore. He said it was the cement dust, but I knew it was tiredness.

'He couldn't sleep at night. He said he was worried about the machines. There were problems. I didn't know what, but he said some of the machines were dangerous.

'He started kicking in his sleep. I got bruises. When I showed them to him, he said it was the machines. He told me he had dreams of fighting the machines. They were getting out of control.

'I begged him to see a doctor, but he wouldn't go. He didn't believe in doctors. He said they were like engineers: they couldn't diagnose the whole of the problem.

'I told no one what was happening. I didn't want to worry your dad. He was busy writing his bird book. Theresa was helping him by doing the typing, and what with looking after you and everything, they had enough to think about.

'They came round the week before Christmas. The book was finished and they were so excited. They brought the atlas with them to show us where they were going in the mountains. We stayed up all night talking and laughing and drinking the wine they'd bought to celebrate. But after they left, your grandfather Frederick said he was disappointed. He'd wanted us all to spend Christmas together.

'We saw them off at Taunton Station. They looked so young and I remember remarking to Freddie how much in love they seemed. Your mother was singing. She looked lovely in her coat. It had a big white fur collar and looked nice with her hair. It was so red, redder even than yours. Your dad looked so handsome in his big green overcoat. They were like Omar Sharif and Julie Christie in *Dr Zhivago* going off to the snow.

'You started crying and Theresa got upset. She didn't want to leave you, poor thing. She was crying and Donald was looking worried. You got worse and worse. You were getting blue in the face and kicking your legs. No one knew what to do with you.

'Freddie took you from Theresa. The train was coming in and

they had to get on it. Freddie found something in his pocket and gave it to you. It was an old egg timer, a lovely thing with coloured sand. Donald had found it in an antique shop. He'd given it to Theresa the first time he went travelling without her. I don't know why Freddie had brought it. Maybe he was going to tell them to take it for good luck. He was a bit soppy like that.

'Anyway, Freddie took you off down the platform and you stopped crying. The train went, and we stood there for ages looking at the track, not knowing what to do. It was sad to think that we wouldn't see them for a month.

'After a few days we got used to it. We liked having you to ourselves, it was like having Donald all over again. We were a bit naughty and let you sleep with us even though you had your own cot. You looked so funny curled up between us like a little piglet. You slept right through the night and it helped Freddie get a good night's sleep. He said the dreams weren't so bad when you were there.

'We started preparing for Christmas. Freddie went up to Mr Wilsher's and bought dry logs and a lovely tree. We put it in the window and I started making decorations for it. I stayed up late, working right through the night. Freddie had gone to bed early. I remember that night he said he'd felt properly tired for the first time in weeks. Anyway, I had just finished the last angel when I heard him coming down the stairs. I thought he was coming to find me. He always missed me when I wasn't there. He said the bed felt too big without me, even when you were in there with him.

'He was in a state. He was crying. He couldn't tell me what it was at first. He just stood there like a little boy clenching his hands into fists. I was worried. I ran upstairs. I thought something had happened to you, something terrible like he'd rolled over and crushed you in his sleep or something. But you were sleeping peacefully with your mouth open.

'I came back down and Freddie told me. He said it was a dream. He couldn't get it out. It was like some devil tormenting him. I tried to take him in my arms but he pushed me away. He said that we had to phone to find out if it was true. But he wouldn't tell me what it was all about. I shouted at him then for the first time in my life.

'He said he was leaving. I told him not to be silly. I made

some tea and he came up behind me and put his head on my shoulder. I could feel his tears running down my neck. He said he was so worried. He'd dreamed that Donald and Theresa were trapped in deep snow on the mountain. It was so real. He could still see it all. Theresa was buried up to her neck and she was screaming to Donald to help her, but he couldn't hear. He was completely buried. More snow started coming down and rocks and great lumps of ice. It was awful. Freddie said it was as though the sky was coming down.

'He went on like this all night, crying and shouting. I thought he'd gone mad. I wanted to call a doctor, but he wouldn't let me. He just kept saying over and over again that he knew it was true.

'We must have fallen asleep in the sitting room. I don't really remember because it was all so terrible. The telephone woke us. I picked it up. As soon as I heard the foreign voice, I knew.'

The tape recorder stops and I open my eyes. I feel disoriented. Where am I? A hospital, but this is not how it was. A doctor, a small doctor with a moustache, now I remember. I was telling him something. What was I saying?

He left her one hundred pounds on the kitchen table and went back to Austria. His brother was still living there. He ran an antique shop. He never wrote. He left her. He left her alone with me.

'You look exhausted,' the doctor says. 'Shall we call it a day?'

— 7 —

It is hot again. The sky is shocked of colour and over the great white lake of sea the seagulls are flying in slow motion as if they are drugged. Two red fishing boats rock gently up and down on the water. From here the boats seem tiny, like pearls of blood on a white belly. One of the fishermen throws out a line in a silver arc fine as saliva and laughs with his companions. The nearness of their voices disturbs me. There is something disorienting about hearing them speak so clearly and not being able to see them. But then all my perceptions are shifting now. I wouldn't be surprised if the fishermen could read my mind.

Odd thoughts. They keep coming and going, rising and falling. Just like the fishing line. Another one skims across the sea. I imagine eating mackerel, digging my fork into the tough brown muscle, and then the taste, not fishy at all, meaty and surprisingly sweet and melt-in-the-mouth. But I don't know why I'm having such fantasies. I feel no real hunger. Food, proper meat and gravy and vegetables, seems to belong to another world, one I left behind long ago.

A hot breeze pricks my genitals. It doesn't matter if I stand naked here. There are only the gulls to make remarks. A herring gull taunts me now with an off-key 'mark, mark, mark', coming in so close I can see all the knife-sharp edges of its feathers. It turns swiftly, making me think of an ice-skater twisting on a blade, and then dives cleanly into the sea near the fishing boats. A moment later it pulls back, beak empty, screaming furiously at the missed opportunity.

I remember the music competition and how that had seemed like a missed opportunity. I thought I would never make it as a pianist and the scar on my wrist was an itching reminder of my failure. But Sergei had saved me from going under. He pushed me on to practise, ignoring my complaints when my part-healed hand swelled and throbbed. 'Pain is in the mind,' he would say as I wept with frustration. 'You must overcome your mind to achieve your dreams. You must forget even that you have a mind. Your body is everything. Your hands and your heart, they are the essence of your art.'

'But it's real, Sergei. The pain is so bad.'

He cuffed me hard on the side of the head. 'Now you have a choice, boy. You can run away or you can fight me, make me feel pain, but will that make your pain go away?'

'No,' I sobbed.

'So what is left to you?'

'Work.'

'Good. At last you are learning.'

I won the competition the next year and jubilantly carried my trophy home. My grandmother was waiting for me in the garden. She hadn't come to the Albert Hall. She said she had nothing to wear. She couldn't go somewhere posh like that in her gardening clothes and anyway she wouldn't know what to say to the other boys' parents. 'They talk fast up there. I wouldn't be able to keep up,' she'd said.

She had cooked a celebration meal, a great golden pie with leeks from the garden and steak. It was the first time I remember eating steak. We drank home-made elderflower wine and then Sergei arrived with a bottle of Stolichnaya. He poured three tiny glasses. My grandmother protested but he ignored her and said that we were not allowed to drink until he had made a toast.

'No Russian drinks vodka without a toast,' he said solemnly, lifting the tiny glass to the light. He put it down again – too close to the edge of table: I had to move it with the tips of my fingers – and began to speak. The toast went on and on. It was like a song or a prayer. I watched his lips move, wondering what the words meant. Was he quoting something? There were no gaps or pauses as in English, just this glorious rolling sound that was closer to music than language. Sergei's eyes were closed and he looked younger, or maybe it was the midsummer light turning everything golden. His eyelids were deep and heavy, the colour of dun leather, and I could see his eyeballs moving, seeming almost to keep time as he spoke. I closed my own eyes and let myself drift on the strange and beautiful sound.

'What, Andrei! You have gone to sleep.'

'No, no. I was listening. What were you saying?'

'Drink!'

'No, I mean, can you translate it for me?'

'It is not possible. I do not know how.'

'But your English is so perfect, Sergei!'

This amused him. He bowed his head graciously.

'Thank you, Andrei, my son Andrei. Come on now. Drink!'

I let him go first. He swallowed his vodka in one gulp and wiped his mouth on his sleeve. I did the same. The Stolichnaya tasted of nothing, but it was so cold and oily it set my teeth on edge.

'Another?'

'No!'

'But you must make a toast, Andrei.'

My grandmother's place was empty. She must have gone to bed during the long toast and I felt a little pang at not saying goodnight to her. At the same time I was glad she had gone because there was a strange warm feeling in my stomach which I quite liked and wanted to keep to myself.

'To Sergei!' I held up my glass. He had filled it up to the top this time. 'For. . . for – ' Now I didn't know what to say. I could think of no words to express what I felt for Sergei and I knew he would make a joke anyway. 'For everything!' I finished lamely and downed the vodka in one.

We carried on drinking. Four, five, six glasses. Sergei was now proposing toasts in English and they were getting louder and louder.

'To Andrei, may you have as many women as you have fingers and toes!'

'What, only twenty?'

'You did not let me finish the toast, rude boy. May you have as many women as you have fingers and toes – in one night!'

'That's impossible. I would die.'

It was strange behaving like a man. I had no idea what sex felt like although I thought it would probably be nicer than doing it to myself with soapy hands, but I realised that it didn't matter. I could pretend that I knew and Sergei could pretend that I was really a man and we could share jokes and Stolichnaya. The boy in me was thrilled senseless by this and I commanded another vodka. Sergei poured and missed the glass. I laughed and licked the stuff off the table. It was great pretending to be a man.

Sergei started talking about a Russian author called Solzhenitsyn who had written something about cancer, but I found it difficult to concentrate as everything was becoming blurred and when I sipped my vodka the glass banged against my teeth. Sergei carried on and on about the Gulag and camps and this cancer ward and was getting quite carried away, pounding his fist on the table, setting the cutlery and plates rattling. Then he started on the time theme again, only this time it wasn't his time that he said had been stolen, it was his soul, his Russian soul.

'Sergei, I want to ask you . . .' My voice sounded thick and sort of older. 'What happened to you in Russia?'

'It's in the past, Andrei. The past means nothing.' He took another slug of vodka.

'But, Sergei, you think about the past the whole time.'

'What do you mean, boy?'

'Your newspapers, you *live* with the past. It's all over your house.'

'That is not the past, Andrei, that is history.'

'It's the same thing, surely?'

'No, I have no past. I have only history. Those papers, you think they mean something to me?'

'Well, yes.'

'They mean nothing. I bought them. Do you understand, Andrei, I *bought* them. I paid a collector a lot of money for them.'

'You've never read them?'

'No,'

'But why?'

'It is enough to have them.'

Years later it all made sense, but not then. I could not understand why having a history was so important to Sergei. What did it matter? He couldn't do anything about it. It seemed crazy to me. Looking back now, I can't believe how ignorant I was.

The following year I went to university and felt even more ignorant. It shocked me to discover how much I didn't know and I set about trying to educate myself as quickly as possible, often skipping music lectures (of course I studied music, I knew nothing else) to read poetry or study the big science books which fascinated me. I delved into Gray's *Anatomy* one day, *Butterflies of the World* the next and in the evenings learned how to drink blackcurrant and lager without throwing up and roll a tight spliff, Then there was sex. I lost my virginity to a philosophy student, two years older than me, and not a virgin.

We met in the student bar. She was wearing jeans and a rugby shirt. Sara was her name. She drank pints and mixed with the First XV crowd. I usually avoided them. They made me feel too tall and too thin, like a white plant grown without light. They were all shoulders and thighs, haunches and big knuckles. A rich smell came off them, a little like roasting meat.

Sara hung around with them but she never really spoke to them. She let them buy her pints and then stood with them drinking in sulky silence. She chain-smoked roll-ups and sometimes she let them light these for her. Once I saw her kiss one of them. It was late at night and the bar was closing. I couldn't be sure it was her because he was blocking my view with his broad rugby player's back. He'd got her in the corner of a wooden bench. All I saw was some hair her colour, a sort of dirty blonde like trampled-on animal straw, weaving from side to side, and a pair of girl's feet in black velvet hippy shoes. I left before they broke apart.

The night we met, Sara was on her own. She was rolling one of her cigarettes at a table. I was going to sit away from her, but she looked up and smiled as I walked past.

'Hello.'

'Hi,' I said. My chest hammered once very hard as she smiled again. She had a wide, curling mouth like a cat's.

'You're the pianist.'

I liked that. As if I were the only one. At the time I was at Exeter University there were several other piano players much better than me. My chest hammered again.

'That's right,' I said but my voice didn't sound like my own. I realised with horror that I was putting on a slight American accent to flatten my Somerset vowels. I coughed. If she noticed, I would pretend I had a sore throat.

'So, why are you here? Shouldn't you be practising or something?' She made a dancing movement on the table with her fingers, which were long and slender and stained with dark-blue ink. Her nails were bitten down to the quick.

'I want to read a letter. From my grandmother. She lives in Somerset.' I couldn't believe I was telling her this.

She wrinkled her nose as if she could smell the country air coming off me. 'Is that where you're from?' she said. 'I thought there was something funny about your accent.'

'Yes. What about you?'

'Yorkshire, lad,' she said broadly, then made her voice posh. 'Harrogate, actually.'

She tossed her dirty-straw hair and blew some smoke at the ceiling. My stomach did a backflip. I offered to buy her a drink. She accepted and that was it. I was hooked. We talked some more and then went back to her room for a pizza. I piled it on thick. I played a Rachmaninov tape which I found in the bottom of my music bag, and then carried out Sergei's three-minute trick on the remains of the soggy cheese-and-tomato crust in the pizza box.

[62]

'Wow, that's really existential. Did someone show you that?'

'No, I thought of it myself,' I said. To cover up my embarrassment I kissed her. She tasted of tobacco and beer and something else, sweeter and exotic like coconut.

She put her tongue in my mouth while I was kissing her. It detonated me and without really knowing what I was doing I slid my hand under her shirt and felt her breast, which was not hot as I had imagined a breast would be, but surprisingly cool and unyielding. She pulled her mouth back and I saw my saliva glitter streaked on her chin, which excited me so much I nearly blew it. My knees were like melting cheese and colours were flashing through my mind in a crazy fairground whirl. She had my shirt off now and her long inky fingers were kneading and pinching the skin on my back. I reached down to my jeans, set myself free, and then went in.

She shouted when I came. My name and God's as if we were one. I couldn't see her face because of all her dirty-straw hair. I raked my fingers through it quite hard, clearing a space around her eyes.

'I think I love you,' I said.

She threw back her head and laughed. I felt everything in me die. Everything went hard and prickly as if crystals in my blood had frozen. I moved, trying to get away from her, but she tightened her grip and jack-knifed herself upright. Now she was crying.

It was close to dawn when I left. I crunched across the frosted grass and took great gulps of the cold air. Before I went into my own hall, I stood looking at the dying moon. It was high in the sky and wrapped in a shawl of soft blue cloud. I shuddered as the moon fell and then went out of sight as the sky closed in. I felt proud but also very afraid.

In bed I opened my grandmother's letter. She had written about her morning at the market. A gust of wind had blown over her stall, scattering her insects and pictures in the street. 'My dragonfly got the worst of it,' she wrote. 'The wings were all torn. I'm repairing him tonight.' She added that the 'home brew', as she called her perfume waters, was selling well, especially to tourists.

She left the news about Sergei until the end. She didn't want to save me from shock, she was telling me things the way they

[63]

happened. Her letters always followed the same chronology, starting with the most recent thing and working back. She had last seen Sergei two weeks ago. She wrote:

I saw him in the High Street and he walked straight past me. I had to run after him. I thought he looked ill. His face was grey and his clothes were in a terrible state. I asked him if he was all right. He said he was, but there was something odd about him. It was like he didn't know where he was. Then I saw that he was blind. It's very sad. I will try to visit him more often, but you know what he's like.

At midday I woke screaming. A terror had got hold of me. I was buried alive in a piano. The lid was too heavy to lift. I screamed and screamed. The students next door banged on the wall.

'Oh, for Christ's sake, shut up, will you! We can't stand it any more.'

Sara and I started seeing each other, as it was called. We didn't do much. We stayed in her room and played tapes, drank wine and fucked. She called it that. I preferred to think of it as making love, but I didn't tell her. I wanted to do things her way. I thought it would make her happy and not leave me. So we drank white wine when I would have preferred red and smoked roll-ups when I would rather have had a cigarette and fucked on the floor or against the wall when I would have liked to do it in the bed. I asserted myself only by leaving her room every night, very late when I thought she was asleep.

One night she sat bolt upright in bed as I disentangled my limbs from hers.

'Why do you always sneak out?' The sharpness in her voice surprised me. 'Do I snore or do funny things in my sleep or something?' Her hair was wild, all matted and knotted from our lovemaking a few hours before. 'I'm not letting you leave until you tell me.'

My heart started to pound. Jesus. What could I tell her?

'It's not you, love. It's . . .' I hesitated, playing for time. 'It's – oh, shit, I'm sorry, Sara . . .'

'What? Do you want to finish?'

[64]

'No!' Now my voice was sharp. 'I don't want that at all.'

'What then?' Her blue eyes glittered in the dark. 'Why can't you spend a whole night with me? I want to know, Andrew.'

Nausea swirled in my guts and I had to lean on the door for support. She sprang out of bed and ran over, pressing her naked body against me and teasing her tongue in my ear.

'Come on, come back to bed, come, come, come on.' This drove me wild when she said it while we were in bed and she knew it. She grabbed my hand. 'Please, Andrew, please. Come on.'

I tried to pull away, but every part of me now wanted her. I could do it. I could stay awake. I would use my old trick, biting on my fingers, on the half moon where it was most painful: it always kept me awake. I let her pull me towards the bed, then I suddenly saw my own bed and heard once more the terrible knocking on the wall. It was getting bad. The students next door were now trying to evict me. I pulled my hand free.

'Andrew, what's wrong? Don't you want me any more?' She started to cry. I couldn't bear it. I put my arms round her and kissed her. I brushed the hair from her eyes and looked deeply into them. I needed her to believe me.

'I will stay all night when I've finished.' She started to speak but I put a finger to her lips and held her tighter. 'I'm working on something at the moment. It's a concerto, it's inspired by ... well, by us. I need to work on it when everything is still fresh in my mind. It's so difficult to get into it later in the day when I'm tired and anyway I want to see you. So that's where I go. That's what I've been doing.'

Her body was soft in my arms and I felt myself weakening. I could stay awake. I didn't have to leave. Her eyes were shining.

'Wow,' she said.

At Christmas Sara went home to Harrogate. I saw her off at the station. She leaned out of the window of the train and we kissed. She tasted of brandy and the peppermint she'd sucked after we left the station bar. 'My father would hate it if he knew I smoked,' she'd told me. I tried to imagine her parents. She said they were middle class, plump and boring. They were retired teachers, but they still did voluntary work. Her mother bred dogs, lhasa apsos.

'Goodbye.'

'Andrew!'

'Farewell then.' I forgot she hated 'goodbye'.

We kissed. The whistle blew. Our lips fluttered in alarm, but still we did not break away. The train sagged and then slowly started to move. Sara handed me a small gold package.

'What's this?'

'Christmas present. Don't open it now.'

The package felt heavy.

'I didn't get you anything.'

'Don't worry. Work on your concerto.'

I held her hand and walked with the train until the end of the platform. She blew me a kiss after I let her go. I stood for a long time staring at the track. An icy wind blew seed husks and a few dry leaves across the rail. An odd feeling suddenly drifted through me, a tingle which was both familiar and strange. I wondered if this was *déjà vu*. What had she said? 'It's like looking into the mirror of your past.' She said she'd felt it the first time she saw me.

Her train vanished. The wind settled down and I suddenly became aware of the station, quiet and huge like a great glass cathedral. The platform was empty. Not even a pigeon came to settle on the narrow grey aisle. I waited for a sound, an announcement, a rumble, a click of heels, something to set me on my way, but the stillness remained. It seemed to grow heavier, thicker. Everything was suspended under the glass dome of the station roof in a perfect calm that anticipated nothing. What lay beyond had gone speeding down the track, never to return. I shivered at the thought and broke the silence with my own ragged breath. It turned to mist in the icy air.

On the train to Taunton, I opened Sara's present. It was a heavy ball of glass, hand-blown, and inside it a blue lozenge of more glass studded with air bubbles like spheres of mercury. I held it up to the window to catch the light. The whorls of glass were a world within a world, an underwater reef which ebbed and flowed depending on which way I tilted the glass. I looked into the ball all the way down to Taunton, holding it against the window to catch the reflections. Trees, fields and streams flashed by in a distorted watery glass blur which eventually hypnotised me into sleep. The guard had to shake my shoulder to wake me up.

Wells was quiet and cold. My grandmother's chilblains were bad and she looked tired. Her eyes were circled with dark-blue shadows and her skin had lost its girlish bloom. She looked strained as if she were resisting something, a pain or an ache, or maybe just the passing of time. Seeing her like this made me realise for the first time that she was old.

She said it was the cold. 'It's got into my bones. No matter what I do I can't keep warm.'

'You need central heating, Nana.'

'Pah! What's wrong with logs?' She threw another one on the fire. It sizzled as the sap began to ooze out. There was a strong smell of resin. The log spat and crackled and sweated furiously but gave out little heat.

'Your logs are wet.'

She said nothing. There was a distance between us and a tiny spark of hostility which fizzed, not knowing whether to explode or gutter out. I felt strange in the house. Too big in my army coat and heavy boots, too stompy and awkward. The walls shuddered and the floorboards creaked as I paced about. I felt as if I could have brought the house down with my own nervy vibration.

My grandmother shivered and sighed: 'I can't bear this.'

A chill gripped me. For a wild moment I thought she was going to tell me she didn't want me here.

'Do you think it will snow?' she said.

I looked out of the window. It was late afternoon and quite dark. The apple tree was still and white. The branches glimmered in the dark as if already dusted with snow.

'I don't know. Maybe,' I said.

'I hate the snow.' My grandmother rubbed her stomach and then her arms. 'I hate it.'

'I'll buy some dry logs tomorrow,' I said.

We ate a silent supper of cold ham and potatoes and frozen beans. I tried to tell her about university, but she didn't seem interested. She smiled, but her mind was somewhere else. She kept looking at the kitchen clock and then out of the window, as if expecting someone or something. My mind drifted to Sara and

I felt a pang. My grandmother pushed the dish of potatoes towards me.

'Eat some more, love, you look thin.'

'I'm not hungry,' I said and put down my knife and fork, too loudly, on the white plate.

'Are you well?' She was looking at me intently now. I knew what this meant. 'Are you well?' was a code. She could never ask directly if my nights were bad.

'Everything's fine,' I lied. 'No problems at all.'

She sipped her tea and looked at me over the rim of her cup. I could not be sure, but I felt that there was a tiny softening of the strain around her eyes.

'That's good,' she said. 'I'll come with you tomorrow to get the logs.' She got up and kissed me goodnight and I smelled the familiar lily-of-the-valley scent of her powder. I kissed her on each cheek and the chalky softness of her skin took me by surprise. I had grown used to harder, more vinegary sensations. I hugged her and she sniffed my hair. I wondered if she could smell Sara.

I looked at the ball before I fell asleep. It was calming to watch the glass pattern contract and expand. I remembered the quiet of the station, the strange feeling of everything being held. I'd been tantalised by it and also troubled. I did not know why.

When I woke I felt something had changed. I got up and went to the window. It had snowed. The garden was covered in thick white folds of the purest snow I had ever seen. I opened the window. The air was warmer than I expected and I leaned out further, feeling a crazy euphoria which made me want to leap from the window. I was so far out I could touch a branch of the apple tree. I flicked it with my fingers and watched, delighted, as the light, bright snow fell in a shimmering shower to the deep bed below. I pulled back from the window and got dressed quickly, pulling on layers of odd clothing, and then I heard a sound from the room next door. I hopped over and opened the door so I could hear better. I thought maybe my grandmother had gone to sleep with the radio on. I listened. The noise was muffled, like the hooting of an owl from a distant wood. She was sobbing.

Dr Chase wants to know about the drugs.

'It was only dope, nothing serious,' I tell him.

'You didn't experiment with anything else?'

'Well, cocaine.'

'What about heroin, LSD, uppers, downers, amyl nitrite?'

'No, none of that.'

'Good,' he says. He makes a note on a white pad. He has tiny handwriting. I can't read what he's written. It doesn't look like words, more like a code consisting of blips and dashes like Arabic. He gives me a small grim smile. There is a tension between us today. Normally he sits next to me in one of the airline chairs, but today he has retreated behind his desk. I wonder if he has done this to make a psychological point: he's firmly in charge, drumming his fingers impatiently on the wooden desktop, while I'm sinking into my chair so deep and comfortable it could be a bank of snow. Deep and terrible.

'Would you say you are a heavy drinker?'

I wonder what he means by 'heavy'. Two or three bottles of whisky a week, was that heavy? I always thought I drank within my limits. I mean, I was never drunk on stage. Well, only once slightly in Berlin, but it didn't affect my playing, added to it if anything, judging by the reaction from the audience: four encores. No wonder that oboeist wanted to punch my face in . . . Dublin? Oh, God, I was very drunk then, but that was afterwards. I wonder if I should tell Dr Chase about the car accident.

'I suppose I was,' I say hesitantly.

'What's normal for you?'

I wonder why Dr Chase insists on using the present, as if I haven't changed, as if I'm still where I was, as if I'm still free to drink and not here in a state of sober suspension in hospital.

'Two bottles, sometimes three. A week,' I say.

Dr Chase's neat face registers no judgement as he makes another note. I wonder if I'm an alcoholic.

'Two, sometimes three bottles a week,' he repeats. We could be talking about bottles of milk, his expression is so bland.

'Yes,' I begin to feel defensive. 'It's not unusual among musicians. I've known others drink a bottle a day.'

Dr Chase lifts his hand. 'Don't worry, you won't be judged on how much you drink, but the court will need to know if you were affected by alcohol or if you have a history of heavy drinking. Unfortunately it can exacerbate sleep problems.'

'I was not drunk,' I say flatly.

'I don't believe you were,' Dr Chase says briskly. 'Don't worry, it will be a minor point. I also have notes on your accident in Ireland.'

I stiffen. I was incredibly drunk then. I passed out at the wheel. I could have killed someone, not just nearly myself. I wasn't charged, although I should have been. They took enough incriminating samples at the hospital. At the time I wondered if the effect of the trauma had somehow mysteriously diluted my urine. But when I found myself in the hands of a charming Irish female doctor who patched up my wounds with lingering attention, I suspected that those guilty phials had received a touch of the same Irish magic. There are other rules for artists in Dublin, confirmed when the doctor accepted my dinner invitation after my discharge. I drank mineral water, she champagne. I could not take my eyes off her blue-black hair, her glittering eyes, the intriguing slopes and curves freed at last from the confines of starched professional white into liquid turquoise silk. The magic lasted through the night . . .

You despicable bastard. How can you think such thoughts at a time like this?

'Will the court need to know about the accident?' I ask.

Dr Chase shuffles through some notes in a clear plastic folder. 'I see you had a brain scan,' he says wearily. 'This may come up, but only to confirm that there was no lasting damage. You see, a blow to the head can also influence sleep, but as you were suffering from a disorder quite clearly *before* the accident, it should not be an issue.'

I relax slightly.

Dr Chase changes the tape. I stare out of the window. In the distance, I can see a gardener pruning the rose bushes with a huge pair of secateurs. The sky is a dreamy blue. My throat

[70]

constricts. There are no clouds, only an endless sea so pure the sky could have just been born. I have a sudden delirious urge to go up in a balloon.

'Were you sexually active at university?'

I don't reply. I'm up in the sky, floating, feeling free. Pure and naked and clean. I've left the darkness.

'Andrew, this is important.'

'Yes, I was. Very,' I say belligerently. Now I want to tell Dr Chase to fuck off and leave me alone.

'I'm sorry, but could you elaborate?'

'I fucked five women a night, drank six bottles of whisky a day, didn't wash, never went to lectures and I fought in the pubs. Will that do?'

Dr Chase rewinds the tape, wiping out what I've just said.

'I know this is difficult. You may feel that you are on trial already, but I do need a full picture of your history. The court may need to contact some of your sexual partners.'

'Christ, why?'

'Well, there are no living witnesses of your sleeping behaviour.'

'I didn't *sleep* with them, doctor. I fucked them.'

'Would you like a coffee?'

'No .'

I have a sudden shocking vision of myself in the dock. I am wearing my performing suit, which is soiled with grime and dust from being kicked and trodden upon. I am dangling, waiting for the hanging. At the same time I am hanging on for dear life, clinging to this last crumpled image of myself. A puppet man with the strings cut. Watching and waiting are the white faces of my first hostile audience.

'Are you sure?'

Yes. I'm sure. I'm guilty as hell.

'Are you sure you wouldn't like some coffee?' Dr Chase says again.

I nod weakly. 'All right.'

He gets up, failing to suppress a slight sigh. Anger buzzes in me again.

'I didn't sleep with them,' I say as he stirs milk into our cups. 'I always left them afterwards. I didn't want to frighten them. I never let anyone sleep in my bed.

'Here.' He hands me the coffee and a box of tissues. Then he leaves me. He takes a long piss in his *en suite* bathroom. Or maybe he just waits respectfully behind the white door. He knows I hate crying in front of him.

I don't sob. I haven't been able to do that yet. I cry silently. The weight of my tears surprises me, the solid heaviness of the moisture which thuds into my lap like a shower of hot stones, soaking my pants around the crotch area. It looks as if I've wet myself.

Now I feel real revulsion. It's not just the humiliating soaking, it's also the feeling of being inside my own skin. The itchiness, the acid burning in the stomach, the restless, shifting agony of having to be here like this. It feels as if all the badness in the world has got under my skin. All the diseases, all the terrible deaths and shitty crime and filth and muck and grime are crawling around just there under my skin. I can feel it twitching and pricking its way along, silting me up with blackness. With absolute blackness.

'Look at this,' I say as Dr Chase comes out of the bathroom. I bunch my hands into fists. 'Analyse this.'

He is momentarily caught off guard and I see something like panic flicker across his face before he checks himself.

'Your self-hate is understandable,' he says evenly. 'But it's important that you learn to forgive yourself. I've been thinking about ways to approach this – '

I swing round in the airline chair. 'I can't bear this.'

'Go on.'

'I don't want to go on, that's the whole point. I'm angry and afraid and sick, sick, sick of myself. I don't want to talk about it. I don't want to forgive myself. How can I, doctor? How can I? You tell me. You have all the answers.'

I'm feeling irrational, wild and out of control. I want to set the airline chair spinning crazily on its axis. I want to shatter glass, overturn furniture, ball up all the papers, the awful evidence of my life, and send them flying around the room like hail. I want to fight. I want peace. Oh, Christ, I want this to end.

'Be a little kinder on yourself, Andrew,' Dr Chase says. He leans forward. There is a sad, appealing look in his eyes. 'There are many people who want to help, but you must allow yourself to be helped.'

'I can't be helped,' I shout. 'You can't cure me!'

My chest is hammering and there is a terrible ringing noise in my ears like hundreds of wind chimes all being played at once. Maybe I'm about to have a heart attack. Good, that would solve everything.

'Would you like to go for a walk?' Dr Chase asks.

'What?'

'Just down to the garden. It might help.'

'Yes, all right. I'm sorry.'

Dr Chase helps me to my feet and half supports me as we walk to the door. The telephone rings. He ignores it and we go out to the corridor. He lets me go and walks a few paces ahead. I follow him slowly. I feel like a sad animal. A toothless circus tiger that has been prodded into submission.

A young Japanese doctor, bristling with pens, rushes past us with a flurry of 'hiyas' and little bows. I shrink from the small ceremony and turn my face to the wall. Now another pair of white coats, a man and a woman, deep in consultation outside an office. Through the glass door I glimpse a computer terminal, potted geraniums and a smart woman talking on the telephone. The hospital feels charged, wired up, busy installing order into the minds of the disconnected. The restless atmosphere, tinged with a smell of new paint and citrus air freshener, sets off a jangling in my nerves.

We pass a television room and there I see my first patients. Three men and a woman, faces impassive in the blue glare of the screen. There is a small pot of plastic flowers on top of the TV and on the floor three overflowing ashtrays and three identical mugs of tea. No one talks. No one rocks or moans. No one even moves. The men and the woman look like wax.

Dr Chase opens a heavy lead-glassed fire door at the end of the corridor. It leads to the hospital garden. I can see a wedge of green, and I hurry towards it.

Outside now, and the trees and grass look blindingly bright as if they've been dipped in some chemical gloss. The birdsong is too sharp, a great zoo screech which makes me grit my teeth. Everything out here seems too harsh, too frighteningly well-lit. Even the air seems to be glaring.

Dr Chase walks to an archway of roses. He stops and clips off a bloom with a small silver pair of scissors which I realise he must keep in his suit exactly for this purpose.

[73]

Through the arch there is a small stone quadrangle with a fish pond in the centre. There are two wooden benches, one on each side of the pond. Dr Chase selects the bench drenched in sunlight and motions me to sit down. He joins me and places his bloom – a perfect white bud – in his buttonhole. He sniffs it once, shuts his eyes and stretches his arms back over the bench.

'That's better,' he says.

I allow myself a cautious draught of the morning. The glare has worn off. The air now feels moist and inviting like a much missed mouth. It feels good.

'Have you ever thought about what happens to the past, Andrew?' Dr Chase asks.

He is still leaning back with his arms folded behind his head. He is not looking at me but at the sky.

'I used to believe I lived for the present.'

'The past may have its own future.' He says this musingly, as if it's an idea he's suddenly plucked on impulse, like the rose.

I don't reply. I am watching a corpulent goldfish gliding around slowly just below the surface of the pond. I concentrate on its mouth, the opening and closing O. It looks as if it's trying to speak, trying to communicate some unfathomable thing. I look for other signs of pondlife, but the great fish seems to be the only inhabitant. The pond water is oily, almost black. A few giant lily pads relieve the gloom, but they are dusty and old, cracked and curling at the edges. A single pink flower blooms, but it looks artificial. There are plump cigarette ends floating in the water. One has a smear of bright red on the filter. I wonder if Dr Chase brings other patients here in times of crisis.

'Maybe the past becomes the future,' Dr Chase says. His eyes are still closed.

'I don't know,' I say and return to watching the fish. I like the way it lies under the surface, both provocative and repellent in its cold, gold beauty, listing slightly on its plump belly as it searches the filthy water with an unblinking, primitive eye. Here's natural order, I tell myself. The rules aren't being broken down there.

Dr Chase is bending down looking for something under the bench. He comes up and in one quick movement tosses a small stone into the pond. With a twitch of a thick gold tail, the great fish dives out of sight. I am left looking at ripples.

'There's your past,' Dr Chase says. 'It forms rings around you.'

I look at the swirls of water and then at my psychiatrist, who is grinning.

'The past never stops, it keeps moving round and round us. It's not too difficult to see how a wave can sometimes engulf us.' He throws in another stone for effect. 'I know this is a very crude demonstration, but it might help you understand how you came to be so caught up in the waves of your own past.'

I nod. But I'm not really interested, I'm feeling too dull. The heat and the smell of the dank pond mingling with the sickly-sweet perfume of the roses is making me feel drugged.

'Our minds pick up the past all the time, but we reject it because we are too busy with the present.' Dr Chase's voice is sleepy, hypnotic. 'The past confuses us, we can't exist on two time planes at once, so we sort of cancel it out. The past then floats around looking for some place where it can come to life again, become present again. It requires a receptive place, a fluid environment untroubled by the demands of daily living – we can't hear our past clearly when we're living from day to day. We get snatches from time to time, fleeting memories, and sometimes we daydream or make up stories to amuse our friends, but most of the time the past eludes us. It waits for a quieter time. It waits for sleep, for the barriers to come down. We roam through the past easily in our dreams and in our nightmares. We believe in it. We accept all distortions and live as if it were now. We do not think we're *reliving* until we wake again.' Dr Chase looks at me. His quivering little face is rapt.

'Interesting,' I say. But I feel irritated at his enthusiasm. How can he expect me to get excited about this? I lean my head back against the bench. The wood is warm against my scalp. I close my eyes and wish I could sleep. I wish I could sleep as I slept before I knew dreaming. I wish I could sleep away the past. In my mind, I see a small boy in a pushchair, laughing and kicking his legs, trying out new words, delighted with himself. He knows nothing about fear. He sees a great golden building surrounded by a cool green moat where ducks and splendid white swans are gliding. The sun glints on the white feathers. The boy laughs and hurls a chunk of bread into the water.

Someone is there behind him to catch him, to stop him falling in. But he has no fear of falling. He does not know there are murky depths. How can he? He is a fish. A free-swimming fish. A fish who swims through the past without fear.

'Your night terrors come from the past, you know that?'

'Yes,' I say wearily.

'Your fear is part of the past.'

'Yes.'

'And now, sadly, part of your present and your future.'

I open my eyes. 'You mean I will always have the terror?'

'Possibly not. There are drugs . . .'

'But they can't wipe out the past.'

'No.'

'Then there is no hope for me.'

'Andrew, there is always hope.'

I close my eyes again. I wish I could believe him.

'Dreams are the strangest phenomena in human behaviour,' he says. 'Although they belong to us as products of our minds, we cannot really control them. We cannot help what we think in our sleep. Every night our dreams send us, in the accepted waking sense, completely mad.'

I feel absolute defeat. I slump back against the bench and look up at the sky. It is a great, soft blur.

'Andrew, I'd like to try some experiments. You are not under pressure to take part.'

I look at him. He is playing gently with his ludicrous moustache.

'What sort of experiments?'

'Well, firstly, I'd like to analyse you in a sleep laboratory.'

'What the hell's that?'

'Don't worry. It's quite painless. We just monitor your sleep with electrodes. Your brain draws a map. You won't feel anything.'

'What's the second experiment?'

'Hypnosis.'

'Can I think about it?'

'Of course.'

He gets up then and shakes me by the hand. It is a curious, almost brotherly gesture, as if we are not psychiatrist and patient but a couple of old friends who have just spent an hour or so chatting about the strangeness of life in a pretty garden.

'Stay a while,' he says.

I watch him walk away, light on his feet, so neat and self-contained. As small and precise as I am large and out of control. He does not even need to dip his head as he passes under the rose arch.

I stare at the pond. The fat goldfish, disturbed by my shadow, dives again. I pick up a small stone and throw it in. I throw another, aiming for the centre of the ripple. I miss, pick up another, throw, miss again. Then childishly I grab a fistful of stones and hurl them as hard as I can into the water.

— 9 —

On Christmas morning we walked through the snow to the cathedral. My grandmother pulled her blue shawl tight around her shoulders and throat and half covered her face. Only her eyes showed, red-rimmed and bright, as she stepped cautiously through the snow. She lifted her boots high and winced each time she set down her foot as if the white powder was caustic.

The snow was deep. At least eight inches had fallen overnight and the sky was a dull metal-grey colour. A chill wind blew across the road, lifting the top layer of snow from the deep drifts on either side. A flurry swirled around my grandmother's head. She shuddered and pulled her shawl tighter.

I took her arm and felt her tremble. Her eyes above the shawl were moist and I felt a sudden overwhelming surge of tenderness. I pulled her closer to me, wanting somehow to protect her. She leaned against my shoulder and we walked pressed together, like a pair of strange lovers, into Cathedral Close.

There was a choir of children singing outside the cathedral. They were dressed in red coats with white fur hoods and red boots which they stamped as they sang 'O Come All ye Faithful'. Their breath formed a single white cloud of vapour over their fur-shawled heads, making them seem like angels caught in a mist. Behind the choir, the cathedral soared, a great golden ship sailing across the snow-swollen sky, swaying with its Gothic passengers, the almond-eyed angels, martyrs and kings and queens. The children finished their carol and coughed and rubbed their hands before starting another, 'Hark the Herald Angels'. Their voices were thin in the icy air. We listened for a short while longer and then walked inside.

The cathedral was warm and lit by hundreds of ivory candles. People smiled at my grandmother as we walked up the stone aisle to a bench near the front. We squeezed our way to a space in the middle of the bench and sat down and unbuttoned our coats. The smell of incense and the steamy dampness of snow melting on coats made me feel suddenly drowsy. I closed my eyes and felt my grandmother shift on the bench. I heard her sigh, then a rustling sound of her thick skirt brushing against her nylons as she went down on her knees. I opened my eyes. She was resting her forehead on the wooden shelf holding the red hymn books and blue prayer books. She was pressing so hard, the wood left a red line across the centre of her brow.

I felt embarrassed watching her pray and looked away. My gaze settled on the great cathedral clock. The strange timepiece with its night-sky background painted with stars, three circles of green and gold, suns and moons and Arabic numerals, had always seemed to me too exotic for a place of worship. The hours and quarter-hours were struck by automata, jousting knights and painted horsemen wielding hammers. One of the horsemen wore a big helmet complete with ears which gave him the strangest appearance of half man, half rodent. The clock had fascinated me for years. It was both a painted nursery toy and a mysterious mechanism of magic and astrology. My grandmother told me it was the oldest clock in England.

There was a Latin inscription around the clock's moon-plate: *Sphericus archetypum globus hic monstrat microcosmum.* One day I had plucked up courage to ask a verger to translate if for me. He said it meant that the clock represented the universe in miniature. I was dazzled by the idea that a clock could mean so much. I asked the verger if the medieval universe was different from our universe. He said he didn't really know but he thought it might have changed a bit.

My grandmother nudged me in the ribs. Everyone else in the

congregation was standing up. I stood up slowly, trying to make it look as if I had been simply leaning forward and not slouched in a star dream. She nudged me again and I joined in the carol. 'Silent night . . . All is well, all is bright.' My grandmother had tears in her eyes as she sang and there was something defiant about the way she tilted her head just a little further than normal, as if she was letting all her sorrow run down her back.

Every year around Christmas it was the same, especially if it snowed. She would remember the avalanche and mourn her son. After she had prayed, she would be more like herself again. But it was hard for her being with me at this time. I reminded her too much of my father. I had reached my full man's height now and my voice had deepened and although my hair was still my mother's strong red, it had lost all the softness and lightness of childhood. I would say things sometimes or gesture in a particular way and she would draw in her breath sharply. At other times she would simply stare at me, bewildered, a distant look in her eyes.

After the service, we walked to the tree surgeon's house to buy some dry logs. My grandmother loosened her shawl and stepped lightly through the snow. Two spots of colour glowed in her cheeks and her eyes darted to the hedges as she looked out for treasures for her pictures.

We drank a glass of port while the tree surgeon, a big, soft-voiced man called Tom Wilsher, packed our logs into three plastic sacks. He offered to drive us home in his van, but I told my grandmother I wanted to walk for a while. She touched my arm before she climbed into the van with Tom and told me not to be too late. She was cooking goose for lunch and didn't want it to spoil.

I went to Sergei's. His cottage looked deserted as if no one had lived there for years. All the curtains were drawn and the snow path to his front door was completely smooth except for a thin spiky trail made by a bird. The cottage seemed so shuttered I thought that perhaps he had gone away. But in the years I'd known Sergei he had never gone anywhere. Not even to Bath.

I stamped my feet on the path. The snow had a thin crust on top which made a fudgy crunching sound as it broke under my boot. I shouted. My voice sounded strange in the snow-thickened air. I shouted again, but the cottage remained silent and still.

I went round to the back. The old sofa was still there, a robin perched on the antimacassar, pecking at the lace. The sight cheered me and I rattled the back door and shouted again. But there was still nothing. I took a few steps back, thinking that I would look for a stone or something to throw at his window, when my eye was caught by a bundle wrapped in a sack. I kicked it. It felt solid. I thought that maybe Sergei had been clearing things out, but I knew he never threw anything away. I knelt down in the snow and opened the sack. Inside was a pile of newspapers tied with blue string. I flicked through the papers and started to shake all over. Sergei had thrown out his history. I couldn't believe it.

Now I wanted to leave. It seemed that he was preparing for something. He wouldn't want me to see him. He would be ashamed. I started to walk away. Then I heard a scraping noise come from a small dark window at the top of the cottage. It was him. He was fumbling with the window latch.

I ran back, slipping on the snow. 'Sergei, you old bastard, it's me Andrew – Andrei!'

He had the window open. Now he leaned out cautiously. He was a wearing a sort of white smock which fell open to reveal his chest. His old man's skin looked pink and tender like a wound. His face was contorted with the effort of squinting to see where I was.

'Andrei!' At least he sounded pleased.

'Were you asleep?'

'I have the flu. It came all the way from Hong Kong.' He laughed and then coughed. The noise was terrible, like the barking of an old seal.

'Can I come in?'

'You will catch it.'

'I don't mind.'

'No, leave it for another time. We will drink vodka.' He coughed again and gripped the windowsill, knocking off flakes of blue paint which drifted down to the snow. I flinched. He seemed desperately ill.

'Have you seen a doctor?' I shouted.

He waved a carbuncular hand. I couldn't tell whether this meant yes or no.

[80]

'Sergei!'

'Go home, Andrei.'

I moved back a few paces and my foot touched the bundle of papers.

'Your history is out here, Sergei, all your old newspapers.'

'Leave them!'

I looked down at the bundle. I knew I would take it home.

Sergei gave another rasping cough and then released a spume of phlegm. It fizzed as it hit the snow. I noticed there were tiny flecks of blood in it, like the merest smear of embryo in an egg yolk.

'Sergei . . .'

'We will talk next time, when this has gone back to Hong Kong.'

'Let me come up.'

'Go home. It's too cold.' Another cough. This was tiring him. It was better to leave.

'All right. Look after yourself. Call the doctor again. Merry Christmas!'

Sergei shook his head as if he didn't know what I was talking about.

I stayed with my grandmother until New Year. The last of the snow melted on New Year's Eve and she was cheerful again. She even made a picture, a winter collage of berries and silver-birch leaves, which she gave to me as a present for Sara. I'd told her that I had a girlfriend one night when we were sitting by the fire. I hadn't intended to, but the smell of woodsmoke had reminded me of Sara. My grandmother had smiled girlishly and asked the colour of her hair. 'Is it red like yours?'

'No, blonde.'

In the last week, the strain between us dissolved and we talked freely. I told my grandmother about Sergei's illness and she said she would visit him. We even looked through his old newspapers together and she became quite animated and started telling me stories of the past. She had a vivid memory and once the stories started they were unstoppable. She told me about the red, white and blue dress she wore on the day of the Queen's coronation and all about the street party afterwards. She knew exactly what

[81]

she had been doing when Neil Armstrong stepped on the moon. 'Making a rhubarb crumble. Can you imagine? Someone was walking on the moon while I was making a crumble!'

It was wonderful listening to her. She talked about the past like an old friend and I found myself wanting to write down the things she said. I was worried that I would forget her stories as soon as I left the fireside where the warmth and dancing light of the flames seemed to illuminate some deeper part of us both. I remembered the sacred ibis, the Egyptian god of stories, and wondered if the old bird was still soaking up stories. Maybe it had become too wise or too weary. How could one creature, even a god, take on the whole history of mankind? It was never ending. The thought occurred to me that maybe each one of us was the sacred ibis. We all carried stories with no beginning and no end. We were the story. The complete history. I wanted to tell my grandmother this, but didn't know how.

We spent New Year's Eve talking over a bottle of port. We were so wrapped up in talk that we forgot to keep an eye on the time. It wasn't until we heard the cathedral bells that we realised the New Year had begun. We went out into the garden and looked up at the sky. The clear ringing seemed to come straight from the stars. We held hands and she pointed out the winter lozenge etched into the blackness. It replaced the summer triangle. I looked at the stars. They seemed impossibly distant and I knew I could live and die thousands of times before I reached one, but just seeing the patterns up there, glittering unchallenged, I felt part of something.

I returned to Exeter feeling renewed. I threw myself into work and my tutors were impressed. Before Christmas, I had been warned I would scrape a third if I was lucky. My performance had been uninspired and my composition ragged and rushed. I had not even bothered to attend theory of music and history lectures and had spent most of my time in the bar or the library, listlessly flicking through magazines. Now I stayed in the music theatre until late at night, practising, reading and composing until my fingers ached and my eyes streamed.

At first Sara was delighted with the change. My new energy fuelled our sessions in bed, which became operatic. I even spent whole nights with her, never sleeping properly – I was too overworked to sleep – but it was enough to stop her wondering about my deeper state of mind. She told me she loved me every day. I told her I loved her too.

We started talking about what we'd do after we graduated. She wanted to spend a year travelling and then start a PhD. I found myself agreeing to go to Mongolia with her. I had no idea what I'd do in Mongolia, but the thought of a vast and limitless space both appealed and appalled. I would compose, I told myself when my stomach contracted at the thought of all that emptiness. I would compose an opera.

Sara started washing her hair every day and gave up smoking roll-ups, which made her put on weight. While I pushed harder at my studies, she seemed to lose interest in hers. She seemed to become softer. I didn't know why. I had no idea that there were degrees to this feeling we called love. I didn't even think about it very much. I accepted our situation, our togetherness, and tried to get on with my work.

Sara became sadder. She said I no longer talked to her. She thought I had lost interest in her. I said that my work had to take priority. She knew I was desperate to get a first. She became depressed. Her own work seemed to mean nothing to her, which infuriated me. I shouted at her: how could she give up now?

Every time I saw her she cried. Her whole body seemed filled with tears, they came from every part of her. There was something magnificent and even brave about her grief. I tried to comfort her but everything I did seemed to make it worse. I began to feel awkward around her. Her grief was relentless, a great flood. I was almost drowning in it. And like any stupid drowning man, I panicked and lashed out. Sara bore my insults and my rages silently. She said I had no idea what it was like to really feel.

I asked her what she meant.

'I always felt there was something remote about you. Something untouchable. Sometimes you're so cold. It's as if you're frozen inside.'

'I'm an artist,' I said. 'I need to withhold part of myself for my work.'

Sara shook her head. 'No, Andrew, it's more than that. I feel

[83]

it's more than that.' She started to cry again. I stared at her helplessly. There was something about the way she'd said 'frozen' that disturbed me.

I worked harder, pouring all my frustrations into my playing as I pushed towards the first. Sara was by now seeing the university psychologist. We didn't talk about her sessions. We didn't talk about anything. We lay in her bed side by side both staring at ceiling, wondering if there was anything we could say.

I got my first. Sara took a second, which I think surprised her. I went to Somerset to celebrate. Sara couldn't come. She had to go home to Harrogate to meet her sister, who had arrived unannounced from India. Our parting was neutral. I kissed her cheek at the station. Her skin was cool and smelt unfamiliar. She kissed me back and then looked away, her eyes glittering. There was no intimacy. We didn't know each other any more. We said goodbye.

— 10 —

Dr Chase has wired me up to his dream machine. I am pinned down, skewered on a high white bed like some sort of ghastly exhibit. Wires criss-cross my naked body in taut lines, all different colours, connecting me to a bank of machines consisting of matt black boxes like a complicated sound system. There are dozens of dials on the system and tiny red and yellow lights, which flash every few seconds.

Dr Chase twiddles one of the dials behind my head, checking it against another small time machine in his hand.

'Everything all right?'

I smile grimly. I am freezing cold. The air conditioner is turned up too high, presumably for the machines, but I don't want to ask him to turn it down. That would mean more adjustments, more fiddling with buttons and dials. I'm so unnerved by all this gadgetry that already I'm close to telling him to stop the experiment. I just want this over with.

Dr Chase checks a wire. 'Right, everything's on line. Sorry, it took some time. This was the worst part; now you can relax.'

I manage a rigid smile.

There are two silver electrodes taped to both my palms, which, despite the cold, are beginning to sweat. I want to scratch them but flex my fingers instead. I look at the white skin of my arm puckered around another cold electrode and a bubble of hysteria balloons. What if something goes wrong? I see my fingers scorched black as winter hawthorn, my head exploding on the pillow in vivid technicolour, my balls shrivelled into two blue sloes stripped of skin – the whole of me hollowed out and stinking of fire.

Dr Chase writes something on a yellow pad. He looks up and frowns absently. He's wearing a white coat today and looks like a real doctor. His brow is corrugated with concentration and his eyes are sharply mathematical. His hands as they check my wires are dry and cool.

The wire connecting the electrode to my prick is looser than the rest. I put it on myself while Dr Chase showed professional disinterest by busying himself with the electrodes on my head. My prick is smaller than I have ever seen it: it looks like a small brown bird foetus curled up softly above my mildly throbbing balls.

'Nearly there. Everything OK?' Dr Chase asks.

'This could be my most explosive erection ever,' I say.

He laughs. I sense he's pleased I'm making a joke of all this. It makes it easier for us both.

'I'm going to give you a sedative and then we'll be ready for lift-off.'

'OK.'

But I turn my head away as he prepares the syringe. I hate needles. God, I should be used to them by now, but I can't bear the terrible small stab of steel breaking through skin. It sets my teeth on edge like no other sensation. A needle prick is a tease, a dreadful feeling. I'd much rather deal with real pain, a solid punch or kick or burn. Something to get my teeth into.

My arm goes dead. I try to lift it up, but it feels weighted to the bed as if it has just been pumped full of sand. My lips start to tingle, then my scalp. It feels as if something is crawling around in my hair, a small mouse, needling its claws against the thin skin, or an insect, rushing madly in and out of the red roots.

Dr Chase pats my arm. His eyes are calm as they hold mine. I

[85]

try to relax, but my nerves are itching to be pulled away from this wired trap. I clamp my lips together and set my teeth.

Dr Chase walks away to the other side of the room to a glass box which I realise is a recording room. His voice is loud and has a metallic edge as he speaks through an intercom.

'Can you hear me all right?'

'Yes, fine.'

I'm surprised I can speak. The tingling sensation is getting worse, and as I articulate the words, my own spittle burns me.

'I know it's difficult, but try to relax.'

I raise my eyes, it seems easier than trying to laugh, but as I try to bring them down again, they seem stuck in my head, stiff like a Victorian doll's eyes.

'Try to breathe normally,' comes the metallic command.

I try to think of something to calm me down. The fat goldfish swims into mind, then flicks out again. Dr Chase says something else, but his words are drowned by a loud buzzing noise right in my head.

'Andrew, can you hear the alarm?'

So it wasn't my imagination.

'Yes.'

I feel tired. I wish he'd stop all this, turn off the terrible black boxes and let me sleep. The room seems to have warmed up. Perhaps he did turn the air conditioner off. I try to focus on him, but he has become a white blur, frantically pushing buttons in his glass box, a dream doctor trapped in an aquarium.

Then he pushes me out on a wide, grey road. I don't know how he does this and I don't question it. I'm still on the bed, but sitting up and a belt is digging into my chest. I'm being carried and I realise I'm not on a bed at all but some sort of stretcher. I can see fields and small black and white shapes on one side of the wide road, which seems to go on for ever. I am enjoying the sensation of being rushed through the night, like an Indian prince on top of an elephant. The view from up here is magnificent, a rolling panorama of grey and green and gold. We pass through a canopy of trees. I can see birds clinging to the branches with tiny bronze claws, their delicate heads buried under wings in sleep. I feel euphoric, enraptured with the scene around me, and I reach out and let my hand brush the leaves. The tiny birds remain asleep and I ache with tenderness for them. They seem so vulnerable and I can see their hearts, no bigger than a seed, beating under creamy down feathers. My bearers slow down. I'm close to a branch and I reach out, intending to softly stroke one of the birds. It seems important that I should show them I mean no harm, that I'm just a passing visitor, a well-meaning stranger in this exotic, peaceful land. But as I reach out, my hand jerks and I knock the small creature from its perch. I'm thrown into a panic and shout to my bearers, who bring me down abruptly, jarring my back. I undo my belt (there is a metal clasp like that on an airline seat belt) and rush over to the bird. It has landed in a pile of white feathers and is completely still. I'm terrified, but as I pick it up I see that the bird is not dead, only stunned. It is soft and warm and flutters in my hand as I stroke the feathers and look into its golden creature eyes. The bird makes no sound. I carry on stroking but the movement of my fingers on the soft down suddenly becomes uncontrollable. My fingers jerk rigid and involuntarily I start to squeeze. I try to release my grip, but my fingers press even tighter, seeking the hot, damp throat, slim as a stalk. Now I'm crushing bone, I can feel it grinding into splinters, shattering into particles and I can't stop. It's as if some dreadful magnetic force is driving my hand. I bite the inside of my mouth, trying to transfer the pain I'm inflicting. The bird's tiny tiger-jewel eyes bulge and I can feel its heart maniacally beating like a hammer in a watch gone crazy. Then suddenly it stops. The bird is a velvet rag in my hands.

The alarm wakes me. I'm confused and the first thing I do is check my hands. They are blue-white and shaking. The whole of me is trembling with great rippling waves of shock.

'You experienced a terror.' Dr Chase disconnects the electrodes from my head. He looks grim. 'Was there dream content?'

I don't speak. I don't want to go back there.

I get up and put on a thick towelling gown, thoughtfully provided by Dr Chase, and walk around the sleep laboratory. The shaking takes a long time to subside. My limbs ache and my mouth feels sore. I recognise the metal taste of blood and run my tongue around the inside of my lower lip. It is rough and swollen. My head feels soft, sort of displaced, like the feeeling after a bout of vomiting or hysterical sobbing or laughter. I turn

[87]

and see Dr Chase in the glass box, holding up a long sheet of paper, squinting at the madness I've just spewed up.

'All right?' He comes out with the papers under his arm. I know he's excited by what he's seen and for a moment I hate him for it.

'We'll go in here.' He indicates a door which I thought led to a cupboard, but it turns out to be a small, windowless consulting room.

There is only one chair, made of moulded plastic. Dr Chase sits in it. I have to hop up on a narrow bed which juts out like a shelf from the wall. It is quite high and I miss my first attempt at swinging on to it. Dr Chase laughs. 'That should be easy for you with your height.'

He spreads out the papers on a metal desk. From my elevated perch, the scribbled graphs look like tribal maps to some secret territory, or mountain peaks caught in a thunderstorm.

My brain drew this. It's surreal seeing in picture form the wild contents of my head. This is the force, the sickness, the ... No, don't, this is a – what did Dr Chase call it? – a polysomnograph and it means nothing.

It means everything.

'Do you want me to tell you what it means?' Dr Chase asks.

I nod.

He starts jabbing at the graph with a pencil, leaving small dots on the peaks and troughs. They are regular at first like a series of fine zigzags.

'Your first sleep phase,' Dr Chase says. 'Nothing unusual here.'

He moves the pencil further along. Here the peaks suddenly jump into tall, thick lines, and then further across to a dark mass of clotted ink.

'Stage Four sleep. Your night terror occurred here,' he says, jabbing at the dark clot.

I look at the frenzied pattern and feel weak.

'If you want a real measure of the terror, look at your heart rate,' Dr Chase says.

'Cardiotachometer, is that the right line?'

'That's the one.'

My heart rate had spiked sharply, rising from eighty beats per

[88]

minute to one hundred and sixty then peaking at one hundred and seventy-six.

I'm horrified. 'It's more than doubled.'

'Astonishing, isn't it?'

'Considering I'm not awake.'

'The equivalent when you're awake would be having an orgasm.'

I glance down to where my prick is hidden under the gown.

Dr Chase knows what I'm thinking. 'There was no erection. Also normal.'

Thank God.

Back in my room, but the experiment is not over yet. Dr Chase has asked me to record everything I remember about the dream. He has given me a tape recorder. I turn it on, speak my name and then play it back. My voice sounds remote as if I'm lost on a road somewhere and calling home. I click off the recorder. I don't want to go over the terror, it's still too close. I can still feel that awful fluttering in my hand, still see those tiny trusting eyes.

I run a bath and watch the water splash randomly from the high-pressure taps. The water foams as it swirls into the smooth trough of enamel. I step into the bath and lie down and close my eyes, but I can see the black lines again. The waves of madness. I feel utterly weak as I realise how trapped I am. I'm at the mercy of those peaks and troughs. I can't control them. The terrible electricity inside me has a mind of its own.

I climb out of the bath. This is ridiculous. I'm going off my head. I wish I could play. No, I don't. I'm never going to play again. Remember that. I know, I'll just go to the wardrobe and look. Nothing else.

I go over and slide open the door carefully as if I'm expecting an animal to be crouching in there. The smell is rancid and wild, like a goat I found decomposing once on the cliff. It's my suit. It stinks to high heaven. Just look at it, remember, nothing else. It's an old suit, 1950s. Good heavy cloth, but soft. I could really sink into this suit. It knows me, this suit. I've worn it for every concert. The jacket arms are long. I always had problems getting suits to fit, and before I was earning enough to have one tailor-made, I had to find one. I spotted it in Portobello Road on the day of my first big performance – I can't believe I left it that late. The stallholder was about to pack up. Very camp, very impressed when I said why I wanted it, very reluctant to give it to me for my price. I finger the cloth. This suit. How could I have wanted to destroy it? She pressed it for me that night. She hung it up in the bathroom and afterwards it smelled of her.

— 11 —

I wake wet. It doesn't happen often and I am surprised to find my hand curled around my prick which is still firm and sheathed in a fine pale web. I try to remember what I've been dreaming, but nothing comes. I lie on the damp sheet, not wanting to get up, feeling weak. I haven't been eating. Nothing for three days except tea and some sugar I crammed into my mouth last night when I ached for another sort of sweetness.

The hut smells sour. I can see mould patches billowing between the wooden beams in irregular greenish-yellow stains, like rotting clouds. A huge fungus has appeared under the window. A monstrous thing, pale golden with laced edges, oozing like some festering animal organ.

I heave myself out of bed. The floor is damp and sticky beneath my feet and cluttered with crusty tins of milk and beans. I know I should wash, but there is no soap and my towel is black with mould. I shove some more dry sugar in my mouth and almost retch as the sickly crystals dissolve on my tongue.

I look at myself in the spoon. My distorted face looms like a bruised mushroom, puffy around the two black holes of my eyes. Shocked, I make myself disappear with my own breath.

I leave the hut and begin the climb down the cliff path. Sweat slithers down my legs and I have to keep stopping to control a lurching dizziness. Red and green light spots swim before my eyes and the noise of the flies and bees is loud and discordant. The dry earth crumbles into silken, slippery dust, rising in a fine red spray which stings my eyes and fills my mouth with a gritty sweetness reminiscent of the dry sugar.

I reach the end of the path. The erosion is worse here. The cliff looks stripped, red and raw as I imagine the face of Venus, closer to the sun than earth. Nothing grows here. A few bleached branches are strewn about in casual bundles like the bones of a small animal. No gorse or greenery, just smooth red earth all the way to the beach where I can see a man hitting a piece of wood with a hammer. The great hopeful ocean of sky above seems a disconsonant backdrop against the stark waste.

The village is quiet and I realise that I don't even know which day it is. If it's Wednesday or Sunday, the shops will be closed. I won't be able to buy any food unless I catch a taxi to Sidmouth. This worries me. The crowds, the noise of crying children on holiday, pushchairs polythened against the seaspray, spilt ice cream, the yellow-eyed gulls plump as white pillows, the astringent smell of fish and chips, music from cars. There will be people walking arm in arm, perhaps lovers. I couldn't face it. And the awful possibility that I might be recognised, a hand on my arm, unfriendly: 'Hey, aren't you the pianist, the one who . . .?'

The village shop is open, but I hesitate before I go in. I know my wild appearance will cause a stir. People are conservative down here. There will be talk.

I pretend to look at the window display so I can check myself properly in the glass. I am much thinner, stringier, as if I've been stretched, and my hair is longer than I imagined and bristles with burrs like the coat of an old sheepdog. My beard has grown down to my throat. I run my fingers through the coarse hair and cringe as I find sugar granules.

Walking into the shop, I am momentarily blinded in the half-light, and stumbling I grope at a shelf. Tins and bottles crash to the floor. The shopkeeper, an elderly man with thick glasses, looks up in alarm. Cursing under my breath, I mutter 'sorry' and pick up a wire basket.

The shop is well-stocked and I buy cheese, bread, two dozen cans of Carnation milk, canned fruit and soup, tea and a glass of Devon honey. The label tells me it is locally produced. I am grateful for the dark as I go to the checkout, where the old man is talking to a woman. I stand behind her broad back and listen to her. Warm local accent. Something about bees. She shows the man a sting on her arm. It is right in the soft place of the inner elbow, a small red nipple surrounded by a lighter circle of pink.

[91]

The woman gently rubs the wound with the tip of her finger and winces. The man asks whether she has tried vinegar.

I am quite happy to wait. Their murmurings are calming and I know they haven't recognised me. They would have said something by now. The shop has a waxy pungent smell of old cheese rind, candles, paraffin and smoked bacon. I breathe it in deeply, recalling the hundreds of other times I stood here, clutching at my grandmother's skirt then, sucking on a Fox's Glacier Mint. I wonder if the old man still gives them to children.

The woman laughs and turns towards me, her eyes lit with curiosity. I bend down to pick up my basket and then a stomach cramp grips me. The contraction is so sharp, I can't straighten up immediately. Another stab and I grab my gut in a panic, and then I feel it. The touch on my arm, almost a caress, a reaching-out stranger to stranger. So strange to be touched after all this time.

'I'm all right,' I say, but my voice sounds hoarse, seized up from too many silent days – and nights, I can't help thinking – oh, Jesus. The woman removes her hand and there is an embarrassed shuffling as I pay for my goods and rush out of the shop into the sun where I stand for a while, breathing heavily. She comes out and asks me if I'm ill. Her scent is warm and heavy, like the honey in the glass which she tells me comes from her bees. I thank her for her concern, nothing is wrong, I say. She nods and walks off down the village, swinging her shopping bag.

Sitting in the sea now, dipping my fingers in the honey and sucking them. The salt stings my legs, biting into the tiny cuts I received during my ragged climb down the cliff, but I don't care. I'm almost grateful for the pain. I heave myself in over the stones and let the waves break over me.

The love of women. I grabbed it once as hard as I now push it away. I had to have it. I commanded it. And I was lucky. Women came to me easily. They were drawn to me, lured perhaps by the well of dark, the frozen centre which they hoped to thaw with warm womanly love. I didn't tell my women about the terror. I didn't need to. They recognised it. It was a challenge for them. They didn't know what they were fighting at the time, and then, of course, neither did I. I had never even heard of terror. I believed what my women told me. I believed in my own enigma.

I got over Sara surprisingly quickly. My joy at achieving the first-class degree overwhelmed any feelings of guilt or remorse as I threw myself into my new life. The life I'd always dreamed of. The life of a famous pianist.

I became famous quickly – some have said too quickly. 'Too much, too soon' was a criticism that nudged its way into most of my early reviews. My pieces were wildly improvised and under-rehearsed, but they always provoked a reaction. In the early days, purists registered their protest by walking out on some of my more extreme interpretations. I was accused of murdering Mozart and carving up Chopin. But I didn't care what people thought. I was flying so high, I believed I was above criticism. The music I played did not belong to Mozart or anyone else. It was my own dangerous creation.

I was determined to break every musical boundary possible and invited fire-eaters, ballet stars and jugglers to join me on stage. Each concert became an event with lights, colour and special effects. The press did not know what to make of me and I was called many things from the 'greatest virtuoso of the twentieth century' to 'monster maestro'. I was devil, angel and snotty graduate all rolled into one. I was mad. I was not going to last.

I didn't care. I was making vast amounts of money, drinking gallons of whisky and rumpling sheets in the best hotels in London, where I lived like a spoilt prince, pampered and protected by my women who glided around my concert parties in shiny black dresses like tame seals. I signed myself over to as many as possible. Even my autograph was promiscuous.

It went on and on. I lived in a rainbow blur, dashing from hotel room to bar to café to dinner party to stage. In between, I rushed down to Somerset, breaking the speed limit all the way in my sparkling silver Lotus Elan. My grandmother was pleased at my success, but she had no idea of the *excess* of it. She didn't read newspapers and had got rid of the television after I left. She lived as she had always lived, quietly working on her pictures, tending her plants, visiting the cathedral, and laughed at my suggestions that she should move.

[93]

'Why should I come to London, love? What could I do there?' she would say. 'It's too late for me to move.'

I left her bundles of guilty cash on the kitchen dresser before rushing back to the city. I hoped she might take some of the money to Sergei. I didn't visit him. I started to several times and once even got as far as his cottage door. There I hovered and heard him playing Rimsky-Korsakov, bravely, beautifully, blindly. But I had to turn away. It was too much. Everything about me was too much.

Did I know it couldn't last? I didn't want to think about it, I was so caught up in the whirlwind of my own success that I had no time for contemplation. I lived at full speed, cramming in everything as fast as possible. I barely had time to sleep. Remarkably, my bad dreams virtually disappeared. I still had occasional horrors, but most of the time I was unaware of them. My sleeping partners told me that I thrashed and moaned at night, especially before a performance, but when I woke I was unable to remember what I'd dreamed. I tried not to think about the past. I convinced myself that if I dwelt on the demons they might come back.

I stopped living in hotels and moved to a musical house in Ladbroke Grove. There were five of us, two male violinists from the City Orchestra who were engaged in a passionate, plate-throwing affair, a black jazz singer whom I rarely saw because he slept all day, and his girlfriend, an actress who was training to be an opera singer. It was a noisy, invigorating time, full of laughter and argument. The house bristled with competition and the neighbours frequently complained. We called ourselves the Loud Crowd and intimidated the local bars and cafés.

I continued to work hard on my reputation both on stage and off. I revelled in the intense erotic power I could whip up simply by stepping from the piano and throwing back my head. I wore my hair in a ponytail for performances and acquired a gold earring. My dress shirts were never ironed – I don't think the house in Ladbroke Grove possessed an iron – and I bought more antique evening suits from the market in Portobello Road. I spent my money on cars, drink and women. Anything my friends and companions asked for, I bought. Designer clothes, jewels, electronics, exotic fruits. One woman – Marianne, Marina, Marcia? I can't remember now – told me her brother had contracted hepatitis while travelling in Malaysia. I paid for her to fly over to join him. I never saw her again. One of her friends, Pauline (I remember this because she had the letter P tattooed on her right breast) told me that M had got married in Malaysia to a boyfriend who had been in jail. It didn't matter. Nothing mattered, I said that all the time. It became my maxim.

In the summer of 1988 I gave a performance at the Royal Festival Hall. As usual when I strode on stage there were cheers and whistles as I gave my trademark low bow, letting my ponytail snake across the floor. It was an intensely hot night and when I sat down my cream silk shirt was already soaked with sweat. Perhaps because of the heat, the audience seemed to take longer than usual to settle down. People were using their programmes as fans and the rustling went on and on, punctuated by dry coughs.

I flexed my fingers, tempted to play their coughs – a trick Rachmaninov had once played on an audience, skipping variations each time the level increased. The coughing calmed to an occasional snort. I began.

The opening bars were too slow and for the first few minutes it was heavy going. Then I began to relax. I forgot the sticky heat and the prickly audience and played, picking up the rolling notes, running with them, speeding them along, making the notes run into one another. Now I collided them, smashing them down hard and picking them up again. A dancer in a black tunic bolted on to the stage. Then another. I hammered the piano. More dancers appeared and then the jugglers with black and silver balls. They wove their dance around me, a black and silver flock of crows, their faces twisted into expressions of agony as they flew across the stage.

The Second Piano Concerto describes Rachmaninov's mental collapse and that night I went down with it. I plunged through the music, going deeper than I'd ever dared before. The great dark well of sound came from some subterranean depth, deeper than myself, deeper than the dark slow-moving river outside, deeper, it seemed, than the earth itself. I was exhausted as I struggled to bring the piece back to the light, forcing my way up the tempo, breathing fearfully. I reached the top and felt a rush, a surge of warmth and then the lights went up, dazzling in their brightness, and I shakily took my bow.

[95]

The roaring sounded to me like the sea. I was facing the sea. It was filled with row upon row of bobbing white faces. Some were waving as they called for an encore. But I could give no more. I backed away and slid behind the curtain, pursued by the whistles and shouts of the clamouring crowd who were now rumbling their feet in a storm on the wooden floor.

I reached the cool of my dressing room and locked the door behind me before pressing my face against the mirror with its untidy fringe of good-luck cards, horseshoes and sprigs of heather. I breathed hard and felt the wires in my fingers and toes relax. The embroidered butterfly my grandmother had given me on my last speedy visit to Somerset was lying on the dresser. I picked it up and stroked the soft wings. She had used green and gold threads and tiny jet beads for the eyes. So many hours of patient stitching. I put the butterfly back on the dresser feeling a sudden and inexplicable sense of loss.

I sat in the dark for a long time. There were voices outside, silvery whispers and giggles and the occasional tentative knock. I waited for them to disappear. I was aching with tiredness and I knew I would not be taking any fragrant, fawning admirer home tonight.

When I came out, someone moved. She was bending down outside my door and when she came up, her face flushed crimson.

'Someone asked me to give you this.' She held up a single white iris. 'I don't know who.'

She was very embarrassed. Her green eyes were all over the place, climbing up the walls, lingering on the dressing-room door, clinging to the iris, which she still held like a spear. I took it from her.

'Thank you.'

In reply, I received a full gaze of green, not so shy now, steady, almost defiant, and in spite of my earlier vow, I felt a flash of my own leap somewhere low. She was small with rough dark hair and a sulky mouth which cried out to be kissed; this mouth had received hurts and wounds. It showed in the swollen ripeness accentuated by plum lipstick. I moved forwards. She took a few steps back, light on her feet, I noticed, with a slightly affected elegance.

'I've got to go.' There was a faint upward tilt to the accent,

[96]

which I couldn't place. She moved away down the hall. She was wearing a short purple shirt with a black jacket slung over her shoulder and tight black leggings which revealed the well-developed, almost mannish muscles in her calves. I watched her legs as she walked down the hall and wondered if she was a dancer.

Just before she left, she turned and threw me an ironic smile. 'You're drooping, you know. You should put it in water.'

Her name was Natalie and the accent was Australian. She'd been brought up in Sydney, where her family still lived the life of beach barbecues, sparkling-wine parties and concerts in the park.

'Imagine life as one big beach ball,' she said. We were sitting outside on the South Bank now, sharing a cigarette, looking not at each other but at the thick black water of the Thames.

'I can't,' I said.

She started telling me about her mother and father. They were hard-working people in search of a better life, which was why her father had sold his building business and emigrated with his wife (she'd kept the books) and spoilt five-year-old daughter, taking them from their red-brick Reading home with its small square garden and creaking yellow swing to a large bungalow with huge windows and a view of the bay in Vaucluse.

'Australia is the end of the world,' Natalie said, flicking ash into the wind.

Her bitterness intrigued me. The women I met never spoke frankly about their childhood. They never revealed anything of themselves at all. But then, I suppose, neither did I.

I offered her another cigarette. She pushed away my hand when I tried to light it for her and reached into her pocket for a box of matches. Her face, illuminated by the match flare, was fierce.

'Why the end of the world?' I asked.

'The sun. It drives you mad after a while. Everything feels too exposed. Not like here. In London you can be anonymous, I mean, you could be anything. Not in Sydney. Everybody knows you.' She pulled her black knees up to her chin and hugged them.

'But you could have left Sydney, travelled around . . .'

She shot me a look of amazement. 'They wouldn't have

[97]

allowed it. They didn't like to let me out of their sight. The only-child syndrome, I suppose. Also I think they were frightened of Australia, the bush and the wild country. The *Abbos*.' She sniffed and took another drag on her cigarette.

'I was their little princess. I spent all my time trying to please them. They wanted me to become a gymnast so I used to put on my suit every morning before school and every evening and go down to the beach to practise backflips.' She hesitated. 'He used to blow a whistle from the house to tell me to come home, and I ran back every time. I was such a *good* girl. The apple of his eye.'

She laughed and rolled her eyes. 'I won tons of awards. My mother polished those bloody trophies every day. You could see your face in them, but I never even looked at them. They didn't seem to have anything to do with me.' She hugged her knees again and I found myself wanting to move closer to her. The cold wind blowing from the river was beginning to get to me after all the sweating on stage. I shuddered.

'I'm sorry, am I boring you?' she said.

'No, not at all.' I shifted just slightly on the bench towards her. I could smell her hair, warm and lemony, and see the frown line across her forehead as the breeze stirred a few dark curls. She wasn't pretty. She wasn't even my type. God, all those mascaraed blondes in black dresses, where had they come from? This one didn't even seem to care that I'd just given the performance of my life although she'd given me a flower. It was lying on the bench between us, seemingly forgotten.

She picked at her nails and stared at the river and then shoved her hands into the pockets of her battered leather jacket. 'I really should go,' she said. 'I need to get the night bus.'

'You could tell me some more.' I paused. 'That's if you want to.'

She seemed to relax and took her hands from her pockets. 'Well, I wasn't good for long. I started staying out on the beach and it caused arguments. He thought I was screwing every surfer on Bondi. I wasn't, but being accused of it made me want to. I just used to go and sit by the fire and listen to everyone laughing and playing their guitars so that I could feel part of something. One night I had too much to drink and this, well, this oaf – oh, it doesn't matter. The details are unimportant. He got me pregnant.' Her eyes flashed. 'They paid for the abortion.'

[98]

I looked at the lights melting on the water and the dark barges swaying against the tide. There was a smell of diesel and rust and musted cloth. I didn't know what to say. I sat and stared into the night and then a train rumbled across Hungerford Bridge, breaking the silence. She opened her pack of cigarettes and offered me one.

'I don't know why I'm telling you all this.' She sucked at the cigarette and blew the smoke through her teeth.

I lit my own cigarette. 'Why did you leave Australia?'

'I fell in love.' She shook her head. 'Another mess. He was married. We were both teaching at the same school.' She stabbed out the cigarette. 'I really should go.'

'What were you teaching?'

'Gymnastics. They didn't sack me, but it was difficult for me to go back there after we were found out.' She sighed and glanced up at the sky. Her small hands were clenched into fists and a minute pulse twitched at the corner of her mouth.

'They paid for me to come over here to sort my life out and, well, I don't know . . .'

'About going back?'

'Something like that.'

We both stared across the river towards the Embankment with its swinging lights and moored blue and white city ships. A party was in progress and voices and music drifted across the water. I turned towards her.

'How about forgetting the night bus and taking a cab home with me?'

She rubbed her face and frowned. 'All right,' she said very quietly.

— 12 —

The hypnosis experiment has failed. I won't go down. Dr Chase asks if he can try again. I refuse.

'I'm sorry. I'm probably not ready for this.'

'Fine, fine.' He's trying to be gracious, but I sense his frustration. His eyes give him away. The challenge has lit them too brightly.

I get up from the padded couch. My head feels clotted, thick and muzzy, as if I have a hangover. It's hotter than usual in here; Dr Chase must have turned up the heat to help send me off. But I failed to follow his directions into unconsciousness. I hadn't deliberately resisted. It was quite pleasant lying on the couch, listening to him chanting numbers backwards. Nowhere near as nerve-racking as being wired up in that ice hole sleep laboratory. But I just couldn't let go. It was as if thick blinds had unfurled in the entry cell of my mind, shielding everything. It was odd. The hypnosis experiment seemed to push me further *out* of myself, not deeper in.

I relax in the airline chair while Dr Chase decides what to do next. The chair is comforting. It's so familiar now, I could be sitting in my own armchair at home. Home? What am I thinking. What home? Whose home? The house where I lived, the place where it began and ended . . . but that's not my home any more. It's shuttered up, draped, closed. Like the rooms of my mind.

Dr Chase gets up and walks over to the window. There is something reserved about him today and he appears deep in thought. For once his hands are still. They are not fiddling about behind his back, but shoved into the pockets of his immaculate grey suit. No rose today. I miss it. Without it he appears too formal, like a headmaster or a lawyer. He opens the window and refreshes himself in the breeze. I hear the thin scream of a lawnmower and smell cut grass.

'Do we really know what terror is?' he says.

I know I'm not supposed to reply. It's an open question. He's thinking out loud again. It used to panic me when he first did this because it seemed to indicate that he knew nothing. It was up to me to give him answers and of course I didn't have any. I thought I was here to find out the answers from him. Now it's different. I trust him. I've seen how similar we are. His work means everything to him. He's obsessed. Look at the way he's standing there, staring out of the window, rocking back and forth as he forces his mind to contemplate the unimaginable. He told me right from the start that we would be working in the dark. Not enough was known about my condition for him to produce a standard analysis of what happened. He couldn't even offer me an explanation. He told me we would have to explore this alone. I was frightened and suspicious. I thought he *knew* and was playing games with me. He was playing Devil's advocate to release my demons for evidence. Now I see things differently. Now I see that we are both possessed.

Dr Chase moves away from the window and walks a complete circle before coming back to the desk.

'Most people never experience true terror,' he says. 'It's such a primitive emotion. It has no place in the civilised, sophisticated world. We've forgotten terror because we believe that we don't need it any more.'

I nod. Dr Chase draws a black circle on the ink blotter.

'Terror,' he says. 'Paralysing fear. A complete surrender. How can we live with that now? Life has become too fast. Terrified people can't live in a speeding world because they can't move. They can only stand there silently screaming while everything flashes past. They cannot even put up their hands to protect themselves. Terrified people can't move into the future because they are paralysed at one point. The point of terror.'

'But how . . . how do people, how did I become terrified?'

'It's a possibility that there is a sort of switch mechanism in the brain.'

I begin to see what this means. 'Are you saying that my switch is turned on?'

'Possibly.'

'It can't be turned off?'

'Perhaps. But we need to locate it first and discover how it reacts chemically. Also we can't switch off certain functions without knowing why they're there in the first place. It would be too dangerous.'

I slump in my seat. It sounds so far-fetched. A switch in my brain for terror. A switch which floods my mind with dark instead of light. Why? Why should it be turned on in me and not everyone else? I'm normal. The experiments in the sleep laboratory showed I was not brain-damaged.

'Why should this happen to me?'

'Andrew, it's only a possibility,' Dr Chase says.

'But it's important to me.'

'I know, that's why I'm working on it.'

Then it occurs to me: this switch idea could be a defence.

'Are you going to use this? I mean, in court?'

'Possibly, but I do have to keep to what is known about your condition, the different sleep phase, your past history and general psychological state. The court won't want to know *why* you feel terror, just how.'

'Is that why you wanted to hypnotise me, to find out why?'

'Partly. Sometimes hypnosis throws up interesting associations from the past, but it doesn't matter. I don't want to push you too hard.'

He gets up, goes over to the coffee filter and pours two small cups. I'm grateful for the hot drink. This talk of terror and switches chills me. I sip the coffee and imagine it melting something deep inside me. Maybe I'm not normal. My first lover told me I was frozen inside.

Dr Chase drinks his coffee in silence. There is no awkwardness, there is too much filling this gap which I realise is some sort of interval.

He puts down his cup. 'A dream is like a theatre,' he says. 'But the dreamer is everything. He is the scene, the player, the producer, the author, the audience and the critic. Have I forgotten anyone?'

'The tout?'

Dr Chase laughs. 'Ah yes, the tout. Jung forgot the tout. But then, all dream performances are free. We don't need touts!'

I sip some more coffee, wondering what is coming next.

Dr Chase leans back in his seat and locks his hands into a pyramid. Sunlight streams in through the window behind him, making the tips of his ears and fingers glow red.

'Let's take the dream author,' he says. 'Where does he find his fantastic story? Suppose he looks in the past. Childhood, travel, family, relationships, sex – the author can do a lot with this material. He can juggle events or leave them as they are. But as they are, they are just replays of an old story, a well-known story, which the audience has seen before. The author wants to excite the audience, show them something new, so he changes the events. Families become lovers, schools become offices, holiday islands become homes. But it's still not exciting enough. The author gets carried away. He adds a dash of the fantastic by removing earthly barriers. The players now have extraordinary powers. They can fly in space and swim underwater without

[102]

needing to take a breath. They can climb mountains without effort and speak foreign languages. They can even communicate with animals or trees. Nothing is impossible. The author is satisfied. He has created a new vision out of the old. The vision may tell us something about the past or it may not. Now it's up to the audience and the critics to decide what's happening. Another version of the story begins.' Dr Chase dismantles his finger pyramid and smiles.

'What happens if nobody turns up?' I say. 'I've cancelled concerts in my time.'

'It's the same with dreams. Most of our performances are wasted because we cannot remember them. It's like playing to an empty house night after night.'

'But what do you really think dreams mean?' I ask. I'm suddenly fed up with all this playing around with authors and critics. I want a straight answer.

Dr Chase sips his coffee and grimaces when he finds it cold. 'It depends on the dream. Big, colourful narrative dreams are important. They can tell us a lot about the past, but equally they can describe the future.'

'How?'

'In dreams our future is a point of time which is not fixed. In dreams, the past and future are one and the same because in dreams there is no such thing as time. Or time as we know it in waking life.'

I shudder. My coffee cup grates against glass as I put it down too quickly on the table.

— 13 —

My grandmother died in her garden, sweeping dead leaves from her lawn in November, the dead end of the year. I did not understand when the hospital telephoned me. How could she have had a heart attack? She was so alive, so fit from all her gardening and there hadn't been any signs. My grandmother had not complained of being ill. She said she was getting slower, but that was nothing. She wasn't slow enough yet to stop. She had more time to give. It didn't make sense. She was only seventy-three.

Natalie insisted on coming with me to the funeral. I resisted, saying it was a terrible start to a relationship. A question of bad timing – it was our first week together after we'd met at the Royal Festival Hall and we'd been in bed, we'd been making love and planning to get drunk. Now I did not know what to do. I was sorry this had to happen to her.

Natalie ignored my protests. 'Andrew?' She touched my arm. She was still wet from the shower she'd been taking when the telephone call came, and I wasn't sure if the drops on her face were water or tears. 'It makes no difference. I would like to be there.'

We went to Somerset to deal with the awful business of death. The funeral was held in a small, damp stone chapel, which smelled of dusty books, musty cloth and mouldy leaves. The rain beat down as we sent her off. It hammered on the chapel roof relentlessly, drowning our prayers, our hymns, our fare-wells. Outside we huddled by the scooped well of earth sur-rounded by flowers in cellophane so misted with rain that the blooms were obscured, and said more prayers. A boy from the cathedral choir read Henry Scott Holland's poem 'Death is nothing at all . . .' I threw a sapphire butterfly on the light elm coffin and walked away before they sent her down.

I sheltered under a yew tree at the edge of churchyard and watched the rain sweep across from the hills in a great grey sleeve. She had gone to earth and I couldn't say goodbye. They had asked me to play something in church but I'd declined. I found the idea distasteful, together with the notion that we had come to this drenched, dark place to celebrate a life. I had nothing to celebrate, I'd told the Reverend. He said that he was sorry.

I watched the rain and then I put my face against the ribbed bark of the tree and felt it burn as I rasped my young celebrated skin across it. Natalie found me. She wiped the blood from my chin with her rain-soaked fingers and led me away. She took me back to my grandmother's house and put me to bed, smoothing the cover and kissing my forehead.

'Try to sleep,' she said.

I lay under the wooden beams in my boy's room with its black

[104]

and white photographs of musicians and actors on the walls, shelves of books and music scores, seashells and wooden drawers still filled with a boy's beach shorts and swimming towels, and listened to the wind roar. The apple tree cracked outside.

'It's only a storm, love. It's only a storm,' I heard her say.

But there was no real time for grief. Death is a demanding business and there were things to be done. The house needed to be sold, things stored away, letters written, files made. I would have preferred to leave things as they were. I thought the house should have died with my grandmother, but unknown to me she had made a will.

One afternoon we had a tense meeting with a solicitor. He came round and sat in her chair. He wore a blue suit and kept stroking his legs with plump hands, a movement which made him appear both extremely nervous and smugly confident at the same time. I disliked him instantly and he sensed this. Beads of sweat appeared on his high forehead, mottled pink by the fire which drew from him a sweetish yeasty smell.

'My client has instructed that the proceeds from the sale of the house should be divided between the cathedral and the music school.'

My client. That annoyed me. My grandmother might be dead, but she still had a name. I crossed my legs and glared at him.

The solicitor hesitated, licking his lips nervously. I said nothing. He returned to the will. My grandmother had left various items of furniture to friends and charities but he reduced her bequests to the level of a shopping list as he ticked them off one by one with a cheap biro which leaked ink down his quivering fingers.

I was the last on the list. She had left me the piano and all her artwork and cottage industries, the perfume waters, the dried herbs and plants. I closed my eyes.

'I'm sorry,' the solicitor said, 'I'm afraid that's all.'

Natalie, who was standing behind me, squeezed my arm. 'Thank you,' she said coldly and went to see him out.

I spent the rest of the afternoon drinking my way through a bottle of whisky, trying to get rid of the nasty taste in my mouth. I was glad that my grandmother hadn't left the house to me. I didn't need the money, and the cathedral having been so much a part of her life, it seemed natural that her house

[105]

should be given to the house of God. I was also touched that she hadn't forgotten the music school. But the solicitor had thought I was disappointed. He thought she'd cut me out. The bastard had almost gloated. He'd recognised me, of course. He knew who I was. His eyes had gleamed, but he'd turned his curiosity into a gesture of mild disgust as he walked into the house, trailing mud on the carpet in his solicitor's stiff black shoes. I poured myself another whisky and toasted him with a curse.

Now I don't know where I am. Is it a cave? It's dark and damp and cold and I can't turn around. There is a smell of earth and underground rain and my heart is beating crazily. My hands and arms glow like white fungi and I realise I'm naked. I try to call out, but my voice seems paralysed. A wave of panic flutters in my chest, my heartbeat is so strong I think the organ might burst. I'm underground and alone and being crushed by my own heartbeat. Terror is coming in a thick yellow wave . . .

I knocked over the tea Natalie had brought me, scalding my arm.

'God, are you all right? You look terrible.'

'Bad dream.'

'I'll make another pot of tea. Here, clean yourself up.' She threw me a towel and watched while I dabbed at my arm. She looked small and distant and faintly despairing. The empty whisky bottle was between my feet.

'I'm sorry. I needed to wipe myself out,' I said.

'Perhaps you should go upstairs and sleep properly?'

'No, it's all right.'

She went out, taking the whisky bottle and the towel. I got up and walked around the room. I felt like walking outside – I was aching from sleeping cramped up in the armchair – but it was dark and cold and I did not think I could bear the smell of rain on earth. I went over to the stereo and flooded the room with music and then turned on every light. Slowly I felt the coolness of normality return.

I told Natalie I had dreamed of death. Her face, pale against her high-necked black dress, flickered with some minute emotion before smoothing once more into calm. She ran her hand through her curls which the rain had coiled into tight spirals.

'Of course,' she said. 'You're bound to dream about it. It's only natural.' She hesitated. 'I expect I will.'

I got up and threw a log on the fire. It hissed and spat and I felt my chest heave as I realised my grandmother had still stubbornly been using apple logs from the leaky shed at the side of the house. She had never even touched the money I left her. I pushed the log deeper into the fire.

'Do you ever dream that you're dying?' I said.

Natalie looked into the fire, her eyes following the small tongues of amber lapping the damp wood from which there came a sound like the mewing of kittens.

'I've dreamed of others dying.' She paused. Her face was shadowed by the flames so that only one green eye glittered. 'But not my own death. That would be terrifying.'

I said nothing. The dream was fading and I did not want to disturb her by reliving it. I did not ask her to explain her dreams either. A part of me was too unsure of her for real intimacy. We were still at the first fluttery, hovering stage of romance with each other, a sort of prelude which I did not know how to end.

The rain storms continued. The worst for twenty years, the radio said. Rivers across the country broke their banks and every night we built big log fires, using up all the apple wood. We bought more logs from Tom Wilsher, who refused payment and patted my arm as we left.

'Your grandma will be missed, you know. She was special. She cured my hydrangea, did she ever tell you that?'

I shook my head, unable to speak.

The rain started coming through the roof and we put out pots and pans to catch it. At nights we slept curled tight against each other. I felt Natalie's flat gymnast's belly rise and fall smoothly against my back and wondered what to do. What if she left me when we returned to London?

In the afternoons we broke off from the house-selling paper-work and escaped to the hills. Natalie was fascinated by the English countryside. She remembered it only vaguely from her childhood and her grandparents had lived in flat Oxfordshire. The roundedness of Somerset appealed to her and when I first showed her the Mendip Hills her face lit up like a child's. This was the 'real England', she said. She liked the rituals of country living, the smallness, the narrow cottage gardens, the heavy thatch, the slow quiet shops where everything was packed in white paper bags, the way everything fitted together.

'It works down here,' she said. 'You know where you belong. Everyone and everything has a place.'

The cathedral knocked her sideways. It was looking particularly lovely the afternoon we visited, lit with lights of deep rose, violet and gold, its fluted folds of stone shimmering like some rare and mysterious eastern silk. Natalie lay belly-down on the grass and took photograph after photograph.

'It's like Ayers Rock, I mean Uluru, with all the different colour changes,' she said, squinting up from her lens. 'It's a much deeper red now – look. It's so strange; it seems to have moods.'

I stared at the great stone walls and was suddenly struck with awe. The cathedral was so much a part of my life that sometimes I forgot to look at it. I'd even come to despise the way it had become a great greedy centre of pilgrimage, luring tourists to its obscene glass altar stuffed with foreign money. But now I felt stirrings of a sort of religious sympathy. Not for a god – I was still ambivalent about that – but for those who'd created it. I imagined the pain, grief and impassioned joy that had gone into making every arch, every flute and fold and winged angel. Looking up into the wonderful blush of colour, I saw that the builders were the true gods. Each stone bore the mark of their worship.

After Natalie had photographed the cathedral from every angle, we went to one of the medieval hotels. We drank warm ale in a dark timbered bar and listened to the soft talk of a group of old men who sat shoulder to shoulder on deep wooden benches. The men began to play dominoes and Natalie whispered that she wanted to photograph them. For her portfolio: she was thinking about taking a photography course in London.

I felt a lurch in my stomach – this meant she wouldn't be leaving – but I said nothing. I knew how easy it was to dream down here. I realised I was falling in love with her, but I also knew that when I returned to London I would be hurling myself into work again. The thought did not excite me: all the dazzle and noise and sweating excess now seemed, here in the deep comfort of the old bar, brash and utterly meaningless.

Natalie touched my hand. 'What is it? You look as if you've just had a shock.'

I looked into her eyes. I'd never felt anything like this, but she wouldn't believe me, of course.

'You should come back here,' I said.

We sold the house to a young family. The father was a carpenter who restored antique furniture. He said the house was the right size, the right age, the right everything. His wife, an exquisite creature with copper hair, walked excitedly around the kitchen with their children, a gold and cream baby girl balanced on her hip, and an older boy. He was dark and serious and recognised me immediately.

'Hello, Mr Schidmaizig.' He held out a small hand gravely. 'I really admire your playing.'

The father looked surprised. 'You know him?'

'He's famous, Dad,' the son said haughtily. 'Mr Schidmaizig is the best pianist in the world.'

It turned out that the son, Stuart, I think his name was, had won a scholarship to the cathedral music school to study violin. When I told him that some of the money from the house would be donated to his school, he was impressed.

'I suppose you don't need it.'

'Well, no, but that's not the reason. My grandmother – it was her house – she left it to the school and the cathedral in her will.'

Stuart's eyes widened. 'She must have been a nice lady.'

We were in her bedroom at the time; the others were inspecting my room. He looked around, and his eye caught her pictures, which were stacked against the wall.

'Did she do those?'

'Yes, she sold them in the market.'

He went over to a picture that I hadn't seen before. 'This one is brilliant!'

It was a snow scene worked in silver, blue and white. A fountain of icicles made from tiny crystal beads glittered next to a frozen lake where two skaters skimmed, their arms linked Russian-style. Behind them deep lilac snow clouds swirled.

I picked up the picture and turned it over. It was dated the previous Christmas, which was strange. My grandmother had shown me all her new pictures then, except this one. I stood for a long time staring at it, and then remembered Stuart. He sat quietly on my grandmother's bed with a picture of a little twig boy. He smiled at me and I caught myself thinking: God, one day I'd like a boy like that.

The next day we started packing. Natalie went to Wells and brought back half a dozen wooden wine crates which she lined with newspaper and some soft white flannelette. We packed the pictures first, layering them with tissue paper and cloth like a great cream cake. Natalie stopped every so often and stroked a butterfly or a cloud, murmuring: 'These are amazing, Andrew, all those hours of work.'

But I found it too painful to linger over the pictures. I saw my grandmother stitching and gluing and stretching. There was so much of her in the mosaics and collages and the work – simple and even crude as it was – moved me in a way a great painting could not.

Natalie found the skating picture. She paused before putting it into the box. 'This one's strange,' she said. 'It's different from her other work.'

She stepped back a few paces to see it better. 'I don't know why, but I find it quite disturbing. Those skaters look as if they're running away from something. And all that ice makes me feel quite shivery.'

'Put it in the box,' I said. I suddenly felt cold myself. She had seen it too – the terrible innocence in the picture.

Natalie suggested we broke off for a drink. We went downstairs and she poured two large whiskies. By now it was quite late and the fire had gone out. She threw some sticks into the grate and blew on the embers. The fire flickered into life again and she shoved in two branches of apple wood. Then langorously she began to take off her clothes.

I watched, sipping my whisky, as she freed herself from a fawn bra and tiny pair of pants unselfconsciously, as if she was simply undressing before taking a shower. She lay before the fire, her arms raised over her head, revealing her mysterious armpits with their tiny beards like the lips of mussel shells. Her small breasts rippled as she shifted slightly and then turned on her side. The firelight illuminated a circle of silvery hair at the base of her spine which set every part of me yearning. I walked slowly towards her and ran my hand down her back. Her skin felt like warm ivory. She shuddered. I took off my own clothes slowly, almost reluctantly. My speedy old self would have ravished her in seconds, but now I felt something in me soften. I didn't want sex with her; I wanted to *play* her. She was the most exquisite instrument I had ever seen.

Afterwards she lay like a child angel with her arms crossed neatly over her breasts, breathing deeply. I put my face in her hair, which smelled of apple smoke. A muscle in my thigh pulsed and she laid her hand on it to calm me. Then she twisted up, caught my foot in her lap and began massaging my toes and ankle with a firm, expert hand.

'You should do some stretching exercises,' she said, bending down and kissing the ball of my foot. 'Relax, there's too much lactic acid there.' She kneaded my thigh and then began to clean me neatly all over like a cat. When I was thoroughly washed she lay back and sighed.

'You taste like a man,' she said.

'How do men taste?' I asked teasingly.

'Men are forests, women are beaches.'

I licked her arm and then my own. Both were salty, hers lighter but more astringent.

'We're both beaches,' I said.

'No. You're more woody.' She buried her face in me.

I grabbed her and pulled her close. Laughing, I said: 'I know you, little beach girl.'

'No, you don't,' she said. 'You don't know me at all.'

I pulled away from her slightly. 'I want to know you.'

She laughed. 'You know too many women, Andrew. I know *that* about you.'

We stayed by the fire and it was afternoon when I woke for the last time. Light was flooding into the room like an echo of the night's firelight. Natalie sat at the piano with my jacket thrown over her shoulders. She was holding the photograph of my parents.

'You haven't told me exactly what happened,' she said when I went up to her.

'Nobody knows. The camera was all they found. There may have been an avalanche. There were warnings, but no one really knows.'

[111]

'Strange that they just disappeared.' Natalie stopped. 'I'm sorry, you probably don't want to talk about this now.'

'No, it's all right. I don't remember anything about them. I was too young.'

'You look like your mother – same eyes, same hair. She's beautiful.'

There was something about her use of the present tense that touched me. I kissed her. Then I surprised myself. I told her I loved her.

We spent the rest of the day finishing the packing. I worked away from Natalie, in my room, while she packed my grandmother's things. I was grateful. I couldn't have faced touching her belongings, especially not intimate things like stockings and underwear, things she would have blushed to see me handle.

I packed up my boy's belongings quickly, not tempted to browse through books or linger over photographs. Now I felt linked to something new, something I'd begun with three potent words. Natalie had not replied. She had simply rested her head on my shoulder. Her eyes, when she looked at me again, were completely clear and still. The intensity of her gaze had sent a shock rippling through me, right to the roots of my hair.

I went downstairs for a break. Natalie was in the kitchen, packing dishes and cutlery, wrapping them in newspaper which she tore off from a great pile on the centre of the kitchen table.

'I was running out, but I found these behind the piano,' she said, indicating the newspapers.

'Not those!' I couldn't stop myself from shouting. 'Don't use any more.'

'What's wrong?' She paused, holding a half-wrapped glass in her hand.

I picked up the paper she was using: a copy of *The Times* from November 1963. The Kennedy assassination.

'They're valuable. They're history.'

She looked at me strangely and then smoothed out the page she'd been using to wrap the glass.

'Well, find me a box then.'

That evening I went to visit Sergei. He hadn't come to the funeral. I'd heard he was sick again, a kidney infection. I took

[112]

him some fruit and a bottle of vodka and banged loudly on the door.

He looked awful, yellow and wizened, and ushered me inside quickly. The cottage was dark and filthy, littered with old food packages and charred pieces of newspaper which he'd been using to light the fire. There was a smell of sour milk and unwashed, sick old man's skin.

I offered him the fruit, but he waved it away. 'Take it home, Andrei. Food is wasted on me.'

As far as I could see in the gloom, he had been eating only cheese and sliced white bread. The cottage looked like an obscene bird table with its crumbs and hardened crusts, which crunched under my feet and pricked my backside when I sat down in the single armchair.

Sergei fumbled around looking for vodka glasses. I offered to help him.

'I'm not a child, Andrei!' he shouted, knocking over a shelf of books which crashed into my lap. I handed him a hardback copy of Bulgakov's *Master and Marguerita*.

'Manuscripts don't burn,' he muttered. 'Wonderful. I fell in love with her too.'

'Who?'

'Marguerita, of course. Brickhead!' He found the glasses and set them down on the suitcase.

'Now, Andrei,' he said, wiping some spittle from his mouth with a filthy sleeve. 'Tell me why you've been such a devil.'

'How did you know it was the Bulgakov?'

'Hah! Now he plays games with me. Because I can *feel*, Andrei. I know how things feel. I do not need to see them. Seeing is superficial. Like your bastard shows.'

'Sergei . . .'

He held up a hand. The warts were still there, like tiny shrivelled walnuts. 'Don't protect yourself. I understand. You make a lot of money now, you drive a fast car, you have women, more than your ten fingers in one night, your face is in all the magazines. Everyone loves you, everyone wants a little piece of you. Everyone wants to smell your shit.'

'Yes,' I said simply. There was no point defending myself.

'So, "Rach brat" – what is this they are calling you? They are daring to mention you in the same breath! Go off and play your rock and roll. Forget Rachmaninov. He has forgotten you.'

'Sergei – '

'Why did you come here, Andrei? Why, to humiliate me? Do you want to drag me outside so I can run my hands all over your car? Do you want to throw your money at me, is that it?'

'Please, Sergei – '

'Shut up! Even the sound of your voice offends me now.'

I stood up. 'Well, I should go then – '

'He has so much pride he will not even drink with me. What am I going to do with you?'

I took a large swig of vodka and sat down in the chair. Sergei raised his glass towards me.

'And he has forgotten the toast.'

I poured myself another and went over to the bookshelf where he was leaning, slightly hunched over. I took him by both shoulders and looked into his blank eyes. He felt frail, a soft pouch of bones, like a dead cat I remember taking off a road once.

'You're right, I have been fucking about. I don't want it any more.'

'Don't speak such words!'

'I'm sorry, Sergei. I want to give it up. It's dead. Finished. I'm not saying I'll stop performing completely – maybe I'll do some recitals – but I've had enough of circus tricks. I want something real.' I dropped his arms and felt ashamed as he slowly rubbed them to get the circulation going again.

'Drink!'

We clinked glasses, swallowed the vodka in one mouthful and slammed the glasses on the suitcase ready for another.

'Now tell me, Andrei. Who is she?'

'What do you mean?'

'You have met a woman. An important one, I think. That is the reason for your change.'

'You old bugger!'

'Andrei, please, you know I do not like sour language.'

'Yes, I've met someone. She's Australian, a gymnast, except she now wants to be a photographer.'

'This is very good.'

'She's strong, Sergei. You'd like her.'

'It is very good that she comes from Australia.'

'Why?'

Sergei said that people who lived in light places like Australia were lucky. The earth was bright on the Australian side. Russia and England were like the dark side of the moon.

'She has never seen snow?' he asked.

'I don't know. She lived in England for a while.'

'Ask her. I do not think she has seen it.'

I did not need to ask. On the train back to London the first soft flakes of the year began falling as we pulled out of Bristol. Natalie looked up from her magazine and her face glowed with surprise. She grabbed her camera and ran up the carriage where, beyond the sliding doors, a group of schoolchildren had gathered. They leaned out of the window with their mouths open trying to catch the snow on their tongues and then made way for her. I heard her laughter. She waved at me to join them.

I waved back. But I could not move.

— 14 —

Dr Chase is away at a sleep conference in America. I miss him. His absence has left a space around me. Without our daily sessions – painful as they are – I feel loose, disconnected from everything. Dr Chase is my only contact with the world outside myself and now I have nothing to anchor me; I'm drifting, not knowing what to do.

I've spent the past three days lying in bed, trying not to think. But now it's driving me mad – not my incarceration here, but the gaol of my mind. I keep running around the edges, through all the bright, banal corridors, trying not to be sucked into the great black no-go area, and it's driving me crazy. I don't know how long I can keep running like this, like a white mouse spinning in a wheel, going nowhere. It's exhausting trying to stay sane.

I could stop the spinning right now if I wanted. My razor now stays in the bathroom. For some reason the hospital thinks I'm less of a suicide risk now than when I first came. I can't understand why. Did they honestly think I would feel better after a few chats with a psychiatrist? Anyway, who's deciding all this? What's going on? I could slash the razor across my veins on both wrists. Then plunge them into warm water – didn't I read somewhere that it helps the blood flow faster? But how long would it take? I could be unconscious for days and wake up in intensive care, my wrists bandaged, a guard assigned on twenty-four-hour watch. No, too risky. The throat, then. But I don't have enough guts for that. Your honour, the accused cannot be with us today because he cut his own throat. The tiny innocent 'own' – there's the horror in that sentence. He cut off his *own* leg. He killed his *own* child . . . *He cut his own throat.* God, what an animal.

I need a quicker, cleaner way. I could use my sheets. My good, heavy cotton sheets, one of the advantages of mental-hospital life: a sheet that is strong enough to hold your weight. But they've got me another way. There's nothing to hang the noose from.

Death by drowning. Easy, I just fill the bath, put my head under and slip away. Who said near-drowning experiences were erotic? Oh, for Christ's sake. Now I have to go and be sick.

I return from the bathroom and pace around looking at the white walls. I know that I'm not going to do it. I can't take the risk that there is something else waiting for me, something more terrible than living – even living like this. What does that make me? A coward.

I flick on the television. I need to send my brain to sleep. But it's the news. The newsreader is grave as he reads this item: 'Two sisters aged ten and thirteen have been found dead on Hampstead Heath. Police are treating it as murder.'

I watch as the horror unfolds. It is a familiar, ghastly tableau: dogs on the Heath, ranks of police, stiff and serious in black outdoor jackets. Now the girls' school, small and grey and forlorn, the playground deserted. Now photographs of them in maroon uniforms smiling trustingly into the camera. The parents appear. They are sitting together on a sofa, huddling against each other as if they are cold. The father, a lorry driver, the newsreader has told us, is staring at the camera as if he is looking at the road. His eyes register nothing. There is no fear, no pain, no anger, just nothing. His wife, pale with tiredness, but still pretty in a bright summer dress, is equally blank as she appeals for anyone who saw the girls on the Heath to come forward. She does not say the names of her daughters. She says 'them'. Just before the camera moves away she drops her head and her husband moves urgently to comfort her. A wave of nauseating shame washes over me. I feel like an intruder into their private pain and, disgusted, I switch off the TV. I pace around. I cannot get these people out of my mind. Their shabby sofa, the terrible room with the photographs in silver frames on the sideboard, the rose wallpaper, but most of all the gleaming trophies . . .

'Mr Schidmaizig!' A knocking at the door.

I awake from a terrible sleep; images of terror rear once more, then fade. What have I been doing? I was out on the Heath, chasing someone . . .

The door rattles again. It's the nurse. 'Is it all right if I change your bed?'

'Hold on.' I stumble around, looking for something to wear, and find my white pants in the bathroom and pull them on. They are wet up to the knees. The bath is overflowing, the hot tap still running. I quickly turn it off and shut the door.

The nurse comes in and the first thing I notice is that her face is sunburnt. This shocks me briefly, not because it's so bad, but because it reminds me suddenly that these people have a life outside of here. Outside these cool, blank walls.

'For you.' She hands me two letters. I turn them over so I don't have to look at the handwriting.

The nurse notices, but says nothing. She brushes past me and begins to strip the bed. I sit down in the chair and pick up a newspaper. Out of the corner of my eye, I can see her making the bed. She is smoothing on a fresh sheet now. The cotton rustles with a coarse sound which makes me think of wind moving across a field of dry summer grass. Now the top sheet. The cotton has a hot chemical scent, not like fields at all, more like alcohol. A rich almond liqueur. Now the pillows. She plumps them, smoothing out all the creases, and arranges them at the top of the bed. Like sandbags. A short while ago, my bed might have become a battleground, stained with blood, but now she's here, like a brave lieutenant, I feel ashamed.

[117]

The nurse walks out of the room with the used sheets and deposits them in a metal trolley in the corridor. She comes back in and heads towards the bathroom. I put down my newspaper.

'I'm sorry it's a bit of a mess,' I say. 'I forgot I was running a bath.'

Her sunburnt face flares a more intense red. Does she think I've done this deliberately, I wonder? She walks into the bathroom and I hear a slight gasp and then the heavy thud of a towel hitting the wet floor.

She comes out. 'It's lucky you caught it in time. What were you doing?'

I'm thrown by this. What was I doing? I don't even remember filling the bath.

'Watching TV,' I say. 'The news,' I add unnecessarily.

The nurse regards me for a moment and I get the impression that she is afraid of me. She is quite young, early twenties, with mild blue eyes and sleek blonde hair pulled back into a short ponytail. The sort of young girl you see on the streets of London all the time. She would have lots of friends to go sunbathing with, perhaps by the ponds in Hampstead, perhaps Brighton. A nice day out away from the hospital, away from people like me. I'm glad for her.

'Isn't it awful?' she says.

I don't know what she's talking about. Ridiculously, I think she might be referring to her sunburn.

'The murder. It was not far from here. It's terrifying, everyone's frightened. We live in a hostel, near the Heath.'

There's a catch in my voice when I say: 'Yes, I hope they find him soon.'

'We're not going to the Heath any more. We were there yesterday by the ponds, lying out on the grass . . .'

I find myself wanting to reassure her, but part of me can't believe that she's confiding in me. She must know why I'm here.

'We're going to take it in turns to sleep in each other's rooms until it's all over,' she says.

'That's sensible.' I feel fatherly. I feel all the things I should feel, but it's making me uncomfortable. I want her to go. She shouldn't be telling me this. There is something awful about her wanting to trust me when I feel in a twisted way responsible for

[118]

the deaths of those two girls. I chased them across the Heath like a madman in my dream, hunting them down like two deer, and the father's staring eyes and the mother's bowed head are all because of me.

'I'm sorry, you have enough to think about,' the nurse says. Then she does something strange. She thanks me.

The door closes behind her and I return to the newspaper, but I can't face it. It's filled with news about the murder. I turn to the letters lying on the bed. Should I . . .? So far I've thrown away every single one unread. I look at the envelopes. One plain, one airmail. I open the plain one first with trembling hands. What am I doing? It's better not to know what people think. Throw it away, throw it away – but I can't.

It's from the Music Society, asking me if I want to renew my membership. I laugh out loud. The letter is a circular with my name written in ink. Who sent this? Who wrote my name? I turn over the envelope. It was sent to my address at Muswell Hill and then forwarded here. Who forwarded it? Who is dealing with my mail? There's no one there, no one at my home. Then I remember: Linda, our cleaning lady and gardener. She is looking after the place. Dr Chase arranged it.

Linda. Will I ever see her again? What does she think as she goes about the house, polishing and dusting? Is she frightened? Does she go in every room – does she go in *there*? I see her: short and mannish, red hands, throaty voice, mud on her knees, unwashed hair. A salty sort of girl. A coper, someone said of her once. The sort of girl anyone could entrust their house to. Linda wouldn't be frightened. She would shrug her chunky shoulders and get on with it. It would be just a job to her, clearing up after Schidmaizig.

I have a sudden urge to call her and ask what it's like. Is the house changed or is everything just as it was? But I know what she'd say. Linda, never a great talker, would not discuss how she felt. She'd deal only with the practical. The letters, the bills, the fact that she needs more money to buy fertiliser for the garden. She wouldn't be able to treat me as a friend. Especially not now, when I'm . . . when I'm dangerous. Even in the past she hesitated whenever we asked her to share lunch with us or talk about herself. She would become twitchy and guttural and make excuses. Linda never let down her guard. She needed money

[119]

and we needed a gardener. It was simple. We had an arrangement. If I telephoned her now and asked her how she was
coping, it might stop her coping. It might make her think about
why she's there. It would upset the arrangement. She doesn't
deserve that.

I turn my mind away from Linda and pick up the second
letter. The bright stamp shows an Australian bird. The sight of it
jolts me so hard I feel as if I've been hit on the back of the head.
I drop the letter in shock.

— 15 —

I dreamed of her last night. For the first time since it happened.
She was lying on a lawn of snow waving her arms up and down
to make the wings of an angel. Her dark curls were brushed with
ice and her green eyes danced, reflecting the gold from a dying
sun. In the dream I was taking her photograph, laughingly
telling her to keep her arms still. She got up from the snow and
ran towards me and I took her in my arms and began to eat the
ice crystals from her hair. I woke crying.

Natalie did not make her snow angel. When we arrived back in
London, most of the snow had melted. All that remained was a
soft grey frieze which hung like a scraggy rabbit-skin collar
around the edge of the garden in Ladbroke Grove.

She was terribly disappointed. She had been longing to see the
city under snow. On the train journey back, she'd talked obses-
sively about photographing the Houses of Parliament, the Natural History Museum and the Albert Hall. Buildings transformed
by weather and extreme conditions fascinated her and she
wanted to work on a series of pictures showing the effects of fire,
flood and ice.

The cold grey weeks which followed the thaw depressed her
and she hung about, fiddling with her camera, dispassionately
photographing odd things: a matchbox on my piano keys, a sheet
of music next to a newspaper, the blue flame of the gas fire. I
was tired and depressed myself and we spoke little. It was as if

we'd returned to earth from another planet and we wandered around abstractedly, avoiding each other.

I was supposed to be practising for a new series of recitals, but the bleak mood sapped my enthusiasm. When I played my fingers felt heavy and disconnected. My mind seemed furred up, thick and foggy, and I wondered if this was the start of a nervous breakdown. The more I worried, the worse I played, and eventually I stopped practising altogether. I told Natalie that we needed a holiday.

She was ecstatic. 'We could go skiing!' She sat by the gas fire, absently pulling out a long thread of wool from a dark-blue sweater of mine that she'd been wearing for weeks.

'I've never been before.' She sighed. 'It was always too expensive in Australia. Oh, let's go! I'm fed up with this city. I feel I can't breathe.'

'I was thinking about somewhere hot, actually.'

She looked down and pulled at another long thread, leaving a hole in the sweater. 'Oh,' she said.

To placate her I said: 'I can't ski and I know if I tried I'd be terrible. I'm not coordinated enough.'

'How can you say that? You play the piano.'

'That's different. I'm sure it's different.'

'Oh, Andrew!' she said despairingly. 'Look, we could do some exercises first. I'll show you.'

She pulled herself up on her knees and bent herself into an S shape with her hands on the floor. She rocked up and down.

'Look, it's easy.'

I felt a sudden stab of envy for her supple gymnast's body. I'd never taken any exercise in my life.

'Come on, try,' she urged.

I laughed, but I felt a splinter of irritation. It was such a little thing, her rocking backwards and forwards like that, pulling at her thighs, but there was a challenge in it. I wondered if she was getting bored with me. I hadn't been much fun lately.

'I've got work to do,' I said.

I began practising with a new vigour, hammering at the piano late into the night. Now I was determined to perform the recitals and the holiday was not mentioned again. I didn't want to go skiing and I didn't want to think about why. The idea was too strange and awful.

[121]

Things became better in February. At the first hint of spring the city began buzzing. The grey tongues of depression left, swept away by fresh, playful winds and the occasional blue sky. I started noticing birdsong again.

The garden in Ladbroke Grove attracted a lot of birds, mainly small greasy sparrows which scratched around in a thick berry bush outside my window. My piano faced the window and I spent a long time watching the birds. I was fascinated by them, a legacy from my father, I suppose. I liked their creatureliness, their small, essential activity as they cleaned and pecked and fluttered. There was something absolutely self-contained about them, which made me feel envious. It wasn't the freedom of flight, it was simply that they needed so little to survive. I began to understand why my father had thought that the study of birds was auspicious.

One day a pair of pigeons came to sit on the sill. Their clarinet cooing made me look up from the piano and I watched as they began to mate in flurry of pink and white and grey. I was transfixed. The female's yellow eyes darted with what seemed to be fear, but then I saw that the male eyes were the same, watchful and urgent. The mating was over in seconds, a brief scuffle to ensure survival.

Natalie came in then. She'd been sleeping and one side of her face was slightly swollen. Her green eyes were glazed like opaque glass. We were loving. She laid her hot head against my neck and murmured something sweet – I don't remember the words, just the sweet softness – and began to massage the knots in my neck and shoulders. She carried on and the massage eventually turned sexual and we coupled on the floor until we were both dry with exhaustion. When I went back to the piano, the male pigeon had returned to the sill. We locked eyes. His yellow bird iris regarded me coolly, seeming almost to mock me. I hit a key hard. The pigeon lifted its wings and flew away.

The recitals were a success. I gave the last one at Kenwood House on the edge of Hampstead Heath before a small audience of about thirty. Natalie looked sensational in a green velvet dress, precisely one shade darker than her eyes, and I remember every male head turned as she stalked in and took her seat at the back. I felt quite light-headed at performing in public again and kicked off with an old Rachmaninov trick – keeping the audience

[122]

waiting for a good three minutes before I touched the keys. The silence during this time was exquisite and their anticipation was so strong I could smell it. Then I started, tripping lightly into Chopin, and the audience relaxed with a collective gasp. I took off smoothly into Bach, a short diversion to Ravel and then finally, luxuriantly to Rachmaninov. It was liberating to concentrate solely on the music without the tricks, the fripperies, the flashing lights and dancers. I came to the end of the piece and felt something in me lighten and take flight as the audience clapped and cheered.

Natalie came up and handed me a white iris. I kissed her on the mouth and let my hand linger on her velvet back. The English Heritage organiser came over with a bottle of champagne, which he opened with such flamboyance I thought he was going to spray me like a Grand Prix driver. Half the audience left with polite congratulations. Natalie and I carried on drinking champagne, encouraged by Mr Heritage, who could not take his eyes off her. A group of music students joined us and asked me to play again. I launched into a melodramatic version of Tchaikovsky's First while Mr Heritage tried to dance with Natalie. He grabbed her around the waist and whirled her about the room. Mischievously I speeded up the tempo as she flew past the piano rolling her eyes. I began a slow waltz and a student asked her to dance. I watched them carefully. The student was pale and seemed in pain. His pale fingers rested lightly on Natalie's bare arm and he closed his eyes as he moved her around with graceful steps.

I ended the waltz and asked his name.

'Julian Crewe.' His hand was dry and cool.

'What do you play?'

'Cello.' He smiled slightly. His high forehead was misted with sweat and he looked exhausted.

'My instrument is outside in the van,' he said.

I asked him to fetch it. He came back and we improvised a Bach variation together. Julian's exhaustion seemed to leave him as he swept his bow across his golden instrument, straddled between his bony knees which poked through the holes in his jeans, conjuring a sound so pure we were all moved to tears. We tried other pieces. Julian picked them up naturally, producing a deep, humming swell that warmed the room. I knew that here

[123]

was a man of genius. The applause faded and one of the other students, a fair-haired boy in a tartan shirt, picked up Natalie's flower which had fallen on the floor.

'A white iris. Quite unusual. What's the significance?' he asked.

Natalie took the flower and put it on the piano. It had wilted and the petals were crushed and brown.

'Oh, I don't know . . .' Natalie seemed embarrassed. 'There's something about the white iris that I like. It looks like a flag. It's a strong flower.'

'The odd one out,' said Julian Crewe. 'Van Gogh's painting of the field of irises. There's a single white flower. It was him, I think.'

I'd forgotten. But of course he was right. The white iris made that painting strange, appearing like a ghost in the blue void. I glanced over at Natalie. She was staring at the iris, her face strangely troubled. To recapture the mood, I started playing again. Some nonsense I made up as I went along and the students laughed and called for more. Someone went out to buy wine and Mr Heritage went off in search of glasses. He said he should have kicked us all out hours ago, but he was enjoying himself so much he didn't care. Later I found out that he'd once played saxophone with a jazz band. We stayed until dawn, playing and laughing and singing. A soapy mist rolled off the immaculate lawned banks of the house as we left. I put my arm around Natalie's smooth velvet waist and pulled her close. We walked through the dew and she plucked a rhododendron for me. She said she had never felt so happy.

After the recital, something changed between us. No, not really changed, perhaps shifted. Before, I'd felt that we'd both been holding back. We'd been brought together in unusual circumstances which had stopped us considering whether we were right. My grandmother's death had bonded us, but we had been too careful with each other, too brave and considerate, and it had isolated us. Now we were easier with each other. We started arguing, not seriously at first, but over minor things. What kind of bread we should buy, whether we should go out for a drink or stay in, which film to watch. It was petty bickering, but in a strange way, it seemed to clear the air.

[124]

The Loud Crowd still inhabited Ladbroke Grove, but I had less time for them. When Natalie first came, we had sat around the kitchen table, discussing music and art and diseases. But after a while the conversations began to sound stale and we retreated to my room. This was at the top of the house and still very much a bachelor's flat, crammed with all my men's things, and dominated by the big black Steinway which I knew got in her way. We both needed more space. She started talking wistfully about setting up a darkroom and unpacking the suitcase she'd uncomplainingly lived out of since our return from Wells.

'It would be so nice to have somewhere of our own,' she said one morning. 'I mean, I like it here . . .'

'But you'd rather not live like a student?'

'Yes.'

'This is getting serious, Natalie.'

'Yes, I suppose it is.' She smiled and picked at her fingers. 'I'm just fed up with being in transit.'

A week or so later I got up, kicked at the mess of twisted clothes and empty bottles on the floor and told her I was going to find us a house.

She sat up in bed and smiled. 'Oh, Andrew,' she said sleepily. 'What a good idea.'

The house was in Muswell Hill, tall and grand and much too big for us, but I liked it instantly, mainly because of the large wooden-floored top room, which was light and airy and reminded me of an aviary. All the rooms had fireplaces, which appealed to Natalie, and there was a large garden at the back. It was quite overgrown with dog roses, thistles, smashed paving stones and one or two crumbling stone statues which I thought looked rather Greek and interesting, but Natalie wanted to clear everything away.

We moved in the following month and she spent the next few weeks decorating, painting everything white, which worried me a little. I didn't want the place to look too austere, but she said she was fed up with poky London places where the stained walls were like maps of the former occupants' lives. Our house, she said, was going to be fresh and uncharted.

'Arctic,' I joked.

'No, new,' she said, paintbrush in hand, looking admiringly at her first great wall of white. 'I want it to look as if nobody's been here except us.'

I didn't help with the decorating. I have no real practical skills – any tool or machine in my hands for some reason always refuses to work. Natalie found this amusing at first, and then irritating. She found it incredible that someone who spent his life flexing his hands up and down a piano could not hold a paintbrush. She tested me by presenting various situations – a cupboard door with a broken hinge, a lamp which needed wiring, a pile of rotten wood in the garden – and mocked me when I pleaded pressure of work.

'So the maestro has no time for the mundane? He's far too grand.' It was a joke, my not helping. I thought she understood. I had moved into the 'aviary' by this time to start composing my first concerto. She couldn't criticise me for doing my job. It was paying for everything after all. Anyway, I didn't expect her to do anything – I always told her to call in an electrician or plumber when she presented me with household problems.

After a while my lack of interest really began to bother her.

'Now we're here, you don't seem to want to know,' she said one day when I came downstairs for coffee.

'What do you mean?' I said, but I was not in the mood to argue. The second movement was giving me problems. I couldn't find a way out of it. I'd made it too dark and complex and she had not been helping with her relentless hammering downstairs.

'I feel as if I'm living here on my own. You could help more.'

'I'm sorry, but I have to work. I can't think about anything else. Call in the decorators if you need help.'

'Andrew, that's not the point.' Her eyes glittered.

'I'll help on Sunday,' I said lamely.

'No, you won't. Julian will be here then.'

'Well, maybe next week,' I said. 'When I've got through the difficult part.'

Natalie sighed and wiped her hands down her paint-freckled jeans.

'I'm sorry,' I said again. I moved forward and kissed her forehead, which tasted faintly alcoholic from the paint.

She smiled tightly and returned to the decorating.

I went back upstairs and tried to get into the piece, but the notes swam before my eyes, which started to stream from the paint fumes. I became aware once more of the hammering downstairs like a faint drumbeat. I tried to ignore it and played on, but the hammering seemed to get louder. Now it sounded like an assault. In a rage, I picked up the noise and played it out on the keyboard, bashing up and down the keys with all my strength. Downstairs we faced each other like boxers.

'For God's sake, can't you leave that until later? It's driving me insane! I can't think.'

'It's all right,' she said icily. 'You needn't have bothered to get so worked up. I've finished now.'

'I'm not worked up. You just don't understand how bloody difficult it is sometimes.'

'Yes, I'm so fucking insensitive,' she hurled back, her voice sounding flat and hard and more Australian. 'I'm just the housekeeper, don't mind me.'

'Natalie . . .' I realised how stupid this was.

'You're a selfish bastard, sitting up there for hours on end while I get on and organise our lives.'

'Well, if I don't sit up there for *hours on end*' (I mimicked her accent cruelly) 'there will be no fucking money to carry on living here. I don't have to keep you, you know!'

She stepped forward. The whites of her eyes had turned red and I could see the beginnings of tears of rage. She still had the hammer in her hand and for a moment I thought she was about to use it. I had gone too far. I shouldn't have mentioned money: it was the one thing that really got to her. She hated living off me.

'Natalie.' I went to take her arm. I wanted to disarm her of the hammer, but she hurled me off with such force that the tool flew out of her hand and went skidding across the floor.

What happened next was like a dream. We both turned slowly as the hammer hit something hard with an awful splintering crack. A shower of tiny silver beads ran across the floor like mercury from a broken thermometer. I bent down and picked up one of the beads, following the silver trail to a large picture which now had a hole the size of a fist right in the centre. The skating picture. I couldn't believe it.

Natalie put her face in her hands and started to sob uncontrollably. 'Oh, God, I'm so sorry, sorry, sorry . . .'

I walked over to the picture. The head of the hammer had

[127]

ripped the ice fountain from the cloth, pulling the beads from their roots, leaving a few threads hanging. The skaters were still intact, but the female skater's boot had been torn off.

Natalie came up and put her head on my shoulder. She felt hot and heavy and there was a strong smell of paint from her hair.

'I wanted to put it up on the wall. I thought with all the white it would look good. I was just banging the picture hooks in.' She stared at me wildly. 'Do you think it can be repaired?'

I bent down and picked up a few of the beads. 'I don't know,' I said.

We got down on our knees and began collecting the beads and tiny crystals, slowly sweeping the floor with our hands as if looking for lost diamonds. Natalie cut her finger on the sharp edge of a crystal, but she didn't complain. She sucked her finger and carried on searching for the beads. When we finished, I saw there were traces of blood on her mouth.

Afterwards we were both still shaken, and Natalie rummaged through the kitchen cupboard for something to revive us. We had no wine or other alcohol: we had both been too preoccupied to shop. Eventually she found a bottle of cheap French brandy which she used for cooking. She poured two large measures and we drank them quickly, leaning against the sink, breathing deeply. We did not speak.

Then Natalie picked up the hammer and went into the living room, where she'd positioned two gold picture hooks on the main wall. I followed and watched as she began taking out the hooks, using the claw end of the hammer. It was difficult. She'd hammered the hooks in too far and when they came out there were marks like two small wounds. She went to her paint pot, dipped in her brush and flicked it over the marks.

'You won't notice when it's dried,' she said.

— 16 —

Dr Chase has acquired blue contact lenses in America. I always suspected him of vanity, but this change of eye colour is unsettling. I can't meet his new eyes comfortably. He is too buoyed up by America to notice – another thing that worries me. I don't want to hear about the conference. Why can't he see that?

He's told me that sleep scientists in the States have discovered that dreams can be influenced by the dreamer. He wants me to try out the experiment. All I need to do is tell myself what to dream every night. Simple.

'I would like to monitor your sleep for a while,' he says.

'But you've already done that in the laboratory.'

'I know, but I'd prefer a more relaxed situation. Laboratory dreams tend not to be so vivid.'

'What do you want to do, come into my room at night?' I'm joking. I can't imagine anything less relaxing than having a psychiatrist watch over you while you sleep.

'Well,' he says very slowly. 'It would only be for a few nights – a week maximum.' The ersatz blue eyes smile. Why, I wonder, didn't he get brown lenses or even clear ones? Is this some sort of experiment too?

'What would I have to do?' I ask. I realise this is fatal. I should just say no and be done with it, but he's appealing to me. He has locked his hands into that familiar pyramid again and he's looking excited. He desperately wants to try out some of the theories he picked up in America on me. And why should I stop him? Why shouldn't I become his guinea pig for a few nights? I'm not much good for anything else.

'Nothing,' he says. 'You just go to sleep as normal and I monitor various responses without waking you. You won't feel anything. After your first phase of dreaming I wake you and ask you to tell me what you've experienced. I'll be recording this into a tape recorder. Then we might try suggesting things for you to dream to see if it works.'

'A week?' I say. 'You're going to stay up and watch me every night for a week?'

'Yes, if you agree. I want to get as full a picture of your dreaming mind as I possibly can.'

'When do you want to start?'

'Tonight. My time clock is completely out anyway from New York so you needn't worry about me not getting enough sleep. I can catnap for the rest of the week.'

[129]

Suddenly he yawns and the blue eyes fill up.

'Damn contacts,' he says. 'I'm test-driving them for an eye surgeon. Apparently they never need cleaning. There's just one problem: they have this blue coating which I think looks rather odd, don't you?'

'I haven't noticed,' I say as I get up from the airline chair and return to my room.

They have caught the Heath murderer. It's all over the papers. Big black inky headlines are triumphantly heralding the end of the hunt. CHILD MONSTER CAUGHT. HEATH HACKER HELD. I read it all with shaking hands. He turned himself in after watching *Crimewatch*. He didn't wait until morning, he gave himself up the same night. I imagine him walking around, smoking (of course he would be smoking a lot and drinking: anything to stop him thinking about the deaths on his hands) and then packing, calmly, slowly, fastening everything up, clearing things away, tidying up his external life: it's the only thing he can control now, everything inside has turned insane.

I read on. He's thirty-five, my age, and lives alone in Kilburn. He was always a loner, neighbours say, 'kept himself to himself'. He worked in a post-office sorting office for a while (lots of time to think, lots of reasons to become even more lonely: other people's letters are the loneliest things in the world). He was slow at school and the other children avoided him, says a teacher who remembers him as 'a solitary child who was not very academic, but very good at drawing'. He liked growing geraniums.

Now he's hacked two girls to death with a kitchen knife and his sordid little half-life is to blame. He's a killer of our times. His sad, twisted little mind belongs to society, a society which has thousands of lonely bastards like him eking out miserable lives. He thinks he's an outsider, but he's not. He's lived an undesirable life, that's all – not an unimaginable one. Now for the first time in his life someone is going to take care of him. He's no longer responsible. Society has at last embraced him. He's going to a place with others of his kind, a warm place with regular meals and people to talk to. He's going to prison for a very long time. Probably for the rest of his life. The little fucker. Why do I envy him?

I leave the newspapers and go to the window. It's raining. The windows are smeared with greasy marks, obscuring my view of the garden. I can just make out the rose-covered arch with its grey veil of rain. I press my face against the window: the glass has a sour cheesy smell and feels cold and oily against my cheek. I stay like this for a long time. The cold reaches my teeth, then gradually the window warms up from my blood. When I pull my face away it's like tearing off an Elastoplast.

I turn on the television and watch the afternoon racing. The excitable drone of the commentator diverts my thoughts away from the killer. I've never watched racing before and find that I quite enjoy it. The elegant parade of the animals, the nonchalant jockeys, the buzz of the crowd, the felt hats and umbrellas, the rain on the camera. It's so quintessentially English, safe yet thrilling at the same time.

I find I'm on the edge of my seat at each race, straining my own neck as the horses speed towards the finish. I start placing bets, choosing horses with pretty names: Spring Prelude, Rainbow Dancer, the Maestro. They all lose. One of my horses falls awkwardly and I have to look away as it's led limping off the course, shivering and covered with ripples of foamy sweat. Like a little boy, I start crying for it.

The next morning I wake up later than usual and the first thing I notice is the chair placed next to my bed. A trickle of fear runs through me when I realise why it's there. I wash and dress quickly and avoid the newspapers. Then I sit down on the chair and try to remember. Nothing. I close my eyes, trying to summon up the night's images, but still nothing comes.

I'm interrupted by breakfast. It's the sunburnt nurse, but her face is better now, still glowing but less vivid, like a pastel rose. I see how extraordinarily pretty she is. She puts the breakfast tray on the cabinet near my bed and I catch a whiff of a fresh perfume. For some reason I think of Spring Prelude.

She smiles a young, easy smile. 'How are you?'

'Fine,' I say, smiling back. 'But I'm sorry I don't think I can manage breakfast today. Well, perhaps just coffee.'

[131]

The nurse puts her hands on her hips and fixes me with a mock-hard stare. 'You should eat, you know, especially breakfast: it's the most important meal of the day.'

'I know, but I'm just not hungry.'

'Well, I'll leave it anyway, just in case you change your mind.' She looks around my room, taking in everything – not that there is much. Her swift, searching glance eventually falls on the papers.

'It's wonderful that they've got him, isn't it?'

'Yes,' I say in a noncommittal way. I really don't want to talk, but she continues.

'At least we can relax now. It was getting a bit much, all sleeping in the same room.'

They were all so frightened of this poor little jerk.

'I suppose it must have been,' I say and to show her that I want to be left alone I absently reach towards the tray and start buttering a piece of toast.

'I thought you weren't hungry,' the nurse says.

Ludicrously, I feel caught out, trapped in some indefinable way. What does she want from me?

The nurse moves over to the bed and starts pulling the sheets off. 'I'll do this now, save me coming back later.'

The toast is as dry as wood and I have difficulty swallowing. I pour myself a coffee and gulp it down.

She smooths on a new sheet, caressing it, making sure there are no ridges to give me bedsores, I suppose. The slight exertion causes two spots of colour to bloom in her cheeks and her perfume seems stronger.

'You're with Dr Chase, aren't you?' she says, picking up a pillow.

'Yes,' I say, sipping my coffee.

She plumps the pillow gently. 'I just want you to know that I think it's terribly sad, I mean, what happened to you . . .'

'Thank you.' I know this is a ridiculous response, but I don't know what to say. I wish she would go.

Changing the pillowcase, she wrinkles her brow as a sharp crease appears across the centre.

'What will you do, I mean, when it's all over? Will you go back to playing again?'

I put down my cup and run my hands through my hair to stop them shaking. 'I really don't know,' I say.

The nurse moves towards me. Now she holds out her hand. I feel nauseous at the terrible *honesty* of this gesture. So heartfelt, so sympathetic and the first female skin-to-skin contact I've had since . . . since then.

She looks into my eyes. I take her hand and she squeezes mine twice rapidly.

'You probably think I'm just saying this, but I've got a feeling it will be all right. I know you're a good person. In a strange way I even admire you.'

'What do you mean?' I ask. I have to ask. How can she possibly admire me?

'What happened to you is the most terrifying thing I've ever heard.' She hesitates and looks around the room and her eyes fall on the newspaper. 'Although you're here with Dr Chase and everything, you're all right. I mean, you're not a real patient. You're not mad or anything and you're able to carry on. That takes incredible strength. I don't think many people would be able to cope as well as you. I don't think I could.'

'What would you do?' My voice is soft, almost a whisper.

'I think I'd – ' Then she stops and exhales loudly. She looks down at her hands. She doesn't want to say it. Why doesn't she want to say it? Does she think it will give me ideas?

'I don't know,' she says and looks at me again. Her lovely young eyes are troubled and shining with a hint of tears.

— 17 —

The sea. Every day now I watch the sea. It's my whole world, this remarkable universe, covering great valleys, mountain ranges and plateaux so remote from me and yet so near. I hear the sea's song first thing in the morning and last thing at night. A day does not pass when I don't gaze at it and now I cannot imagine what it must be like to live without its hiss and suck and pull and mesmerising colour. Today the water is the palest grey. I stand at the edge wondering if I should let the wind take me just as it took the empty bottle I hurled off the cliff a few moments ago. The bottle contained red wine and when I launched it, a few drops spurted from the neck like blood from a pierced vein. I hope I didn't hurt anyone.

An old woman walks her black Labrador along the beach at seven every morning. I know her movements intimately. At the third DANGER sign under the cliff, she always pauses to light a cigarette. She stays leaning against the sign until she's smoked it. Then she carefully buries the butt and walks to the circle of rock pools, where she pauses again to collect a specimen or two. Sometimes she brings a metal detector, which she sweeps from side to side like a blind woman's white stick.

I have never seen the old woman's face, but I know it's not a face that smiles at another in the evenings. I intuit this from her attitude to the dog. Her impatient heckling when it rests its great black belly on the stones like a landed walrus. Up here her shouts and curses are strangely refreshing.

I've missed her today. She must have been and gone while I was drinking my wine. It was not good wine. It had a nasty peppery taste and stained my mouth blue. The old man in the village shop said it was the best he had yesterday. It was that or same fizzy strawberry drink or cider. No whisky, which was what I went for. The space on the shelf which had contained the bottle of White Horse I'd bought – was it two days ago? – was still empty.

The old man had spent a long time wrapping the bottle of wine in more layers of brown paper than was strictly necessary.

'Careful you don't drop 'e,' he'd said, unsmilingly handing me the thick padded package, which I quickly put under my arm.

I said nothing. It was too early to be buying wine. Not yet nine. The bread under my other arm was burning me, the white tissue paper peeling off like sunburnt skin.

I gave the man a tenner and he fumbled about in the till looking for change (too early for tenners). I felt uncomfortable. The transaction was taking too long. The man was stalling deliberately. He was looking at me, taking me in with his myopic eyes which ogled me from behind his thick glasses like two fat grey fish pressed up against the wall of an aquarium. I shifted about and tried to step out of his vision by pretending interest in a rack of yellowed greetings cards. He paused in his duty of finding my change and watched me. A muscle in my back twitched. *Did he know who I was?*

At last a greasy fiver was pressed into my palm and I was able to escape. But as I left, he said something. I couldn't hear what. His words were blurred by the tinkling of the shop bell and I walked away quickly without looking back.

I drank most of the nasty red wine and then woke in a fever just before dawn. The image of their pained terrible faces took a long time to fade. Their silent grief. It was just as it was except I was sitting at the piano and not pacing around. They were as still as they had been, not quite touching each other, both leaning slightly forward on the white sofa. They looked painted there. They filled the room like a pair of bloated figures by Edvard Munch. I was facing them. I saw the horror in their eyes, but they looked past me into space, each enclosed in their own capsule of pain. They were themselves and yet they weren't. There was something familiar about them, something *else*. And then I remembered the murder on Hampstead Heath. The two sisters knifed to death. They looked like their mother and father.

To blot them out, I grabbed the bottle of wine by my bed and drank the rest of it down. It tasted sour, and then, unable to stop myself, I ran outside and threw up all over the grass. I retched and retched to the accompaniment of a foul flock of gulls which buzzed around me, seeming to home in on my distress. In a fury, I picked up the bottle of wine and sent it spinning towards the sea.

Lillian and Peter. I first met them at our wedding. Well, it was *their* wedding. I wanted something small and unfussy. The local register office, a lorryload of champagne, music and as little food as possible. I saw Natalie in a *café au lait* beaded twenties number, me in my antique performing suit. Julian Crewe as best man, Sergei playing something sublime . . .

We got what they called the works. They organised it all: it was their present to Natalie and their project. They were so passionate about it, we could not refuse, and their arrangements became so frighteningly complex that only they could have undone it all.

So it was Muswell Hill's Victorian church, Bach's 'Jesu, Joy of

Man's Desiring' played on a fading organ, hats and dyed chrysanthemum buttonholes. Natalie wore an overblown chiffon and lace ensemble, white of course and horribly scratchy. It didn't suit her boyish figure and caused her to wail piteously: 'I look like a man in drag.'

I was in a grey morning suit teamed with a hideous scarlet cummerbund and bow tie, hired from Moss Bros. I balked at wearing the top hat, which I deliberately left behind in the limousine, and at getting my hair cut. It was the first thing Peter said to me, after giving me the once-over at Heathrow: 'Well, I suppose you music boys have always worn it like that.'

Peter treated me as if I were Mick Jagger. On the one hand, awed and fascinated by my success; on the other, slightly nervous and disapproving. His eyes kept track of Natalie, jealously following her around before suspiciously flicking back to me again. I could tell he was having difficulty matching us up.

The morning of the wedding Peter insisted on going to the pub. I tried to put him off the idea. The nearest one was a noisy little bar off the Broadway, popular with the local gay crowd, and run by weaselly-looking men with crew cuts. Peter, with his Australian tan which made his bald head look like a shiny leather ball, smart-on-holiday clothes and 'my daughter's getting married today' jocular manner would definitely seem queer.

He ignored my suggestion that we have a drink at home. 'I'd like to catch a look at the local colour,' he said. 'Stuff of life, isn't it?'

He sounded *very* Australian. More so than his wife, in whose soft voice I could still detect a hint of Oxfordshire. He played the role of the professional expatriate who has decided that his country of exile is superior and feels smugly sorry for the poor bastards who didn't have the nous to get out when he did.

Peter, of course, had left the mother country at *exactly* the right time. He'd sold the Reading semi when house prices were *going through the ceiling*, and, after buying his Sydney replacement, had enough spare cash for a sailing dinghy. Now things were different and new immigrants were having a tougher time of it. When he told me this he laughed and patted his solid knees smugly. 'You know, mate, some of the poor bastards are having to rent.'

The dinghy gained Peter entry to the Darling Harbour Yacht Club, which he told me was about as easy to infiltrate as the Oxford Conservative Club.

'You know I was bloody lucky, got in at exactly the right time. People with forty-two-footers are being turned away now.'

Peter had even *got in* at the right time for the weather. 'Skin cancer,' he said, as if his years in Australia before skin cancer became an issue had somehow given him immunity.

Now Peter was back in Britain, everything was a point of interest. From the price of things (always more expensive than Sydney, except shoes, which he bought rather a lot of) to the cars (everyone drives 'Jap' down under) to the central-heating system, which he spent an inordinate amount of time investigating before the wedding.

In the dark, noisy bar, Peter bought me a pint of Fosters. I despise lager and would have preferred, on that morning especially, to be drinking whisky. He sipped his Fosters as if it were nectar, making a great haaah after each mouthful. I thought he was about to launch into one of his monologues about the difference between Australian lager in Britain and Australian lager in Australia, but it soon became obvious that he wanted to tell me something man to man.

He leaned over the sticky fake-marble tabletop and gripped my arm hard. I suddenly had this ludicrous image of us arm-wrestling. The modern equivalent of a duel, I suppose, with his daughter as the prize. He'd easily beat me. He was nearly twice my age, but he had twice my strength. Natalie had definitely got her hard-muscled gymnast's body from her father. But he was not lean like her. He was stocky and chunky and mahogany brown like one of those fighting dogs they keep trying to ban.

His pugilistic face was only slightly softened by emotion when he said: 'She's not the easiest of girls. I suppose she's told you all about the *business*?' I assumed he meant the abortion and the married man. 'But she's got a good heart. And if you ever think about hurting it, I'll hurt you – '

I started to speak. I don't really remember what I was going to say, probably something to show him that I was on his side, something like: 'That's all right, mate, I'd deserve it. I'd expect you to thump me,' but he cut me short.

'I haven't finished. Not that I think you will.' He laughed and swilled some more Fosters. 'You don't look the type to me, but you know I just love that girl more than I love my own life. Can you understand that?'

Tears were streaming down each side of his face now, but he made no attempt to wipe them away. I felt a mixture of fury and pity. Part of me would have liked us to have intelligently acknowledged each other as enemies. We could have carried on disliking each other in a cool, distant way, never referring to it, never even acting on it, just carrying on through the years accepting the division. In-laws lived liked this all the time.

But he had spoiled it all with his open warning. The bloody masculine ritual, the hard hand on my arm, the pints of lager which turned my stomach. He should have kept his mouth shut. I could have endured hating him in silence.

And there was another thing. He thought I was queer or 'a bit AC/DC', as he put it.

I should have guessed when we were still in the bar. One of the crew cuts came to clean the table and, recognising me, stopped to tell me that he just 'adored me' almost as much as he adored my 'gorgeous playing'. I had to sign a beer mat to get him away from us. I didn't dare tell him that I was getting married for fear of prolonging the encounter. Peter watched all this, his bad dog eyes moist and sort of triumphant as he gave little non-smiles at the crew cut, who totally ignored my future father-in-law.

'Very friendly, wasn't he?' Peter said when the crew cut left.

Julian Crewe, of course, confirmed it. By now he was quite ill and the disease had given him the appearance of an exquisitely feminine young girl. His face looked made out of near-transparent bone china and his new outline was freakishly elongated, as if he had been stretched by the effort of remaining in the transcendent state between life and death.

He had made a great effort for the wedding and arrived dressed in a slightly frayed antique costume consisting of an Edwardian cream shirt and dun breeches. He carried an elegant black cane which made him appear even more like a ghost from the romantic past.

Julian certainly spooked Peter, who greeted him with a look of sheer horror. We were back at the house by then and I was slugging whisky while Peter fiddled with our video recorder.

I let Julian in and we embraced for a long time. His sick body was thin and warm and quivering. As I held him, I felt painfully conscious of my own bulky health.

'Thank you, Julian,' I said as we pulled away. I wanted him to know in advance how much his coming there, like this, had touched me. I wanted to say more. I think I might have even been on the point of telling Julian I loved him (we men *never* tell our friends this until they're dying) when I became aware of Peter standing in the hallway behind us.

I turned round and saw his dark fighting face twitching with shock or embarrassment, it was difficult to tell which.

'Peter, meet Julian, my best man.'

Julian languidly offered his hand and Peter hesitated for a few seconds before taking it. Fury boiled inside me. But of course he didn't know then, it wasn't that. It wasn't the disease that made Peter check himself before he took that misty white hand. It was what he'd seen: the emotional embrace.

I could have explained. I could have told Peter that Julian was dying of AIDS and that I didn't know and didn't care whether he was gay, because he was my friend. My best man. But I didn't want to inflict this on Julian. So I said nothing and the three of us then sat in the white sitting room for an hour. After the first fifteen minutes, during which Peter interrogated Julian on his work and family history, there was nothing left to do except wait. Julian, who had suffered under Peter's intense questioning like a suspect at a police inquiry, nervously picking at his shirt and looking to me for rescue, closed his eyes and seemed to fall asleep. Peter returned to fiddling with the video recorder.

I stared at the wedding cards on the mantelpiece which looked as if it had been dusted with pink and white sugar. There was one dark card in the midst of all the confectionery. A black and white photograph of Moscow in the fifties. The card was from Sergei, who was too ill to come to the wedding. The message read: 'Respect your future.' Feeling a sudden spasm in the pit of my stomach, I got up, went to the kitchen and carved myself a piece of dry bread.

What a strange time is the waiting period before something

momentous. Nothing can ever fill that time, no thought or emotion can bridge the gap between now and then, between waiting and the moment when something will happen to change us. How much of our lives do we spend simply whiling away the hours, minutes, seconds, waiting for *it* to happen? A flight to take off, a concert performance to begin, a birth, a death, a marriage? Waiting is supposed to be preparatory, but why is it that we never want to prepare, we always want to get the event under way, get things flowing again, get it over with? Waiting, we say, is a waste of time.

And yet as I waited in my kitchen, dressed in my horrible grey suit, chewing my dry bread, glancing at the clock, knowing that I was coming close to *it* – in Peterspeak the Big Day, the Happiest of My Life – I was not wasting time. I was aware that in this waiting space, in this brief intense time, there was a strange, buoyant freedom. Now, if I chose, and only now, I could change everything.

Natalie's lips, when I kissed them for the first time as her husband, were astringent. Later she told me it was some unguent Lillian had given her to stop her lipstick bleeding, but the feeling at the time – we had just risen from the altar – was like kissing a plaster Madonna and finding her real.

The weight of what we'd done also hit me. The grave ritual of the church marriage ceremony had never really awed me as a spectator, but as I kneeled in the fine, sweet-smelling dust as the main performer after the incantations, the sign of the cross, the warm hand on my head with Natalie beside me like a mysterious angel, I felt not like a bridegroom but a sacrifice.

The rest of the day passed in a sick blur of sweet champagne. There were so many people I didn't know, so many tanned, healthy, smiling faces belonging to aunts, uncles, cousins and step-people that even Natalie didn't know she had, that I felt even more conscious of my role as an offering. People kept coming up to me and poking me, as if they wanted to check that I was *really him* – the famous pianist they'd all been told about.

I spent a lot of the time in the gents' and it was there that I heard the 'AC/DC' remark. I'd been dancing with Natalie – she showed me up on the dance floor, gliding about like a swan while I floundered like a trout – and needed to catch my breath.

Peter was there, legs arrogantly splayed as he peed. I wanted to look, childishly I needed to see if his prick was bigger than mine, but I resisted. He was talking with a guest whom I did not know.

'. . . arty-farty.' This was all I caught to begin with and came from the guest.

Peter laughed and shook his prick efficiently. 'If he wasn't marrying' – he checked himself – '*married to* my daughter, I'd say there was something a bit AC/DC about him. Deffo.'

'Jesus,' said the man.

Fortunately, a long white-tiled partition hid me from them. I backed away and returned to Natalie. I didn't tell her what I'd heard.

Peter and Lillian stayed on at our house after the wedding. I felt I hardly saw Natalie. And we were just married, for God's sake. But she told me that she couldn't live with the guilt of not involving them in her new life. They expected it. If she turned away from them now, they would never let her go.

She sailed through it all quite well, back in little-girl role, letting her mother fuss over her, flirting with him, and in turn making them hot milky drinks before they went to bed, or 'turned in', as Peter called it. She was abstracted with me and fully involved with them. There was nothing I could do except wait.

During the days, the three of them toured London. I was able to escape the sightseeing by pleading pressure of work. I returned to composing, but it was difficult to concentrate. I found myself being sucked into their routine even though I had a very good excuse. Peter liked me to work, it proved I was somebody famous.

Lillian got up extremely early every morning. She was very short-sighted and always dropped things in the bathroom. My feet crunched glass when I went to take my shower. Then she would move noisily through the house, stumbling on the stairs, knocking into things – breakfast was a concerto – and the disturbance would propel everyone else out of bed whether they liked it or not.

But Lillian's appearance did not suggest she was a noisy person. Her thin, powdery face, neat bobbed hair and slender legs and arms were quietly elegant. Her voice was soft – unlike her husband's – but not quite calm. There was a element of desperation about her. Lillian looked as if she worried a lot.

Her relationship with Natalie was competitive but not combative. It must have been difficult knowing that it was her daughter her husband was really in love with. Lillian gained her victories by indulging Natalie so much that it pulled her away from Peter.

'Let's leave the girls to it,' he'd say when Lillian had sprung yet another elegant trap – a hair-perming session in the kitchen, strawberry washing or a trip to Hennes – not realising that he'd been cuckolded again. He'd drag me into a corner and try to talk to me about sport, and when I protested that I had to get on with some work, he would cock his head like a wily turkey. 'You need some colour in your face, man.' Then he would try to punch me in the gut.

I never knew what Lillian thought of me. We never spoke. We had conversations, about day-to-day matters and what they'd seen in London on their sightseeing excursions, but that was all. If ever she found herself alone in a room with me, Lillian became ill at ease and always started doing something – cleaning a table or watering a plant – so she wouldn't have to look me full in the face. I often thought that if someone had asked Lillian what I looked like, she wouldn't have been able to answer.

But we did have something in common. Lillian was a somnambulist. One night when I was composing late, she came into the aviary. She startled me; even Natalie never came up there late at night. Lillian's eyes were open and she was smiling, the sort of soft, indulgent smile that some people reserve for babies and young animals. She was wearing a white towelling dressing gown and her hair was mussed up – the first time I'd seen it looking anything other than immaculate – and on her feet were a pair of Peter's shoes. This made it difficult for her to walk properly and she slid about the room like an ice-skater.

'Lillian?' I called her name gently, knowing from my own experience that an abrupt awakening was awful.

She carried on smiling and sliding about the room. I watched her. I had never seen anyone sleepwalk before, odd considering that it was so much a part of my life, and I was fascinated. She looked mad, but also in control at the same time, *serenely* mad. For the first time, I appreciated the fear felt by wakers. It was a tremor sparked by the single clear thought: what if she's not the same when she wakes up?

'Lillian,' I tried again, but still she didn't respond. She stood in the middle of the room and looked down at the ridiculous shoes. There was something dreadful about seeing her so exposed and I suddenly realised how embarrassed she would be if she woke to find herself here, alone with me.

I got up from the piano and gently led her down to her own room. As I opened the door, a volley of grunts from Peter hit me. I could see his hard-boiled head lolling back on the pillow, his mouth open, his chest rising and falling. I smelled their intimate sleeping smell, a mixture of dusty suitcase leather and river fish, and felt suddenly ashamed. I pushed Lillian inside quickly, hoping she'd find her own way to the bed, and shut the door. I found I could not compose any more when I returned to the aviary.

'It's a bit like you, really. She sleepwalks when she's under stress,' Natalie said the next afternoon. We were walking in the park. I had the beginnings of a migraine and wanted to clear my head.

'But she's on holiday.'

Natalie stopped and looked at me incredulously. 'That just gives her more to worry about.'

'What do you think will happen to them?' I said. I don't know why I asked this. I knew the answer already.

'Nothing, of course.'

We walked on in silence. I was enjoying being out in the park despite the migrainous feeling. Or maybe because of it. Migraines make me unusually sensitive to colour and light – often one colour dominates – and the effect can be extraordinarily beautiful. I remember this afternoon as a moist, exhilarating green.

At the pond we stopped just as a spectacular dragonfly came swooping in to land.

'It's not long now,' Natalie said. 'They're going back the day after tomorrow. You've been wonderful. I love you.'

I was trapped in the green of her eyes as she kissed me on the mouth.

*

Lillian and Peter left, but we found it difficult to relax with each other. Their presence in our house had unbalanced us and they had moved our things. Magazines I'd left lying around the floor turned up in drawers and all our cups, plates and dishes had been stacked in order of size by a bored and inquisitive Peter, possibly to make up for the carelessness of his wife, who had smashed every single drinking glass in the house.

Natalie and I took to walking in the park to escape the house, or maybe it was the orderliness of just being married that we wanted to get away from. We were both reluctant to slide into the routine of work so we walked hand in hand through the park, gazing at the trees and the clouds, blinking in the sun as if we'd just woken from sleep. Natalie took photographs of me as I watched the swans and geese fighting over the sodden crusts of bread drifting on the water.

'I always want to remember this time,' she said. 'it seems important. I don't know ... it's more than being married. Andrew, I feel as if we're on the brink of something, something bigger than even us.'

I smiled at her, but a small buried part of me felt a twinge of fear. I returned to watching the swans. They seemed to be a couple and dipped the sinuous white ropes of their necks in unison into the olive water. A bubble of fear surfaced once more with the swans and I threw a pebble into the water to scare them away. Nothing will happen, I told myself as the swans glided like two ghost yachts into the centre of the pond. Nothing.

Natalie said we should go on a honeymoon. 'Not for long. I don't want to go abroad or anything, I know we're both too busy, but let's just spend a few days away.'

I asked where she had in mind.

'Somerset. I'd really like to go there again. Maybe you think I'm being romantic, but that was where we first came together. I want to go back there to see if it was all real.'

We drove down in the Lotus. Natalie wore a floral scarf and dark glasses and a light-blue dress. She sang Joan Baez songs at the top of her voice as we cruised across the silver-green plains of Wiltshire, passing isolated Stonehenge, sealed in its wide circle of wire like some dangerously contaminated building.

'You've got a great voice. I didn't know you could sing.'

[144]

'Ah, there's lots of things you still don't know!'

I braked slightly as we pulled up behind a tractor. 'Like what?'

'Like, um . . .' She laughed and adjusted her scarf. 'Like how much I adore you.'

'How much do you adore me?' I speeded up. I was enjoying myself, the sun and the breeze and this teasing bright mood.

'I adore you, I adore you,' she sang in her Joan Baez voice. 'I adore you more than my own life.'

The tractor driver put out his hand and I overtook, sweating slightly as I eased the Lotus out into the road under a canopy of trees. Natalie leaned back in her seat, her face relaxed as she watched the sun flickering through the leaves.

We stayed at a hotel in Glastonbury with a view of the abbey. Natalie went off on her own to photograph the ruins while I downed a few whiskies in the dark bar and tried to avoid talking to the hotel owner. Unfortunately he'd recognised me when we arrived and immediately started fawning all over Natalie, touching her arm in a familiar way which set my teeth on edge. She had smiled her sweetest smile before telling him that the only thing we needed was to be left alone.

The owner seemed flustered. 'But you must have champagne!' he said theatrically. 'I will send up a bottle.' He tapped the side of his nose. 'On the house.'

'No, thank you,' Natalie said charmingly. 'We don't need any stimulants at the moment. We have each other.'

I had to fake a sneeze to stop my laughter.

I ordered another whisky and sipped it slowly as I waited for her. I knew that she'd probably be gone for some time, at least until after sunset. She'd once told me that light was precious. 'It's always changing. It's so frustrating, but also exciting at the same time. Don't you think it's marvellous that there will never be another day lit like this?'

I'd agreed, but I couldn't really share her enthusiasm. There was a part of me that felt quite envious that she worked in the light whereas I spent so much time trying to make sense of the dark.

We visited Sergei later that evening. He seemed thrilled that we'd come and made a great show of plumping his stained cushions and sweeping books and crumbs off the suitcase table.

[145]

He even managed to make tea, clattering about in the lean-to kitchen at the back while Natalie and I squashed into the big armchair and waited.

Sergei bought out a bottle of vodka with the tea and apologised that there was nothing to eat.

'I would have made an omelette. With cabbages! You know they are still growing in the garden.'

'It's all right,' I said. 'We've already eaten.' The hotel owner had insisted we dined on lobster thermidor with in-season vegetables followed by cherries jubilee and coffee and brandy on the house. Consequently I felt a little sick.

'But Andrei, you have never tasted a Russian cabbage omelette.'

Natalie laughed and Sergei turned towards her. 'Your husband is so bloody spoilt!'

'I know,' she said, shifting around in the armchair to make more room for herself. 'He's got a lot to learn. His grandmother did everything for him.'

I felt my face flush. 'You've embarrassed him now,' Sergei said. He was trying to get the cap off the vodka bottle, but seemed to be finding it difficult.

'Sergei, give it to me,' I said.

'Shh!' He put a finger to his lips. 'I hear something.' We both looked around.

'What?' Natalie said. 'What did you hear, Sergei?'

Then he laughed and patted his chest as the laughter turned into a crusty cough. 'I hear, little Natasha, the wonderful sound of your voice!'

Natalie eased herself from the armchair, went over to him and offered him her small brown hand. Sergei took it and pressed it between both his warty palms.

'You are strong,' he said, 'but you are gentle.' He raised her hand to his lips and kissed it. 'You are welcome in his life. He needs someone like you and he needs to know it. You must show him.' He dropped her hand and then asked if he could touch her face. 'I see you,' he murmured as his hands fluttered over her eyes. ' Vivace, you have music in you too. Never forget.'

'Good,' says Dr Chase when the tape stops. 'At last you seem to be confronting your anger.'

I say nothing. I'm simply relieved that the American experiment is over. The first night I dreamed of the Heath killer after Dr Chase had suggested focusing on the word 'speed'. The killer was riding a racehorse called the Maestro but instead of whipping it to the finish line, he was hacking it to death with a knife. The dream disturbed me so much, I asked Dr Chase to stop the experiment, but he told me I had to face my dream fears before I could control them.

The second night, when my catchword was 'love', I had a peaceful, intensely erotic dream in which the sunburnt nurse was doing something very soothing to me in the hospital rose garden, actually giving me a blow job, but I didn't tell Dr Chase this, neither did I reveal her identity. I just said I was with a woman who *felt* familiar. The third night – catchword 'water' – I dreamed I was walking by the sea with an old woman and a fat black Labrador.

Dr Chase leans back in his chair and stretches his arms luxuriously over his head. He seems in a strange, loose mood today, and I wait, expecting him to launch into one of his extravagant theories.

'How about a spot of lunch?' he says.

This throws me. 'I've just had breakfast,' I say stupidly.

'I thought we could go for a drive. I always think better when I'm driving.'

I feel afraid. I want to come up with a string of excuses why I shouldn't go, but can think of nothing that sounds reasonable. I get up and walk around. Dr Chase watches me. I feel self-conscious pacing about his room like this; his domain where he usually walks about puzzling me out. Now we're going somewhere else, the balance has shifted.

The invitation to lunch is not as spontaneous as it seems. He planned this. The clothes arrived yesterday: a pair of jeans, too big for me now, and a green T-shirt, which smelled intolerably of home. The clothes were packed in brown paper. Odd that, but practical. Very Linda. No note, but then what could she say?

'Are you ready?' Dr Chase asks.

'I think so.'

He smiles reassuringly. 'It will do you good to get out.'

I smile back and feel an unexpected rush of warmth towards him. Where would I be without him? Probably collapsed somewhere. Drunk or dead in a doorway.

He hesitates before leaving and reaches into his jacket pocket. Dark-blue suit today. The colour suits him. He looks less camp, somehow more in control. Authoritative. Another odd thing: I've rejected authority for most of my life, but now that I'm in trouble, I'm taking comfort from it. The doctors, the police, the lawyers and soon the judge. My life in their hands. There is still enough maverick left in me to feel twitchy at the thought and I wonder: is this like praying when you know you're dying?

Dr Chase finds what he's looking for in his jacket – his gold horn-rimmed glasses. I'm glad when he puts them on. Those blue contacts were ridiculous.

We pass the sunburnt nurse as we walk out across the crunchy pebble drive. She smiles at me in a familiar way which makes me cringe.

'Going somewhere nice?' she inquires, head on one side. The sun has lit her hair brilliantly. I'd forgotten how lovely some blonde hair appears in the sun – like a mysterious cloth spun by angels.

'To lunch,' says Dr Chase briskly. He is jangling his car keys, anxious to be off.

'Enjoy it – it's such a beautiful day,' she says brightly.

She terrifies me, I think as I sink into the leather and soap interior of Dr Chase's Jag.

We drive through Hampstead High Street. This feels like the first time I've been out in years, instead of weeks. Six weeks I believe I've been cut off, but a lot seems to have happened in that time. The people seem bigger, bulkier and taller, for a start. And less rushed, as if their increased mass and height has somehow slowed them down. We nose past a few street cafés where these new big people are squashed into white plastic chairs, their brown plump legs and arms placidly arranged, squelching out of too-small clothes. Everyone seems to be wearing leather shorts and high-necked black shirts with no sleeves. And they are smiling. I have never thought of London as a smily place before. Think of smiles and you think of the Philippines or Sri Lanka – airline-ad places, not prickly, tight-arsed London where people go about as if being prodded by invisible poles. But today London has become Sri Lanka. There is even some tropical-sounding music playing. I wind down the car window. The smell is foreign too, rich and spicy; the familiar smell of old animal fur that I always associate with London is overwhelmed by this new exotic aroma. I wonder what it is. It seems to be more than just the food smells coming from the cafés and restaurants lining the High Street. It is, I suddenly realise with a shock, the smell of being alive.

'It's amazing how this place comes alive in the summer,' says Dr Chase.

I glance across to the driver's seat. For a moment, I almost forgot he was there.

'Hampstead is such a *statement*,' he says. 'But I like it in the summer. It's less hard-edged, more naive.'

'Do you live here?' I ask. How strange that I don't know. I simply assumed that Dr Chase *would* live in Hampstead, the psychiatric village with Freud's old place within consulting distance.

'No, Kent.'

'*Kent?*'

'I like the drive. I do my thinking when I drive.'

What's he thinking now, I wonder? That he's got his prize patient in his Jag, taking him out for a trip to make him feel better . . .

'I did a lot of thinking about you when I was in America,' he says, neatly changing gear. We're out of town now, on top of the Heath. *He* hunted here, the hacker. This is his country. I feel a little shiver of fear and then disgust at thinking about it again. I'm obsessed. Why can't I take my mind off the little bastard?

Dr Chase overtakes a Volvo. 'It's essential that you learn to take control again.'

'That's impossible,' I say. 'I can't control something I don't understand.'

We've left the Heath now and Dr Chase is pushing the Jag

[149]

faster, taking corners efficiently as we move away from the city. Would he be able to drive so well if our roles were reversed?

'You understand more than you realise,' he says. 'Last night was important. You dreamed what you decided to dream.'

'No, I dreamed what you told me.'

Dr Chase laughs, a short exclamatory Ha!, as if I've caught him preparing something before he's ready for me.

'You can suggest your own catchword in the future. I very much hope that you will. The point is, you *can* influence your unconscious. You just have to persevere.'

'Is that your cure?' I ask suspiciously.

'No, it's not a cure. There is no cure for your condition, but you can learn to direct it. It just needs practice.'

I look out of the window. Trees and fields flash past in a haze of soft summer green. Everything out there continues, I tell myself. A tree will replenish itself every year – until someone cuts it down. Or it is killed by disease. How strange that trees are subject to viruses, or is it bacteria?

We pull into a pub, a low building covered with ivy. There are not many other cars in the drive, but I feel nervous. What if I'm recognised? Could the management order me off the premises? No Dangers to Society here please, even if they are accompanied by psychiatrists.

I'm in the gents' now, biting my fingers, trying to stop a full-blown panic attack. I saw a woman with short dark hair and muscular legs by the bar. I was buying matches – I had to smoke: Dr Chase had just given me the date for my first court appearance. She was ordering a vodka and orange, and she smiled at me. Her face was friendly but unfamiliar.

Someone has smeared shit on the walls. A dirty protest. But what do SAM, IAN and JOSÉ have to fucking protest about? They're in control. They can take the shit from their arses and smear it on the wall just because they feel like it. They're not shitting themselves with fear.

I return to the table and drink whisky, my fourth. The woman has left. Dr Chase tells me I have nothing to worry about.

'All the evidence is in your favour. You should get a fair hearing.'

'I'm not worried about that. It's going through it all again that terrifies me,' I say, lighting another cigarette.

'I know, I know, but the judge will probably be keen to hurry the case along. He will understand how distressing it is for you.'

I take a long drag on my cigarette.

'The jury should be sympathetic – I'm hoping there will be more women than men – but they could spend a long time deliberating. Some of the concepts are quite difficult for the layman to understand.'

'Do you mind if I have another whisky?'

'No, go ahead,' Dr Chase says. He hands me the money – I didn't have any cash in hospital – and I thank him. I feel like an adolescent out drinking with his father for the first time.

The pub is filled with weapons. Guns, hunting knives, rusted farm tools, a crossbow and other implements are suspended from the dark beams on wires, casting sinister shadows. This is a man's pub, a cavernous place which smells of overcooked meat and leatherette and hums with fighting talk of business deals, farming quotas, local politics ... trials. The yaps and barks of men who drink.

I've no idea where we are; somewhere in Buckinghamshire, I think. Dr Chase seems quite relaxed here, which is odd. I wouldn't have taken him for a Buckinghamshire farming-pub man, but then I was surprised to hear that he lived in Kent. Perhaps he regards these pubs as places where he can catch up on some psychological field work. People behave so strangely in pubs. They must be a psychiatrist's dream.

There's an argument going on round the other side of the bar. Two men, both wearing the same brown corduroy and check-shirt uniform, are talking about the Bomb. One has told the other that he built a shelter during the Gulf War, which, despite local objections, he is not taking down.

'You have to be prepared,' he says, red-faced and puffed up like an old cockerel. 'The Arabs will nuke us one day, it's coming to that . . .'

The other brown corduroy is exasperated at his clone's stupidity, but is not handling it very well. He's had too many beers and needs a fight.

'No, it's the travellers I want nuked. Why should I worry

about Arabs when I've got home-grown filth on my land? I want them off!' He bangs his fist on the bar.

The first corduroy staggers backwards, clipping the paw of a collie which lies sprawled at his feet. The dog lets out a screech then thumps its tail in apology. The corduroy bends down and fondles the dog's ears.

'There's no respect any more,' the second corduroy says.

The first man looks up from his dog. '*He* respects me,' he says, gently kicking the dog in the ribs with the toe of his boot.

The second corduroy takes a slug of his pint. 'No morals.' Then he notices me waiting on the other side of the bar. He turns to his companion and shock flickers across both their faces. They stop talking. United now, they stare.

— 19 —

I went for a swim this morning. My first since I've been here. I needed the break and thought the walk down to the beach would stop me drifting. Lack of sleep (I'm writing all night long to finish this in time) is making me feel light and disconnected. This morning I hardly knew where I was. It was as if I had slipped out of myself and become a spectator. I watched myself make tea, annoyed that I spilled the milk down the front of my trousers, then walk outside and stumble on a small ant hill, spill tea on the grass, rub it abstractedly with my foot, then go back in and find my pen and hold it up to the light for a long time before putting it down without writing anything.

Entering the water was like plunging through glass and the salt burned my eyes. I did not go out far – my thin pianist's arms are not made for swimming – just to the point where I could feel the edge of the great shelf of stones. Beyond this there was the black drop down into the deepest part of the sea world, the unfathomable depths, the mystery. The old boyhood fear came rushing back as my feet probed the tantalising edge, sending showers of stones and tiny shells cascading into the darkness.

I was exhausted when I pulled myself out, my legs raw and bleeding, ripped by the rocks. I lay on my stomach and buried my face in the cold, wet stones. The sea washed over my legs, stinging as the salt seeped into my cuts. I began to weep, silently at first, then not caring, letting my cries become shouts as I banged my head on the stones.

This was how she first saw me. I scared her and she came over with the metal detector poised like a javelin.

'What are you doing?' she said.

'Drying.'

'Oh, I thought you said dying.'

She was wearing earphones and she fiddled with the battery on the metal detector to switch it off. She cocked her head and looked at me sternly. I was half naked (a scrap of underwear saved her from having to confront my sea-shrivelled prick) and still bleeding from my wounds, which the dog immediately homed in on as if I were a piece of raw meat.

'Gwaaan, geterway,' the woman growled at the animal as it lunged at my face in a frenzy of licking. 'Buggerarf!'

The black Labrador sat down and watched me through excitable yellow eyes. I shifted from my prone position. The animal stank, foul and fishy like a dead seabird, and I stood up, mainly to escape the smell, but there was something else bothering me. I had the feeling that I had been here before. It was somehow linked to the nauseating smell.

'Nasty,' she said, looking at my cuts. 'You shouldn't swim here: the rip's too fast.'

The sea rolled up the stones in fast oily waves which caused the dog to make piteous little whines. I moved towards it and it growled. I saw that it was sitting on my clothes.

'Samuel!' The woman, glad of an excuse to abuse the animal, yelled at it. The dog rolled off my clothes lazily, oblivious to the malice glittering in his mistress's eyes, which were a peculiar steely grey colour, reminding me of London pigeons.

In fact, there was something pigeon like about the whole of her. She was short and proud with a plumped-out chest like an old-fashioned bolster. Her face was beaky thin with wispy grey hair and large eyebrows like white feathers. She had improbably small feet, clad in what appeared to be a child's pair of yellow wellingtons.

I stared at these strange feet as I pulled on my clothes, which now stank of wet dog.

The white eyebrows jerked together. 'You live up there?' Another jerk, indicating the cliff.

I shrugged and looked around for my shoes. She found one and pushed it over using her metal detector, a strange contraption, a spacewoman's walking stick.

'Do you ever find anything?'

'You mean treasure!' She laughed, a curious hooting sound, which made me regret asking. 'No, I certainly don't find that.'

'Well, what *do* you find?'

'Knives,' she said, sweeping over the stones with the detector. 'Fishing knives, kids' knives, kitchen knives, I'm always finding knives. And hooks, of course, lots of hooks. I have a fine collection of hooks.'

'What's your best find?' I asked.

'I haven't found it yet,' she said. 'When I do, I'll stop looking.' She gave me what she thought was a smile. It was an expression I'd long associated with old Devonians, a sort of bunching-up of the lower face without opening the mouth. It was complemented by a long hiss out of the side of the mouth.

'Won't be long before all this lot comes down,' she said.

I followed her gaze. The red rock face was more ravaged than ever and pocked with spots of chemical blue and green, vividly disfiguring like the first sarcoma on a beautiful face. Halfway up, a great ledge had fallen, leaving a raw wound of pink earth. The rock seemed to be disintegrating not from the wind and rain, but from some sickness within.

'You wouldn't think a thing like that could die, would you?' The woman's eyes appraised the cliff and then she pulled them away. 'Terrible,' she muttered thickly. She picked up a piece of driftwood and threw it at the dog.

'Cmoawn, yer lazylump.'

The beast struggled to his feet, dug his claws into the stones and opened his dripping mouth in a great fishy yawn. The woman pattered daintily over in her yellow boots and roughly cuffed the dog on the side of the head. He responded by licking her arm in a paroxysm of affection. I received another bunched-up hissing smile and the sense of *déjà vu* returned. It was possible I'd seen her before. She was roughly the same age as my grandmother. Perhaps they'd met when I was a boy. People

[154]

always stopped and talked to each other down here. It was a reflex of country living, as automatic as avoiding eye contact on city transport systems. But the woman showed no sign of recognition and now she had indicated that she was anxious to get away by switching on the metal detector. I left her to her treasure-hunting and turned back towards the cliff.

It was like a disease, the terrible raw slipping away, the secret exposure and the shock of seeing something whole fall apart and crumble to dust. The act of creation in reverse. I watched it happen to Sergei, the gradual decline as the throat cancer sucked the life out of him, gathering momentum as it weakened him to the point of no return, the point where there is no life, only sickness. I was there at the end. I held his hand, held on to life, while he slipped past it like a cat sneaking through a crack in a door.

Sergei suffered the pain without complaining, refusing hospital treatment until the very end when he was drifting in and out of consciousness. They offered him morphine but he refused. He said he wanted to experience his moment of death. It was what he'd lived for, after all. He wasn't going to be cheated out of it by drugs. So I held his hand, squeezing hard, not caring if I was hurting him. In the still white hospital room there was only the pressure of my hand on his as I willed him not to go and pushed him on simultaneously. At the end, his fingers stiffened around mine and he opened his eyes. I had only ever known them murky. But now they were clear.

Afterwards I went to his cottage, breaking a window to get in. The smell was obscene, like warm stagnant water. It had permeated everything. The Russian books, the suitcase table, the bundles of stained sick man's clothing, even the piano. A whiff of it hit me as I lifted the lid, intending to play a requiem for my old mentor. But I hesitated, knowing that he would have despised me for it. My maudlin trawling through his cottage would not have impressed him.

I could not help wondering how it had been, during those last dark days when he'd known that it was ending. What did he think about as he waited? Did he remember his childhood, the piano in the grand flat in Pushkin Square, where he was taught by a beautiful woman with a broken back? A tram knocked her down, he had told me, when she was on her way to play for the Bolshoi. A gentleman, stunned by her beauty, lifted her off the road. He should have left her there, the doctors told him when the traction irons were taken off months later. She would never walk again. The gentleman married the woman, but Sergei never met him because five years into the marriage the gentleman suffered a heart attack and died. The gentleman was twenty years older than the woman. She shouldn't have married him, a lot of people said. She should have turned him down and he should have left her on the road. All the pain they suffered . . . Was it worth it for five years? Sergei thought she was right to take her chance of happiness. He even thought about marrying her himself. He would lie awake in bed at night composing romantic proposals and he bought her roses from the market in the Arbat. She was kind to him, he said, and she was still beautiful, dark-eyed with tawny hair and the palest skin he'd ever seen. His Masha with the pale hands, whirring like two featherless wings at the wheels of her chair. He loved her to her veins.

I wandered around the cottage picking up books and setting them down again. The last time I'd come he'd told me his history. His voice was almost gone and I had to bend close to hear him. I shall never forget the sweet smell of death that even then – three weeks before he went – lingered on his breath.

It started with his arrest on 20 December 1937 for 'anti-Soviet activities', the term Stalin's secret police gave to Sergei's first orchestra. It wasn't really an orchestra – that was another, separate offence – just four musicians in a Moscow flat. One night they played Beethoven too loud and too long, infuriating the old man downstairs, who denounced the lot of them. Sergei spat at his door as he was led off in the black afternoon to join the conveyor of the great terror.

The guards deprived Sergei of sleep for a week. They kept him awake by throwing cold water in his face and beating him with the leg of a chair. The 'confession' they extracted committed him to twenty years' hard labour in a gold mine in Kolomyya.

Sergei tried to commit suicide by swallowing the glass from his spectacles (the glasses were not replaced and he believed this was why he eventually went blind) but the guards found him and forced their fingers down his throat to make him vomit the glass. He tried to kill himself many more times by going on hunger strike, but the guards always saved him. Sergei's teeth were broken by their brutal force-feeding.

He asked the guards why they were making him live his death, but they had no answer. They were simply following orders to keep him alive. Sergei's activism – he tried to scratch compositions on his cell wall with a piece of glass saved from his spectacles – led to prolonged periods in the punishment cells, where his diminishment began. Deprived of light and warmth, he withdrew deep into himself, believing that he could kill himself by simply ceasing to exist. He brainwashed himself by repeating one word over and over in his mind, blocking all sensations of memory and feeling with his mechanical repetition of the word. It filled his sleep and his dreams, the one word repeated silently over and over again. He never varied the tone or pitch, never played games with his word or chanted it aloud. He simply spoke it in his mind and the years passed.

He did not remember leaving the cell and going back to the mine. It was all the same to him. He was an automaton with one word in his head. He still spoke when he was spoken to and ate and excreted and lay down at night, but he felt nothing. He saw nothing in his mind. The word was his wall. Each time he spoke it, he added another brick.

He did not remember escaping. Someone helped him, but he did not know who or how or even why. He woke in a forest with his word and carried it with him across a white field. He did not remember the weeks of travelling across Czechoslovakia or what happened when he reached Germany. They told him the facts later. He simply woke up in a sunny room one day. There was a piano under the window. A great Steinway, glossy as black oil. The lid was open. He sat down and began to play his word. His music, music, music . . .

— 20 —

It's strange to witness others deciding your fate. Although I must be here to take part, I feel excluded. I'm not really involved. I'm

[157]

like a child creeping about on the stairs while the serious talk goes on below.

The talk right now is extremely serious. For me, most of all, as it concerns my life, but also for Dr Chase. He has brought me this far, and if I fail, he fails. Dr Chase is determined that this will not happen. So is Michael Laurence, my lawyer.

Mr Laurence is going to save me from something I honestly do not believe I deserve to be saved from, but I can't let him down. Not at this late stage. Not now the court has accepted my plea of not guilty.

'Is there anything you wish to know, Mr Schidmaizig?' Mr Laurence asks. He has a soft voice, melodious, not a courtroom bark at all, and I find myself wondering if he sings.

'Mr Schidmaizig?' he says and this time there is an edge to his voice. I hear its authority and feel a tingling, almost of relief. People will listen to him. They will also admire him. Blond and square-shouldered, Michael Laurence is extraordinarily good-looking, like an Olympian athlete.

I stare at him, not knowing what to say. Mr Laurence casually flicks through some papers. My papers. It's all there: the scraggy past, which Dr Chase has refined into precise paragraphs; the terrible dark dreams which will become, for the benefit of the jury, illuminations. This is my history. The past will decide my future.

'You're quite confident . . .?' I falter.

'Of course,' Mr Laurence says and lays his hand lightly on the papers as if blessing them. 'We have an excellent defence.'

'Insane automatism,' says Dr Chase. 'Your actions *appeared* to be insane, but you were not responsible because you were behaving automatically.' He sees my clouded expression. 'You're not mad, Andrew!' Now my doctor and my lawyer laugh cosily.

'I feel mad,' I say.

'You are not responsible for your mind when it acts automatically,' Mr Laurence says briskly. 'Your mind is innocent. *You* are innocent, Mr Schidmaizig.'

'I feel guilty.' I watch them exchange glances. I know this is foolish. I shouldn't be saying any of this, but I can't help myself.

'Psychological guilt is not the same as legal guilt,' says Mr Laurence. 'I'm very much aware of the terrific strain you've been under, but believe me, it will be over soon.'

'It won't ever be over,' I say. 'I am guilty for ever.'

My blond defender looks at me with a touch of desperation. Please don't do this, I can tell he's thinking. Don't condemn yourself before I've had a chance.

Dr Chase intervenes: 'You're not innocent, but at the same time you're not to blame. The law on automatism is difficult to understand and of course "insanity" is a loaded word, but it doesn't really mean anything, at least not to the medical profession. The court needs definitions and I'd prefer to think of your condition as an abnormality of the mind, not insanity. It's a bizarre and terrible situation, but Michael is right. The case won't take long. You must just bear with us.'

I laugh. I can't help it. It was the way he said 'Michael'.

Dr Chase gets up and pours us all a small cup of coffee. The familiar smell percolates a sense of reality and I begin to feel calmer.

I sip my coffee and look around the room. I stare at the certificates on the wall and the files on the desk and feel the smile creeping back again. Laughter bubbles in my throat, but it's not a pleasant sensation. It makes me feel out of control.

The paranoia of the accused. Dr Chase and Mr Laurence must have seen this thousands of times in their professional dealings with the desperate (he's *smiling*, for Christ's sake! They all do when it comes to this), but they are determined not to show it.

They turn to the papers. I watch their light-blue suits merge as they ignore me and get on with the business of saving me from life. I excuse myself and return to my room.

More flowers have arrived, including a huge bunch of tight yellow rosebuds, a basket of freesias and some white tulips. The nurse has left the flowers on my bed with a pile of cards. There are about a dozen, all the same size like birthday cards. I open them. They are from fans and the messages are all the same: 'Good Luck', 'Best Wishes', 'Thinking of You'.

The card I know will hurt most I leave until last. I put it on the bed, turned face down so I don't have to look at the handwriting, and go to the bathroom for a glass of water. I would prefer whisky for this but since that's impossible, I've got to have some sort of substitute. I let the tap run for a long time before filling my glass. Then I dry my hands on one of the big, soft white towels and return to the bed, where the card is lying like a grenade. My hands shake uncontrollably as I pick it up and tear it open.

It's brutish, as expected. From him, supposedly representing both of them, but only Peter could have written: WE ARE COMING. I WISH IT WAS TO SEE YOU HANG.

I drop the card on the floor and reach into the bedside drawer for a cigarette. There, I find the near-transparent aerogram with the Australian bird stamp. A pink-crested galah. Lillian's letter.

I light a cigarette and look at the galah. It mocks me. Lillian had written that they were going to stay away. 'We cannot take any more pain,' she'd said.

The letter had been filled with pain. Misspelled, rushed and confused, it had torn her up to write it, as it had torn me to read it. I cannot recall the exact words, just the incoherence, the quavering lines, the stops and starts, the confusion. Lillian would have composed the letter in secret, perhaps in the bathroom, or on a numbing bus ride through a Sydney suburb. Even on the flat golden beach. But of course she wouldn't go there now. Too many reminders. Too much pain.

There is pain in Peter's card, but it is different. His pain is violent. Granular fighting pain. I wonder if he will try to kill me when he sees me.

I chain-smoke my way through the packet of cigarettes, lighting the tips from the butts, and then screw up the packet and throw it in the bin. Then I take all the cards and letters and tear them into shreds. I look at the bin. I can see odd words on the torn paper – 'best', 'love', 'pain'. I stuff the bunch of roses on top to cover them up.

Someone knocks on the door. I ignore it, knowing that whoever is knocking will just walk in. The knocking comes again, a little louder now and accompanied by someone calling my name.

I get up, irritably, and fling open the door. The sunburnt nurse is standing there, her face half hidden by a huge array of flowers.

'I'm sorry, I couldn't open the door with these,' she says. She sounds slightly out of breath. 'They just keep arriving. All your fans, I suppose . . . There's more downstairs.'

The cellophane around the great bunches of pink and white and yellow blooms crackles like static electricity as she walks into the room and looks around for somewhere to deposit the load.

I don't help her. The presence of all these flowers and their sweet, cold perfume is obscene.

The nurse goes into the bathroom. There is a sound like a heavy silk dress falling as she dumps the flowers in the bath.

'I'll go and get some vases.' Her face is flushed and I notice one cheek is brushed with gold flecks of pollen. 'Oh, I almost forgot.' She reaches into her pocket. 'More cards.' She fans them out playfully before tossing them on the bed.

While she fetches the vases, I take the yellow roses out of the bin and put them with the others in the bath. Seeing them there makes me feel queasy.

The nurse comes back, arranges the vases on the window ledge and makes towards the bathroom.

'No, don't – I mean, I'll do them later.'

She hesitates and looks confused. 'There's one . . .' Then she goes off to the bathroom and comes back with a single white iris. 'I got this for you. I read somewhere about your good-luck flower. I didn't have time to get a card. I just, well, you know . . . I just wanted you to know that there was one from me.'

'Thank you,' I say, taking the iris. It feels cold in my hands and I cannot bear to look at it. Quickly, I put it in the nearest vase, but it's too tall and topples out and falls to the floor.

'Oh, we should cut it,' the nurse says.

'No, it's all right. I'll arrange everything later,' I say. Then I thank her again.

She steps towards me. I turn away and face the window. I feel her arms come up around my neck. Her skin is warm and faintly sticky from the flowers. The silky crown of her head presses in the space between my shoulder blades.

'Good luck,' she whispers.

She pulls away. I feel as if I've been dipped in ice.

The dark time. The flowers are still in the bath and the tap is dripping rythmically on the cellophane with a soft crunching noise which sounds like an animal being hit by a wheel. But I won't get up and twist it off. It's a mild, almost welcome torture compared to what's happening in my mind.

[161]

I've been calling up substitutes, superimposing them on the framework of my life, to see how they would deal with this. But they are resisting. They won't play this game. Sergei has just mocked me and called me a coward. He would have succeeded in killing himself. There are no guards around to force him to live. Plenty of glass, look at all those crystal vases. Why am I such a fucking coward?

Julian Crewe? Julian died an honourable death. A pure death after a blameless life. Julian suffered but he never complained. Not even when the disease turned him mad.

My grandmother. Leave her out of this.

Peter? He wants me dead. He wants to see me swinging from a noose. Peter is looking forward to seeing justice being done.

It always comes back to *him*. I can't get him out of my mind. He's doing this now, lying in a cell – this is a cell, don't kid yourself – wondering how it happened, hearing their screams, seeing the blood thick as velvet on the knife. Then the shock and glorious ecstasy of being *wanted* for the first time. Seeing his Photofit on TV. Watching the scared faces in the shopping mall where he has become a star. Now he remembers the dog-damp smell of the Heath in his clothes, in his hair, in his lungs . . .

The little fucker has got his mother's photo up there on the wall. The police let him take it from the flat in Kilburn, along with his drawing pad and the little icon of the Virgin Mary. But the police drew the line at the geraniums and felt sick when he cried and said they'd die. Still, he's forgotten the geraniums now. He's completely relaxed, a little too full after his vegetarian meal, arms behind his head as he lies on his bed trying to figure it all out . . .

He's also looking at a painting by some sad lunatic and the cracks in the ceiling and trying not to throw up at the smell of rose and freesia perfume. In the drawer by his bed is the unfinished concerto that the police let him bring and a wedding ring.

Now he appears in the mirror, wild and red-eyed, his jaw choppy and scabbed after savagely cutting off his beard in the bath. The hair fell like grains of red earth on to the pile of flowers which made him think of wreaths in a huge, white casket. He snipped with the sharp hospital scissors, wanting to carve down to blue bone, but not having the stomach for it.

He returns to his bed where he lies all night, sweating in a

[162]

fever of fear, cursing, then praying to the god he's never believed in, going over and over and over.

Morning comes and he walks to the door, half asleep, and sees Dr Chase standing there. He rubs his eyes, confused, believing that he is still dreaming. Dr Chase takes his arm and leads him back into the room. He sits him down on a chair, orders coffee, and then tells him:

'Andrew, I think you should go home.'

— 21 —

Linda has left the hall light on. I am grateful. I could not have coped with walking into darkness. On the hall table there is a pile of mail: brown envelopes on the bottom, white on the top. I wonder why these have not been forwarded to the hospital. The smell of lavender and beeswax reminds me: I am expected here.

I go straight to the kitchen. Out of habit? Or is it because I know it is the brightest place? The kitchen is unnaturally clean. The white-tiled floor has been waxed and my shoes squeak as I walk around, nervous and inquisitive – like an intruder.

The surfaces are bleached neat, cleared of any signs of inhabitation. No packets of food, jars, keys, tickets, discarded programmes or sheets of music – the disorder I remember. Linda has wiped it all away.

On the round wooden table is a note: 'Dear Mr Smith.' I smile – it was a joke between us that she could never remember how to pronounce, let alone spell, Schidmaizig so we told her to call us the Smiths.

I hope you are feeling better. I have done everything I can here. The grass needs cutting, but I had to leave it because the mower is not working again. Lots of flowers came, but I took them to the old people's home because I was not sure when you would be back. I hope you don't mind. I will be staying with my brother in Manchester for a while. Please could you send my wages there.

Linda.

I turn the note over. On the other side is the brother's Manchester address.

I feel calmed by the ordinary formality of the note. 'I hope you are feeling better.' 'I hope you don't mind.' So practical. So Linda. She would have written exactly the same if I'd been recovering in hospital from an illness, a heart attack, say. But maybe then she would have left the flowers. There is, however, a lie in the note. Linda knew exactly when I was returning.

The kitchen is at the back of the house so I cannot see whether Dr Chase has left or not. I suspect he is still sitting outside in the Jag, perhaps listening to some music, perhaps just thinking about the sad loser who got out of the car and smiled, pretending that he could cope with this.

I go to the window and look out at the garden. The grass is long, but not unkempt yet. Not wild. Not as wild as when we first came.

Do you remember standing here? I was behind you with my face in your hair, which smelled of lemons. Warm Mediterranean hair. Your back was taut against my chest and I could feel all your tightness, all your muscular longing. You wanted to go out there and start digging, get your hands dirty, make this patch yours. Ours. I thought it should be left. I liked the wildness, the cracked stones, the shards of glass and terracotta, the roses like seaweed. 'It's interesting,' I said and felt your enthusiasm suddenly harden and become still, felt it like a missed heartbeat. It was such a little thing, an unintentional act of malice. It cast a shadow, but you smiled it away. You said you didn't mind.

There are leaves all over the grass now. Amber, khaki, red, green – the colours of a battlefield. No wind stirs them up. The leaves are dead. Fallen. I should go out and sweep them up. I should leave this window which smells of meths and go out and get my hands dirty. It would be good to make myself tired. I could build a bonfire. But London people despise bonfires and I must do nothing that disturbs.

This kitchen is bright as a swimming pool. Everything has been polished, sanitised. What am I doing here? I open the cupboards to find out – oh, God, another thing. This used to make you laugh. I'd come down, numbed and incoherent from composing, and open a cupboard.

'What are you doing?'

[164]

'Just looking.'

'For what, what do you want?'

A sense of the ordinary. That everything was still there and had not mysteriously realigned in my absence. Now I look again and find jars and tins and musty cardboard packets of spices. Coriander, cumin, cardamom, memories of disastrous and exquisite blendings. Labels, jams made by friends, baby food left over from other people's visits, decaffeinated teas. A bottle of olive oil, a present from Santorini. A packet of hair dye. 'Is it chestnut or just orange? Be honest!' Vanilla and cooking chocolate.

'Don't eat that, it's six months old. There's Bournville in the fridge.'

I stare at the tins and packets, but I feel nothing. The cupboards are dead. Cabinets containing museum pieces.

Now I become aware of the silence. The *noise* of it. The humming and buzzing and ticking of the kitchen machines. I have never noticed it before, this minute household racket, this insect sound, which must go on in modern houses all the time. By modern, I suppose I mean places where young people live. The only truly quiet houses I have ever been in have belonged to the very old.

I go to the fridge. It's the centre of the noise. The pitch changes from an aggravated hum to a gentle whine as I open the door and peer into the sickly yellow interior. The thought crosses my mind: are fridges designed that way, screaming to be opened all the time, providing a nice little power surge each time they are silenced? The cold white shelves yield a vacuum-packed half-moon of Edam, a half-pint of milk and a carton of fresh soup – coriander and carrot – and, oh, Christ, a bottle of champagne.

Linda, Linda. Why did you have to be so loyal and leave it there? Why didn't you steal it? You could have shared it with your brother in Manchester. You earned this bottle. You deserved something to mark your escape from here, your newfound freedom, your future. You should be drinking champagne now, letting it dissolve the nasty taste left in your mouth by the strangest job you ever had.

Had she bought it . . .? No, too soon, control it, take your time. Take a few deep breaths. That's it. Breathe harder. Down on the floor now. Head between the knees. You're here. You're here 'to come to terms with what happened'. Fuck you, Dr Chase. I'm not fucking ready for this. Put me back in hospital. Bastard for bringing me here in your sweet-smelling Jag, sweet-talking terms all the way. 'You must allow yourself to grieve. You've been holding back. You must go back in order to go forward.' *Time heals. Time heals. Time heals.*

But first I must come to terms with time.

I pull myself up from the floor. Whisky. I am mad for it. There must be whisky. There is always whisky. But not in here. I must go into the white room to find whisky. I'm not ready for that. I look inside the fridge again. It's a raided drug cabinet, medicine-free, save for the champagne. I take out the bottle, feeling its cold weight tug at my diminished hospital arms, and dig my thumbnail into the gold foil. A sharp pain as the wire catches under the nail, but I twist it off and ease out the thick cork. A pearl of blood drops on the immaculate floor. Mustn't make a sound, mustn't think about what I'm doing. There is no ritual. No ceremony. There is only cold alcohol. I hold the foaming bottle over the gleaming sink and catch sight of my face in the taps. My new beardless, white, criminal face. The machines hum louder. They scream at me as I take my first drink.

It's good champagne, Linda. It would have been a nice present for someone who's worked so hard. You must have been cleaning and polishing all week. Not a smear anywhere. Not a trace. Normally you weren't so anxious. It was never like this. You left mud on the kitchen floor. Another joke. We always knew when you'd been. You left prints from your size nines. Big stomping, capable Linda prints. I miss them. I miss you. Not fair. I'm going to have to do this alone.

Linda, how long did it take you to get the place so clean? So straight, so innocent. So *uncriminal*. You must have done it straight away. You couldn't have stayed here with it like it was. You would have cleaned up soon after the police left. It would have been the best thing to do. You wouldn't have wanted to stay here surrounded by the mess of reminders.

The champagne tastes like cold metal. The neck of the bottle is thick and heavy against my teeth – a brutal way to drink champagne. Good.

Linda, you angel. You didn't deserve this. I should have called in someone else, someone from outside, a professional in a blue overall, someone anonymous, someone who knew nothing of the history. I take another slug of the champagne, feeling it fizz like acid against my teeth, and then sit down at the table and write out a cheque for five thousand pounds.

I take off my shoes. They are a distraction. I don't want to hear myself. My steps in this house are too painfully familiar.

The floor is cold under my feet. I leave the kitchen and walk up and down the hall. I touch the walls. They are also cold. Cold and firm and slightly damp like chilled meat. I pass the central-heating box and flick on the switch. A dull buzzing starts up, a droning like a lazy summer fly. The switch glows red. Water starts sloshing through the pipes as the circulatory system of the house starts to flow, reminding me that I am resuscitating the past. I flick off the switch. This is unbearable.

I go into the white room. Sergei's old clock is still marking time on the mantelpiece. I note the time: four o'clock in the afternoon. No man's time. The time when the world would stop, I used to think. I told my grandmother this theory when I was fifteen. She laughed and said it was because I was always hungry then, coming home from school. Transition time. Not morning. Not evening. Not twilight. Not dawn. Not the beginning. Not the end. Four o'clock. Preparatory time.

Sergei believed in the theory. He always hated four o'clock. In the Russian winter it was as dark as midnight at four o'clock.

The time when the forbidden orchestra comes up the stairs to practise.

Four o'clock. It's the real time. This surprises me. Not the time, but the passing of time since I was last here. Since I stood in the middle of this room with the crackle of police radios coming at me from all sides like machinegun fire. Since I went down on the floor, felled with confusion. Not the afternoon, but the middle of the night.

You must go back in order to go forward.

This room is also clean. Preparatory. The polished wood floor sticks to my bare feet. Now my feet are sweating as if I've been running. But it is cold. From my knees upwards I feel a chill. I want to close my eyes and walk out out of here, but in other places it will be worse.

The white curtains are drawn. Who did this? Linda? Did you keep them closed all the time? You wouldn't have wanted people

[167]

to look in from the street. And there were a lot of people out there at one time. Journalists, swigging from bottles of mineral water, photographers, draped in black hardware like assassins, and silent, stern police. The journalists and the photographers received instructions from mobile phones. Lethal and obedient, they waited, like a shooting party, firing off a few rounds for fun at a neighbour. 'Hey, hey, did you know him? What sort of life did he lead?'

The police wrapped me up in a grey blanket. Like a racehorse. Like a newborn. Like a pop star. They pushed me out gently at first, like an offering. Then the police got rough. The scream of outrage from the mob made them nervous. I was pushed hard against the car. Inside my blanket cloak, I fought to free myself, struggled to rescue my arms from the soft, choking folds. Then a hard blue arm sought mine and I was clamped. Three, four, five seconds while they opened the door and I held my breath. Just before I stepped inside, I felt a last rush of warmth from the mob shored up behind me like swimmers in contaminated water. They were drowning in it. Appealing. 'Pleeese. Just. Just. Pleeeese . . .' Then I was inside, inhaling the dry, bad air of the police car. It smelled of fish and chips, sperm and high-tar cigarettes. Gagging air. I wanted to open the window, but we were still in the war zone. A tank was trailing us. A block-windowed TV van. No siren; no noise from the car, except the radio guiding us in like air-traffic control. The officer beside me was breathing hard. Clenched, tense breathing, forced through the nose. Serious breathing for when no one knows what to say. Beyond his breath there was leaded petrol and warm metal. A smell reminiscent of school trips. A sense of excitement and deepest, darkest dread. No colour. No light. No sun coming up. It was sundown at dawn. Time was dying. It was going into reverse, painting everything backwards. Layer after layer of colour began peeling off. Streets, houses, dogs, men, turned from grey to pearl to pale to blank. Everything retreated. The fibres from the grey blanket flayed me like asbestos. Now I was streaming allergic tears. A light flared in the darkness and one of the police handed me a high-tar cigarette.

I heard they offered you a lot of money for your story, Linda. More than five thousand pounds? A lot of money, Linda.

My story. It begins and ends here. Here in this white-walled room, this gallery of echoes.

'Take your time,' the police officer said. We sat here, on this sofa, knees touching. I remember that point of warmth. I clung on to it, as if this alone could save me. The policeman was young, younger than me, with small hands like a boy's. Bitten nails. The skin all around his fingers was chewed and mangled too. It looked as if a rat had attacked his hands. No, this was where he went instinctively, compulsively to help him deal with rats. Red hair, brighter than mine. As short and neat as mine was long and mad and covered in my own vomit. The smell of me must have made him ill. The nearness of me, of what I'd become. I was stinking. Shivering and stinking and afraid. But the police officer didn't flinch. He wrote my name in rounded letters, as though my name was his first adult sentence. This completely humiliated me. This was when I started to slide away, down from the sofa, the soft, surreal, white sofa, to the chemical hardness of the polished floor.

My story doesn't begin here. This is where I first told it, where I first heard it, but it doesn't begin here. My story begins up there, in another room. In the room where I can't go. Let me drink. Let me drink myself into oblivion. Let me be at peace.

'Take your time, sir.'

Have you any fucking idea how hard this is?

I'm very drunk now. Sick drunk. I found a bottle of green charteuse. Bad, oily, nasty. Smelling like flowers that have been left too long in water. The sickest thing anyone could drink. I found the bottle at the same time as I found her photographs. They were in a large art folder which Linda had tidied away. The folder was on the bottom shelf of a cupboard we used for storing all those useless things that no one knows what to do with: cotton reels, broken picture frames, mugs, newspapers marking some occasion. I found a copy of *The Times* with a picture of Margaret Thatcher on the front. She was in the back of a car, a tear in her eye. 'A funny old world,' the headline said. Old world. Now everything belongs to the old world. Centuries ago. Thatcher is a dead film star. Her glamour collects dust here in this cupboard, this old glory hole, along with the dried flakes of marijuana in a film canister, the abandoned tapestry, the velvet hair band, the invitation to a Christmas ball – antique shreds, bits and pieces of the ephemeral past.

I look at the photographs. They are all black and white, taken in Paris and London. The first one is a Parisian café scene. An old man is seated at a round table, reading *Le Monde*. Next to him, a beautiful young woman has lowered her newspaper to the level of her exquisite cheekbones, suggesting an Arab mask. Her eyes have a lustrous, pearly quality as they gaze out at the world while her unknown companion stares into it.

The second photograph is from London, showing a smear of pigeons like a dirty lace curtain in front of the Albert Hall. My hand shakes as I turn this picture over and find another French portrait. This one shows a train leaving an empty Metro station.

I hear you.

'It's not art. Just snapshots. I've taken what was already there. It's easy.'

'They're beautiful. You're beautiful!'

'They're not what I wanted them to be. This is not how it was. I can't seem to get it.'

'You will. Don't be so impatient. You're still learning.'

'You don't understand. Technically these pictures are good, I've learned that much, but there's something missing, something I saw but couldn't reach.'

'I know.'

'What do you think it is?'

'I think you're trying too hard to find it. I think you should show these and let others decide what they mean. Take a risk.'

'I don't know if I'm ready.'

'Well, what's the alternative? You'll just carry on taking picture after picture until you find the mysterious X factor – or not – and then what? You have to show some of the process – the progress – or you'll end up not showing anything.'

'Crap, Andrew. You're talking total crap. *You* won't show anything until you're ready. What the hell have you been doing for the last six months?'

'Experimenting.'

'So, why can't I experiment?'

[170]

'This is ridiculous, Natalie. We're not in competition.'

'Aren't we? You have no idea, have you?'

'Of what, for Christ's sake? What are you talking about?'

'Us. The way things are now. The way you shut me out all the time.'

'I'm working, you know that. You know it's important to me. I need this time. I thought we agreed on that!'

'Don't shout. It's all going wrong. I know you need this time, but it's hard for me to let you have it. I hate myself for it at times. I wish I could be more gracious about it, but I can't. Sometimes I feel that I don't exist.'

'You're spoilt, Natalie, that's your problem. You want it all ways. You want me, but you don't want me to do what makes me happy. You want to achieve something yourself, but you're not prepared to put yourself on the line for it. You want –'

Screaming. 'You don't know what I want!'

'Natalie!'

'No, listen to me, I want to tell you.'

She told me she was lonely. It was the saddest thing I'd ever heard. She was frightened of how lonely she felt. But it wasn't my fault. She knew how important my work was and she felt guilty about distracting me from it with her own needs. But there were times when she felt she could go mad and I wouldn't notice. I was too far away, too remote for her. She began to cry. She wanted someone ordinary, someone to sit down at the kitchen table with and talk about plans. She liked planning. I hated it. She wanted something to look forward to. A goal.

'Something bright in the distance. Something we can strive for!'

I asked her if she wanted to leave. She cried some more and said of course she didn't. Then she told me she'd had an affair in Paris.

I did the worst thing I could have done. I got up and left her. I went upstairs to my aviary and worked on my concerto. It wasn't going well. It hadn't been going well for months – for the same reason that she was having trouble with her work. It was the last movement. It wouldn't take off. I couldn't lift it, couldn't make it go anywhere. I couldn't find the mysterious X. The music was like a lump of lead in my hands. And in my mind there was only

[171]

fear. Why didn't I console her? Because I was frightened. I was frightened of not being able to get it right. The concerto was my life. It was everything. If I got it wrong, I got everything wrong.

I didn't believe her about the affair, of course.

— 22 —

Dawn. No, earlier than dawn. I'm too frightened to sleep here. Too many shadows. Too many memories, whispers, cries and shouts; throughout the long night they seemed to rustle in the walls. The muslin curtains were white ghosts bending towards me in the breeze and I felt wings on my face, horrible cold wings, light and sinister as drifts of snow. I kept moving my hand to brush them away. I saw images: Natalie and me holding hands, window-shopping on a rainy December night. Natalie bending to tie her shoelace, her laughing face illuminated by golden Christmas lights. I could see myself riding a bicycle alongside a shuffling old man who kept telling me to ride on and forget him. My grandmother singing a song as she threaded a string of amber. Trees, rocks, clouds, but most of all snow. Thick pouches of it. I couldn't see the snow, I could only feel it, soft and clogging in the darkest crevasses of my mind.

Now I'm shivering. Blasts of cold are whipping through me, setting up a shuddering that is so strong I think my teeth might smash. I get up from the white sofa and go to the kitchen. I need coffee. Something, anything, to take away this awful cold.

The coffee still smells fresh as if the packet has just been cut. *Carte Noire.* She liked this brand. She brought it back from Paris every time. I pour the coffee into the glass cafetiere and fill it up with boiling water. I stir the coffee with a spoon and take the cafetiere to the table. The plunger makes a sucking noise as I push it down. I pour my first cup and try to stifle a sudden stab of pain as I realise I've made enough for two.

I sip my coffee and look across the wooden table to the empty seat. This is where we talked. Where we had our first real talk after our first night apart. I'd come down from my aviary, numbed and hung over after spending the whole night composing with a bottle of Jack Daniel's for inspiration, and found her here at the table, drinking *Carte Noire* and drying her hair.

'I've decided,' she said.

I said nothing. I knew this game. She always played it. She liked an element of suspense. I was now supposed to say 'Decided what?' and she could then present me with whatever she had decided with a bit more of a flourish than if she'd told me straight. It normally amused me – it was such a female thing – but that morning I felt too sick for games.

She had put on a fresh, white linen dress and her curls were still wet and ringleted from her shower. She looked like a little girl dressed up for a birthday party.

'I've decided,' she said again. But this time she looked me in the eyes. I felt a *frisson* of fear. Had she decided to leave?

'I'm going ahead with the exhibition,' she said.

I raised my coffee mug in salute.

'No, wait, I must go back *there* . . .' She flushed and rubbed at her curls vigorously with a white towel. 'There are some things I missed, gaps to fill in . . .' She trailed off and looked around the kitchen. 'I need to sort some things out,' she said.

I looked down into my mug and caught sight of my own reflection. I watched my lips as I asked: 'Is he French?'

'Yes,' she said and carried on drying her hair.

I watched her rubbing at the curls. They were almost dry and springing around her head in perfect, glossy spirals. She looked so young and fresh and pretty. So deserving. I saw a dark, wiry French boy with smooth skin and large hands. A laughing boy who turned up at her hotel every morning on a scooter, drank red wine with her at lunch and then took it from her lips in the afternoon. He had exotic plans for the future. He spoke of the little restaurant he wanted to open in the sixteenth arrondissement. He would run this for a couple of years to make enough money to move to Mauritius, where he had a friend who . . .

'Andrew.' She dropped the towel and looked at me fiercely. 'I want to have a baby. That's really what I decided last night.'

The morning she left for Paris we made love without protection for the first time. I was tender to start with, but she impatiently dismissed my caresses and urged me on. Her legs gripped me hard as she slid on me and pulled herself up, arching her back

[173]

like a magnificent cobra. The fawn skin of her muscular arms grew tight and hot as she became a thousand hot pulses twitching above me. I was dazzled and afraid. She seemed to be both punishing herself and freeing herself. She gripped me tighter. She wanted me to impregnate her, to fill her up, to close up the gaps. I released into her and she cried out and then began to weep softly. I stroked her hair and held her. I knew that at last she had found something to strive for.

I didn't go to the airport. I watched her dress and pack. She was shivery with nervous excitement and kept running back from the wardrobe to kiss me. I stayed in bed, propped up on a bank of pillows, smoking, wondering if we'd succeeded. Part of me hoped greedily that I was now taking root somewhere deep inside her. I wanted her to carry this with her in Paris, this small, warm, half-formed potential. A seed of hope. But I recoiled at the thought. Had I given her hope simply to ensure that she stayed with me? The idea was hideous.

She kissed me on the mouth. She smelled of leather and going-away.

'Don't be sad. I'll sort it out in a few days.'

I waved my hands, not dismissively, but to show her that I understood.

'I'm sorry,' she said. She ran her hands nervously through the curls. 'I shouldn't have told you. It was cruel.'

'No, I've been cruel. I didn't realise that I was shutting you out. It's been difficult.'

She laughed, 'Well, at least you can work in peace for a few days.'

She kissed me once more and I had to resist an urge to pull her back down on the bed, to start making love to her again, to confirm what we'd started.

'I've got to go,' she said and pulled away, still holding my hand. She looked down at my fingers.

'Unless . . . you don't want me to come back.' The fierce look was back in the green eyes.

Of course. She wanted me to say it. The act of love hadn't been enough.

'Yes, I want you to come back.'

She touched my cheek once swiftly, and then was gone.

The door banged and silence followed, quick and heavy. I didn't weep. I left that to the French boy.

She fades. I get up from the table and wander around the kitchen, trying to calm an agonising wave of longing. It's madness, recreating her like this. I must get out of here. I'll go insane if I stay here. Dr Chase, you've got no idea how bad this feels. I can *smell* her, for Christ's sake.

I leave the house and start walking down the road. The sky is clear and frost glitters on the asphalt. It's a glass-clear autumn morning but it gives me no pleasure. I feel only a stabbing pain in my chest from the sharp cold. I pull up the collar of my coat and walk on. I turn a corner and quickly flatten myself against a prickly green hedge to avoid two boys on bicycles. One of the boys shouts as the bicycles fly past, wheels hissing like steam.

'Watch it, old man!' I put my head down. Old man. I'm thirty-five, for God's sake. But I wonder how they know that I'm at the end of my life.

I reach the supermarket and hesitate before I go in. Its homely sloping roof, red sign and great black and white clock are suddenly disturbing. There's something about the supermarket that reminds me of Highgrove. Maybe it's all the glass and light. Maybe it's the people inside. I can see them milling around, a mass of doughy faces. What if one of them recognises me?

I step back a few paces and knock into a woman who is holding a collection tin.

'Could you spare some change, please, for children with leukaemia?' She shakes the tin.

I remember the nurse shaking my sedatives. I dig in my pocket, find a five-pound note and fold it in half before wedging it into the tin.

'Oh, thank you so much!' The woman touches my arm. 'That's so kind.' I shake her off and walk towards the automatic doors.

Panic flutters in my chest as the doors suck shut behind me. I'm trapped inside now with all the white faces gliding around, pushing silver trolleys which glitter edgily. Children are crying and there is a warm smell of fresh doughnuts. I grab a basket and walk up an aisle. A young woman in pursuit of a column of spaghetti brushes my arm and apologises. I smile, but fear is now twitching inside me so badly that I'm sweating with it. I can feel it running down my neck and legs. I shouldn't have come in here.

I move around the aisles, looking for the quickest route to the drinks bank, and almost collide with an old man who has dropped a jar of marmalade. He stares at the mess in a blind confusion. I feel I should help him, but don't want to draw attention to myself. I walk around him. The poor old bugger stares at me with frightened eyes. He doesn't know what to do about this tiny zone of chaos he has created. He can't walk away and leave it. He is paralysed as he waits for rescue. The other shoppers look at him with pity and disapproval, but nobody moves to help him. He stares at me again, appealing, and now I have to take his arm and steer him away from the broken glass. He clings to me and I feel a sudden wave of revulsion at the sight of his twitchy old man's fingers clamped to my coat. A smiling assistant comes towards us with a huge sweeper of grey rags. Relieved, I pull away from him.

At the drinks bank, I select a bottle of Jack Daniel's and take my place at the nearest checkout. There is a couple in front of me. They have wine, bread, cheese, an avocado and chocolate in their basket. Food for lovers. The girl keeps resting her head on her lover's shoulder and making little mewing noises. They are both darkly beautiful. French. 'Salaud!' the woman says teasingly as the young man playfully tugs her long black hair. 'Salaud!' I close my eyes, trying to shut out a sudden dark rush at pain.

'Monsieur!' says the dark young man. Handsome, so handsome. I wonder if Claude was this handsome . . .

'Monsieur!' He points at the empty console. I put down my solitary bottle and thank him. They both smile at me. Their smiles are identical: white teeth, wide mouths with moist wanton lips, uninhibited. The bottle of whisky falls over – why do they always do that, keep the console spinning when you have only one item? I scowl at the assistant as I pay.

'Well, thank you!' she snarls in reply.

The heavy feel of the bottle swinging in its plastic bag against my thigh is comforting. I walk up the street, taking great gasps of cold air, feeling a prickling sensation as the sweat on my back and legs begins to dry. No one gives me a second glance as I walk up the hill, past the Victorian church (I was *married* here . . . no, don't) and the arc of tall houses with pebble-dash fronts. I pass glossy BMWs and Volvos in too bright colours; child's paintbox red, summer green and flashy gold. The cars rest on drives of immaculate gravel, clean as new graves. Some of the houses have boxes of geraniums on the window ledges end ornamental trees sprouting from more gravel. In one garden, a sulphur-crested cockatoo preens itself on a stand. The creature squawks a mocking insult as I walk past.

I turn into another street. There are FOR SALE signs everywhere, bright and cheerful like carnival flags. It seems that today all of England is changing hands, selling up, moving on, seeking new futures. I pass a butcher's and almost black out on the pavement. Pheasants and rabbits are hanging upside down from large hooks, their bloodied beaks and mouths leering towards me. At the back of shop I can see racks of pearly carcasses, swaying monstrously. The sight makes me want to retch.

I enter the park. The great blue-green pool of grass and sky is empty. Everyone is too busy selling or escaping to come here. I walk across the grass to a bench. The sun has come up and I loosen my coat to let in some warmth. Something glitters on the bench, a tiny bronze plaque. I read the inscription: 'Ralph W. Stillings 1943–1978. Remembered with love.' That's nice, Ralph. It's nice to have something like this. A memory of your short life. A bench-mark. Lovely setting. Let me tell you what I can see. You don't mind, do you? You see, I'm a little crazy and playing games like this helps take my mind off things.

Right, the grass – fresh and green and sprinkled with beech leaves like brown paper stencils. Big blue bowl of sky, opaque on this clear, cold October morning. A row of weeping silver-birch trees by the lake. A plane flossing the sky above a pair of black crows, competing with the noise. Fah, fah, fah, fah. A golden retriever running across the park, its tail a ragged banner in the wind. Two small boys on mountain bikes like a pair of tiny pedalling ants. It's a great day, Ralph. In another life, another time, I might have got to know you. I could have told you why I'm here, why I'm grieving, why I'm so crazy, and you could have told me about your life. You could have told me everything, all the dark things that keep you awake at night. It would be all right because we'd never see each other again. The past wouldn't matter then, nor the future. We could talk, there would be so much to say. A whole lifetime of talk. But hold on a minute, Ralph, we're being interrupted already. Someone is coming. Someone is walking up to our bench.

'Fark!'

He sits down heavily beside me. Too close. He is wearing a heavy army greatcoat, a little like mine. His hair is long and tangled, like mine, and his eyes are wild and red. Oh, God.

'Can you spare some change for a cup of tea, squire?'

I dig in my pocket, feeling for a heavy pound coin, but there is only the light silver shingle of fives and twenties. I give him all I have.

'Cheers!' The paw which takes the money is filthy, scored with deep brown lines like rivers on a sepia map. The eyes greedily ogling the silver are the same colour brown. His hair is coarse and thickened at the ends into matted tails. This man smells like shit.

'Cheers,' he says again. But he is clearly disappointed. He has counted the money and realised that he's going to have to ponce a lot more before he can get to the off-licence.

'For a minute I thought you was . . .' He trails off and squints into the distance, sniffing the air lightly like a dog.

It's a ruse. I know he's seen it, but he won't look at it yet. The Tesco bag at my feet. The telltale bottle bulge. He shuffles his feet, which are encased in clompy army boots threaded with bright orange laces. Tap, tap, tap. Shuffle, shuffle, shuffle. I watch his feet but do not move. The tapping tattoo speeds up. Still I do not move. Now he edges closer to me on the bench. His smell is obscene, sour and sulphurous as if he's been sleeping in a drain. He puts his face close to mine and smiles. I see broken-down teeth, the colour of old amber, cracked lips and grey spittle and remember the brilliant supermarket smiles of the French couple. I had wanted, just for a moment, what they had: the lovers' picnic, the teasing embrace, the mock admonishment. *Salaud!* Now this tramp wants what I have: clean clothes, a pocket full of money and that bottle. If I give it to him, will it change anything? Will it stop him wanting to be me? He might

[178]

hate me for it. Smug bastard: he's so loaded he can give it away . . .

I bend down and reach into the bag. The shit-brown eyes fill with tears. I twist off the cap and quickly stuff the neck of the bottle into my mouth. The warm liquor trickles down my throat, soothing, lulling, cradling until it embraces my stomach. I take another long swig. He's on the edge of the bench now, quivering with excitement, with panic. Then I offer the bottle to him. He reaches into his pocket, pulls out an immaculate white cotton handkerchief and preciously wipes the rim. His eyes are closed as he takes the first sip.

A quiet pattern is established. I take a long swig and hand the bottle to him. He dips his head in acknowledgement, mutters 'Bless you,' then takes his own, smaller sip. He is not greedy with the whisky; he does not even appear to enjoy it. There are no aahs, no moans of pleasure, no comments on the superiority of the brand or my decision to share it. He is simply and methodically getting drunk.

A light rain begins to fall. We carry on drinking, faster now. My head feels soft and the acid churning in my stomach has calmed to a warm pulsing. I feel strangely peaceful and wonder if I should stay here. I could sleep in the park with this silent companion tonight, this friend who has asked nothing of me and who is (although he does not know it yet) sharing something terrible and vital.

I allow him to take the last sip. Then I turn to him and grip him hard on both shoulders. I look deep into his muddied face and see fear flicker and then acceptance. I feel a deep kinship with him and a crazy, drunken, woozy urge to tell him I love him. His acceptance is the forgiveness I crave.

He puts down the bottle and smiles at me. He thanks me and pats my arm, not on the skin but on the top of my overcoat, and moves slightly away from me.

Hot whisky tears start streaming down my face. Everything turns black; the grass, the trees, the sky, the bench and my filthy companion all merge into darkness. I look into the dark and see only my own shadow. My own black self.

'What do you want?' it says.

'I want to tell you something,' I reply.

'Fark! I thought you was . . .'

'I want to tell you . . .'
'Go on then.'
'I killed my wife.'

— 23 —

'You are Andrew James Schidmaizig?'
'Yes.'
'Aged thirty-five. Your address is 57, Cranwell Road, Muswell Hill, London.'
'Yes.'
'You are a musician and composer.'
'I was a piano player, your honour.'
'A piano player. Very well, as you wish. You are accused of murdering your wife Natalie Ann Schidmaizig (née Fraser) at 57, Cranwell Road, Muswell Hill, London on the morning of 15 June 1994. How do you plead?'
'Not guilty by reason of insanity because I was asleep at the time.'
'Thank you Mr Schidmaizig, you may stand down.'
'Mr Wesley-Cope can you please outline the case for the jury.'
'I'll begin by reading a tape-recorded statement the defendant gave to the police.'

'I arrived home late. I don't know the time, but it was after midnight. Yes, it was definitely after midnight. I'd been performing at the Albert Hall. It was the first night. The press were there, stiff in black dinner suits and stiff little smiles. "Nice to see you back, Mr Schidmaizig." Smarmy bastards. It was awful. I had two pints at the bar, maybe three, I can't remember. I was nervous. I'd had a bad night in Liverpool, terrible review. Anyway, it went all right at the Albert Hall. I've always liked playing there. It's a warm place, comforting and the audiences are usually kind. It went all right. I mean, I think it went all right. Two encores, maybe three. I don't know. I'm having trouble remembering. I don't know what I'm saying . . . everything is chaos. I don't know what I played. Just the encores. The cheering and the clapping and the terrible bright lights. Photographers. One hailed me a taxi. I had the window open all the way home. I was looking at the stars and thinking . . . I don't remember. The sky was huge, studded with medieval stars, like a lovely old tapestry. I got home. I was starving. I ate the remains of a chicken. Sucked all the meat off the bones. Performing always makes me ravenous. There was a bottle of champagne in the fridge. I thought about opening it, but it would have been a bit strange to celebrate on my own so I decided to leave it until morning. I thought we could have a champagne breakfast. I'd tell her all about it then. If she could manage it, the champagne, I mean. She'd been sick all day. Really bad, just constant vomiting. I was worried about her. She couldn't come to the concert of course. She said she would go to bed and if she was still sick in the morning, she would call a doctor. I went up to bed. My wife was sleeping. Oh, Christ, she looks so beautiful when she's asleep. Like a dark angel. I lay down beside her. No I didn't take off my suit – I'm still wearing it, for God's sake. She stirred and murmured something. I can't remember what she said. Something about the window, I think. It was a very hot night. I must have gone to sleep. I don't remember. All I know is that it suddenly turned cold. Ice cold and there was this freezing wind. It was so strong I couldn't see. I had to shut my eyes to the wind, but I could still feel it in my ears. It was like being punched. And there was this dreadful ringing, a horrible clanging noise of iron striking flint. Everything was white. Things were being churned up. Awful white things. Shapes. Rocks. I could see white rocks. They were crashing down a great mountain and then there was this terrible crying. It was Natalie. She was lying at the bottom of the mountain almost completely buried in snow and she was crying out to me to help her. I couldn't see her face, only her hair, which was not dark, but red. It was spilling out on the snow. I moved towards the redness, it was like a trail. She was trapped, she told me. She couldn't move. The snow had pinned her down. She couldn't feel her legs and she thought her back was broken. I had to pull her free. She told me to get the rope. There was one lying nearby. She told me to put it around her neck. And I did and then . . . Oh, Christ! Fuck! oh no, no, no, no. What have I done?'

[181]

'Thank you, Mr Wesley-Cope. What happened next?'

'The defendant telephoned the emergency services and asked for an ambulance. He told the controller that there had been an accident involving his wife. He was confused and distressed and had difficulty relaying the correct information to the controller, who repeatedly asked Mr Schidmaizig for his address. When the controller asked the defendant about the nature of his wife's injuries, he replied: "I think she's stopped breathing. She was choking, but now there's nothing."'

'I believe an ambulance arrived forty-five minutes after the defendant's telephone call. An inappropriately slow response some of you may think, but we are not here to try the London Ambulance Service.'

'Quite, my lord. The defendant was very distressed when the ambulance arrived and it became apparent that Mrs. Schidmaizig had stopped breathing. She was dead.'

'I'm sorry to interrupt, Mr Wesley-Cope, but do we have the time of death? I think it would help the jury to know that straight away.'

'Yes, my lord. From pathology reports, Mrs Schidmaizig's death occurred at 4.15 a.m. on 15 June. The defendant telephoned the emergency services at 4.27 a.m. on 15 June.'

'So it would appear that Mrs Schidmaizig was already dead by the time the ambulance arrived, albeit forty-five minutes after the emergency call?'

'Yes it would seem so, my lord.'

'Please continue Mr Wesley-Cope.'

'Mr Schidmaizig was informed by the ambulance crew that his wife was dead and was asked what had happened. The defendant was unable to reply at first as, according to the ambulance team, he suffered a severe shock reaction and had to be administered an injection of valium. At this point the police were called.'

'After the injection?'

'Yes, my lord. I understand that the defendant's reaction was so extreme that he was in danger of harming himself.'

'I see. Do please continue.'

'Two police officers arrived. Police Sergeant Robert Shaw and Police Constable Martin Dudley. Sergeant Shaw attempted to interview the defendant, but this proved impossible as Mr

Schidmaizig was still in a state of extreme shock. Sergeant Shaw went upstairs where he found Mrs Schidmaizig lying on the bed.'

'I think Mr Wesley-Cope, it would be useful for the jury to know how she was lying.'

'Mrs Schidmaizig was lying in a horizontal position at right angles to the top of the bed. Her head was not on the bed, but hanging free over the side.'

'In his statement, Mr Schidmaizig referred to a rope. Was anything of this kind in the room?'

'Yes, my lord. There was a cord around Mrs Schidmaizig's neck.'

'What sort of cord?'

'I call for exhibit A ... this cord, my lord. It matches Mrs Schidmaizig's dressing gown.'

'And how was this cord arranged Mr Wesley-Cope?'

'Sergeant Shaw reported that the cord had been wrapped twice fully round Mrs Schidmaizig's neck. The two ends of the cord were hanging loose on the floor.'

'Thank you Mr Wesley-Cope. Sergeant Shaw then telephoned for a police doctor, I believe.'

'Yes, my lord. Dr Anthony Newman arrived at the Muswell Hill address fifteen minutes later.'

'Faster than the ambulance service I see.'

'Dr Newman's home is not far from the defendant's. In Highgate, I should inform you, my lord.'

'Ha! A journey easily accomplished at five a.m.'

'Quite, my lord.'

'Do continue Mr Wesley-Cope.'

'Dr Newman examined Mrs Schidmaizig and confirmed that she was dead. He also attended to Mr Schidmaizig.'

'There was no one else at Mr Schidmaizig's home?'

'No. The police reported that there were no signs of forced entry. Mr Schidmaizig and his wife were alone.'

'Mr Schidmaizig was taken to the police station?'

'Yes, he was interviewed at Muswell Hill Station where he remained until Dr Alan Chase was called.'

'Dr Chase? He is the psychiatrist who admitted Mr Schidmaizig to Highgrove Hospital?'

'Yes, my lord. Mr Schidmaizig was released on bail, but due

to his uncertain mental state it was suggested he went to Highgrove.'

'Thank you, Mr Wesley-Cope. I now propose a short recess before you call your first witness.'

— 24 —

My hands are shaking so much I have difficulty lighting my cigarette. My twentieth of the morning – thirtieth. Perhaps even fortieth. What does it matter? There is nothing else to do now except smoke. This tiny room is filled with smoke. Dry, chemical, criminal smoke. The walls are yellow with it and greasy. You could scrape the nicotine off with your fingernails. I wonder how many people have been here before me in this bonfire shell, this waiting room for the accused. But we are not the accused, we are merely defendants. We are not allowed to be active: we cannot rush to the battle lines and attack. We must remain silent while our lawyers war, our prosecutors and our defenders. This is their time now. We, the accused, must be passive. We are not guilty. We are proving our innocence by keeping our mouths shut. Our stories, our sorry, reckless histories, will say it all.

How many defendants have sat in this almost sealed cell? (No, it is completely sealed – look at the uniformed guard on the door reading the *Daily Mail*, the absence of a window, the solid walls.) Dozens, hundreds? How many men have sat in here, twitching, smoking, biting their fingernails, praying that their stories will work out all right in the end? That the end will not be the end. In America there are rooms like this with tiny hidden gas taps. At the whisper of a valve, the defendant becomes the condemned. A clean way to deal with the criminal. Stop the guilty breathing. Kiss him with gas into oblivion. I wonder if they would kill me in America. Maybe I would get the electric chair. I've read that it takes longer. The body is shocked, but still alive. It takes a few minutes – how long, I can't remember – before it starts to burn from the inside. Which organ would go first? The heart, it would have to be the heart. In my case, I'd ask – could you ask, would they let you, would they give you the right to choose? – for the lethal charge to be adminstered directly to my head. Straight to the brain.

This is a room for the condemned. Look at the formica-topped table, the knife marks, the lines of filth in the gouged plastic and the table's buckled metal legs. The strange carved inscriptions: AMYL TA DEP, CCP and BNP, the sign of a cross, a swastika next to a heart. A slash of kisses.

I never thought it would be like this. I imagined waiting rooms with newspapers and comfortable chairs, imitation plants and a humming coffee machine. Not this graffiti-scrambled hole which stinks of ash. Not this shit-smeared ceiling (yes, some fucker went to a lot of trouble to deposit an excremental CUNT up there) or the sound of laughter and the slamming of doors outside. It echoes the slamming in my head. The clanging craziness. The clamour that I can calm only by shifting my concentration to the cacophony in my guts. I'm shitting blood now. I saw it smearing the sides of the filthy bowl in the gents' first thing this morning. Two thin red threads. I was surprised at how much it shocked me, seeing my own blood like that. It made me realise that there was something left of me to take.

'Cigarette?'

My fingers are still warm from stubbing out the last one, but I take a fresh one all the same. I'm surprised to see Dr Chase smoking.

'Are you feeling any better?' he asks.

'Yes,' I lie. He deftly flicks a small gold lighter at my cigarette.

'Stomach all right?'

How does he know?

'Yes, fine.' I take a deep drag on my cigarette.

'The next part is going to be unpleasant,' he says, blowing smoke at the ceiling. I wonder if he's noticed the CUNT.

'When did you start smoking?'

'I've always smoked, just not in the hospital.'

'Pressure of the job?'

'Something like that.' He takes another drag and blows the smoke away from his face. Smoking doesn't suit Dr Chase. He holds the cigarette too daintily, like a fine pen. He inhales again. 'Andrew, I think it's going to be all right. The jury are mostly young, that's a good sign.'

'Why?'

'Younger people tend to be more understanding of psychological cases. They are less suspicious of the mind.'

'But it's mostly men. You said before that it would be better to have more women.'

A sound of rustling paper in the direction of the guard makes us both suddenly self-conscious. I turn and look at him. He is unwrapping a chocolate bar, not greedily, but in a nonchalant way as if to let us know that he's not in the slightest bit interested in what we are saying. He's heard it all before, and worse. I watch him bite into the chocolate. There is no enjoyment in his thin-lidded eyes, no moisture on his lips as he bites and chews. The rhythmic crunching makes me think of thick boots tramping across mountain snow.

'Ah, Michael.'

My blond defender walks in, smelling of aftershave. He seems too big for the room and the court costume on him is so theatrical I almost want to laugh. The wig caps his head neatly, its light straw colour emphasising the aquamarine of his eyes, and the black gown falls in graceful silken folds from his shoulders. He looks like an impresario checking out the dressing rooms.

'Andrew.' Mr Laurence – I cannot think of him as Michael – touches my shoulder lightly in greeting. 'Everything all right?'

'Yes,' I keep lying, but I haven't taken the oath yet. I try again. 'How long will this . . . this recess be?'

'Not long, we're due back on shortly. After Wally has finished his Darjeeling.'

'Wally?'

'The judge. Thomas Wallace-Evans. Bit of a joker, but you'll get used to it. You mustn't take offence at his pettiness. The jokes about the ambulance service and all that. He likes to appear dotty. It's a good cover and it gives him more time to take notes. He's bloody sharp underneath it all.'

'What about Wesley-Cope?'

'Tough. We call him the Terrier. He doesn't let go easily.' My lawyer smiles and then touches my shoulder again. 'Don't worry. We're going to be just fine with our nasty little terrier. Alan will see to that.'

Alan and Michael. My doctor and my lawyer. My professional saviours. Now they turn their attention from me. They have business to discuss. Insane business. They have tried to explain the laws of insanity and automatism to me, but I haven't been able to take any of it in. I'm not sure what's happening. It doesn't have anything to do with me. I simply have to be here, like an exhibit. Exhibit A. God, that was awful, seeing it. The limp silken cord, the colour of summer peaches. And watching the Terrier handle it with a nasty sneer, as if it were dog dirt. It was the way he took it from its plastic package and held it up to the jury. You see this? This is what he used, the monster. A piece of her own clothing. Such depravity! I wonder what I will do when the dog prosecutor starts leaping for my throat, when he starts sniffing out all the foul places where my insanity hides. Will I break down? Will my guts give way? Will I even be able to speak? How do other men do this? What did that fucker from Kilburn do? Did he face the jury defiantly or hang his head in shame, looking down at the boots which tramped his trail of madness across the Heath? Did he falter or speak eloquently as he enjoyed the finest time of his diseased life? The time when everyone looked at him, all of them. They couldn't take their eyes off him. All those women. Seven on the jury. Did he feel a shiver of pleasure as he stood in the dock? Your honour, it was like this: I killed because no one cared.

Your honour, it is like this: I killed because I cared for her.

'You are Linda Kesley, aged twenty-six, and your address is 49 Old Park Road, Manchester?'
    'Yes.'
    'You worked for the defendant, Mr Schidmaizig, for three years, I believe?'
    'Yes. I was employed as a gardener and cleaner.'
    'Did you enjoy your work, Miss Kesley?'
    'Yes, I did.'
    'Mr Schidmaizig was a fair employer?'
    'Yes, very fair. But Natalie, I mean Mrs Smi . . . um, I'm sorry, Mrs Schidmaizig, usually made all the arrangements. You know, when I was supposed to come in and that.'
    'And it was Mrs Schidmaizig who usually paid you?'
    'Yes.'
    'How much were you paid, Miss Kesley?'
    'Well, it was five pounds an hour, the going rate for cleaners.'

[187]

'And how many hours a week did you work for the Schidmaizigs?'

'Well, usually five, sometimes more.'

'So, generally you received, let's say, twenty-five pounds a week from Mrs Schidmaizig?'

'Yes, that would be about right.'

'You never received, let's say, more than thirty-five pounds a week, even when you worked extra hours?'

'Well, no.'

'Did Mr Schidmaizig ever give you money? Independently of his wife, I mean?'

'Well, yes, but . . .'

'Call you tell the court how much money you received from Mr Schidmaizig?'

'Well, it was quite a lot. I was shocked. I mean . . .'

'How much, Miss Kesley?'

'Five thousand pounds.'

'You worked for other people, Miss Kesley?'

'Yes.'

'How much would you say you earned a week from all your jobs?'

'Well, it was usually about sixty pounds a week.'

'So five thousand pounds is a lot of money for you?'

'Yes, of course.'

'How did you receive this . . . this windfall from Mr Schidmaizig?'

'In the post. He sent me a cheque.'

'Was there a letter, a note or anything explaining it?'

'No. But some of it was my salary.'

'How much?'

'I don't know. We didn't make an arrangement. It was difficult . . . I was just looking after the place while he was away.'

'How much would you have expected to receive?'

'I don't know. I was only there two weeks. Perhaps a hundred, maybe a little bit more.'

'But certainly not five thousand pounds?'

'No, as I said, I was shocked.'

'Why were you so shocked, Miss Kesley?'

'I don't know. It just seemed a lot of money. Well, I mean, I didn't have to do much at the house and all that.'

[188]

'Why do you think Mr Schidmaizig was so generous?'

'Maybe . . . oh, I don't know. I really don't understand why he sent me so much.'

'Now, Miss Kesley, I want you to cast your mind back to when you were working for the Schidmaizigs in the summer. You came to the house three days before Mrs Schidmaizig died, is that correct?'

'Yes. I worked for three hours, mostly cleaning. Mrs Schidmaizig was out in the garden taking photographs.'

'The jury might like to note that Mrs Schidmaizig worked as a photographer. And she was a very successful one too, I understand. So, Miss Kesley, you were cleaning. What were you cleaning?'

'I was cleaning the sitting room. It was in a bit of a mess.'

'Can you describe what sort of mess?'

'Well, some furniture had been overturned and there was a broken bottle on the floor. Mrs Schidmaizig had cut her hand on the glass, trying to clear it up.'

'What was the nature of this bottle?'

'It was a whisky bottle.'

'Did Mrs Schidmaizig tell you how the bottle had come to be smashed?'

'She said something about Andrew, I mean Mr Schidmaizig, getting into a state.'

'What did she mean by "getting into a state"?'

'Well, I don't really know. I think she meant he had smashed the bottle when he was drunk or something.'

'Drunk! Miss Kesley, be very careful now. Did you ever see Mr Schidmaizig drunk?'

'Well, he used to act a bit strange sometimes. And sometimes I could smell it.'

'What could you swell?'

'Whisky. I could smell whisky.'

'How was his behaviour strange?'

'He acted as if he didn't know I was there. I asked him something once, I think I wanted the keys to the garden shed, but he didn't answer me.'

'Why do you think he couldn't or wouldn't answer you?'

'I don't know. I thought maybe it was because he was drinking.'

'Did you have much contact with Mr Schidmaizig when you were working at his house?'

'Not really. I mean, I didn't see him that often. It was usually when he came down for a coffee.'

'When he "came down", Miss Kesley. Where was he?'

'Working upstairs at the top of the house. His music room was up there, but I never went in. It was the only room I didn't clean.'

'Why didn't you go in there? Had he asked you not to?'

'No, he never said, but Nat, Mrs Schidmaizig, said he didn't like his things to be disturbed. Especially when he was working.'

'You had a good relationship with Mrs Schidmaizig?'

'Yes, very good.'

'You were her confidante, I believe?'

'Her what? I'm sorry, I don't understand.'

'I apologise. You were her friend. She shared her feelings with you.'

'Not all the time. She was very busy, you see, but sometimes she got worked up.'

'"Worked up", Miss Kesley. What do you mean?'

'Well, she would be upset some mornings.'

'How was she upset?'

'She looked like she'd been crying a lot.'

'Did she talk to you about what was upsetting her?'

'Sometimes. Sometimes she talked about her marriage. Well, it was more about men in general, really. She used to tell me to stay single as long as I possibly could. She said there were very few understanding men in the world.'

'Mr Wesley-Cope, forgive me for interrupting, but I think Miss Kesley will find the majority of men in this court to be exceptionally understanding.'

'Quite, my lord.'

'Do please continue.'

'Did Mrs Schidmaizig ever talk to you in detail about her relationship with the defendant?'

'Well, once we had a really long talk. She said that she didn't think Andrew would care if she packed her bags and left for Australia. She gave him three days before he would even notice she was missing.'

'And what was your reaction?'

'Well, I laughed. She was joking.'

'Did Mrs Schidmaizig often make jokes about leaving her husband?'

'Well, it wasn't for real. I could tell that she really loved him.'

'How could you tell?'

'Because she got upset that he didn't pay her enough attention. She wouldn't have minded if she didn't love him.'

'Very astute, Miss Kesley. Now, was Mrs Schidmaizig upset on the morning of 12 June when you arrived for work?'

'Yes. Well, I could tell she had been crying.'

'Did she say anything?'

'She apologised for the mess – she'd only just got up – and she said something about it being a long night. And the thing about Andrew, the defender, I mean, getting into a state.'

'Did she elaborate? I mean, did she tell you why he was in a state, as you put it?'

'She said it had to do with his work.'

'Did she say anything more?'

'Well, it's difficult to remember exactly what she said. I think she said something about a bad review. You know, in the newspapers.'

'She didn't show you this review?'

'No, but there was a newspaper on the floor in the sitting room. It was all torn up. I think that was it because she asked me to throw it away and normally I saved all the papers.'

'Did she say anything else?'

'Well, she was ranting on a bit. She was quite angry, I think.'

'Not joking this time?'

'No, definitely not joking. She was too upset to joke.'

'What did she say?'

'She said that she was going into town to book herself a flight to Australia. One-way.'

'Are you sure she wasn't joking?'

'She didn't sound like she was joking.'

'And then what happened?'

'She went out.'

'And that was the last time you saw her?'

'Oh, no, oh, oh . . . Look, I'm sorry. It brings it all back.'

'Take your time, Miss Kesley, you're doing extremely well.'

'Yes, that was the last time I saw her.'

[191]

She was buying a ticket for Christmas and it wasn't one-way. That was a joke, Linda. You didn't understand her humour. I didn't understand it myself at times. She used her humour to shock. To make me listen. I was always being accused of not listening. I had a talent for it, she said. My ears were the most selective she had ever encountered. Linda, we were *both* going to Australia. We argued about it, I admit that. I wanted to leave the trip until after the New Year. Christmas was not a good time. I had too much work. Everyone wants to hear music at Christmas. I had a full diary, for God's sake. It would have been difficult to rearrange things. We argued, that's all. That's not a crime. I was upset and I had a few drinks. Oh, I don't know how many, why is this court so obsessed with figures? 'How much did you say, Miss Kesley?' God, as if I was trying to bribe her, pay her off in some way, what was I covering up? Look, you know how arguments can turn nasty after a few drinks. It was the Liverpool review. I was upset about the review. Bastards. What was it? 'Schidmaizig was scratchy and unpredictable' . . . and, oh yes, this bit killed me: 'He left it all to the last movement, ending with an overblown, embarrassing finale which failed to lift him out of what was undoubtedly the worst performance of his career.' Ha! So, I got pissed. Who wouldn't? I got pissed out of my tiny mind. I think I even pissed on the review after Natalie tore it up. We were laughing then, look, there was nothing bloody sinister about it. We were laughing and I had her in my arms and she told me it didn't matter about the review, it didn't matter about anything because she loved me and she had something wonderful to tell me. She started dancing around the room – she was quite drunk, whisky sent her a little mad – and she did a cartwheel just to see if she could. She said she was worried about getting out of shape. She did the cartwheel and knocked over the whisky bottle. It smashed on the floor, we didn't clear it up because she was in my arms again and – oh, God, oh, Christ – she told me that she was going to have a baby.

'My lord, I wish to call Anthony Frank, the pathologist who examined the victim. I refer the jury to photographs of the injuries sustained by Mrs Schidmaizig. Mr Frank, would you explain?'

'The jury will notice that across the neck is a linear red line approximately fourteen inches long by a quarter of an inch in width. There is scabbing along this line which indicates the application of some sort of friction.'

'This line or mark, it is similar to a rope burn?'

'Yes.'

'And how would a rope need to be arranged to produce such a mark? Would you mind demonstrating, Mr Frank – I apologise to the jury for the crudeness – with this piece of string around, let's see, perhaps the neck of that glass water vessel?'

'Like this, with the rope pressing in a line against the side of the bottle.'

'So an assailant would have to be coming from behind with a rope to cause such a mark?'

'Yes.'

'And how much force would be required to mark the skin in this way?'

'This is difficult to say precisely, but a fair amount of force.'

'A fair amount. A stronger force than, say, pulling on a large dog straining at a leash?'

'Yes, stronger than that.'

'Were there other marks on the body?'

'There was some bruising on the left side of the neck and I also noticed the presence of petechiae, small purplish spots on the neck and around the eyes.'

'These petechiae, what did they tell you?'

'Petechiae are small haemorrhages which can occur after vomiting or crying. They also occur when force has been applied to the neck area, such as in strangulation.'

'You came to the conclusion that Mrs Schidmaizig had been strangled?'

'The petechial haemorrhaging was indicative of asphyxia and loss of consciousness which occur in strangulation, yes.'

[193]

'Were there any other signs?'

'There were marks on the tongue. In strangulation cases, the tongue is often bitten towards near death.'

'Mr Frank, you found that prior to her death Mrs Schidmaizig had been in good health?'

'Yes, excellent health. She was an extremely fit young woman and three weeks pregnant at the time of examination.'

'Thank you, Mr Frank.'

We were loving. Her skin was soft and supple as suede. I told her and she laughed and grabbed a handful of my own dry, meagre flesh. 'But you're letting yourself go!' We lay there in the moonlight and there was magic in the air. Her face was ethereal, somehow wiser without being older, more beautiful than I'd ever seen it. I was in awe and yet I felt calm with her. It was as if we were meeting again after a long absence. We were careful with each other in our lovemaking. Careful not to disturb with exaggerated cries or caresses, careful not to build the crescendo too high – careful not to leave everything until the last move-ment. I concentrated on the small points of her, her nails, pearly in the cool light, the pale underside of her arm, silky as a young fish, the girlish fine brows which widened slowly to uncrease the thin vertical line that had become a feature there, the coral bones of her neck and the gentle anemone of her sex. She was both mermaid and ocean bed, flowering mystery, so strange now with a little fish floating in her belly. (How big would it be? Smaller than an ear, maybe?) I stroked the velvet planes of her back and she started to drift off to sleep. I listened to her breathing and there was a little catch, almost a stifled sob each time she inhaled. I kissed her on the corner of her mouth, which twitched into a smile. Her breath was warm, salty and still faintly alcoholic. 'I can't wait to show you the jacaranda trees,' she said.

'I swear by almighty God that I shall answer truthfully any questions the court may ask of me.'

'Thank you, Mr Schidmaizig. Now, tell me, did your wife ever mention someone by the name of Claude?'

'She did, yes, but it was a made-up name.'

'A made-up name? I take it you knew Claude was her lover?'

[194]

'Well, she told me during the summer that she had a lover in Paris, but later she said she'd invented him to make me jealous.'

'And you believed her?'

'Yes, I believed her.'

'Why did you believe her?'

'Because . . . she's my wife, no, because I wanted to. I wanted to believe it wasn't true.'

'So, you weren't sure whether your wife was having an affair or not, Mr Schidmaizig?'

'I suppose not. I mean, how can you ever be sure?'

'What about telephone calls, letters, was there anything to make you suspicious?'

'Suspicious, for God's sake. I'm sorry, your honour, but my wife is not on trial here. No, I was not suspicious. She told me everything, there was no reason to check on her.'

'Miss Kesley has said that someone using the name Claude Michel Fleur telephoned your home on a number of occasions.'

'I am unaware of that.'

'It seems that you were unaware of a number of things regarding your wife, Mr Schidmaizig. The police found the name Claude Michel Fleur with a Paris address in your wife's address book. They followed it up and were told that Mr Fleur had gone to Australia, where your wife told Miss Kesley she intended to travel alone. What do you make of this?'

'Nothing. Claude was probably a friend.'

'A *friend*, Mr Schidmaizig?'

'She used his name, that's all.'

'Oh, come, come. She told you she'd had an affair in Paris, Claude was living in Paris and suddenly he flies to Australia. Your wife was planning to leave you, wasn't she?'

'No! We were going together. We were going out to Australia in the New Year.'

'Three days before she died, your wife told Miss Kesley that she was booking an airline flight to Australia, one-way *before* Christmas, which indicates, don't you agree, that she was planning to leave without you?'

'I don't know. Maybe we were both going before Christmas. I can't remember. We hadn't sorted the dates out. Before or after, what does it matter?'

[195]

'It matters a great deal, Mr Schidmaizig. Your wife is dead.'

'She had given him up or made him up ... I don't know. She was pregnant with our child.'

'That is not confirmed. We are still awaiting results of genetic tests.'

'She gave him up.'

'Your wife travelled to Paris frequently for her work, Mr Schidmaizig?'

'Yes.'

'And I believe her work was exhibited here in London at the Photographers' Gallery to some impressive reviews. I have one cutting here. I won't read the entire report, but it is a very flattering tribute to your late wife's work.'

'Yes, she was very excited.'

'And you weren't?'

'I'm sorry?'

'You weren't excited about her success because you were preoccupied with your own work?'

'That's not entirely true. I was preoccupied, but I remained supportive of her work.'

'How, Mr Schidmaizig? Did you attend your wife's first exhibition?'

'No, but I was planning to.'

'You were planning to. When were you planning to?'

'After I'd finished my performances. When I'm playing, I find it difficult to concentrate on anything else.'

'Your work takes precedence over everything else in your life?'

'It did. I am no longer working.'

'But at the time, Mr Schidmaizig, at the time of your wife's first exhibition, you were too engrossed in your own work to pay attention to hers?'

'It seems like that.'

'Yes, it does seem like that. Your attitude towards your work caused arguments, didn't it?'

'Well, sometimes.'

'Were they violent arguments?'

'No.'

'You never struck your wife or harmed her physically?'

'No, of course not – what is this?'

[196]

'This is an attempt to find out why you killed your wife, Mr Schidmaizig. Why you put a cord around her neck and strangled her to death.'

'I was unaware of what I was doing.'

'I put it to you that you murdered your wife in cold blood. You were jealous of her success, which was compounded when you discovered she was having an affair.'

'That's not true.'

'Let me read something which is already familiar to you, Mr Schidmaizig. A review of your own work, published in the week your wife died. Again, I will not read out the entire report, but tell me what you make of this, Mr Schidmaizig: "It is always unbearable when an original performer loses his way, especially when the performer is still young ... This was not a triumphant comeback."'

'It was the worst performance of my career, I think you'll find that's how the review ends. Mr Wesley-Cope, my work is not on trial here.'

'Mr Schidmaizig, I see that you remain sensitive to criticism.'

'No, my work is no longer important.'

'Ah, but it seems that it's still important enough for you to defend it! Your work received some pretty damning criticism just before your wife died. I would say that is important. Thank you, I have no more questions.'

My doctor and my lawyer piss with me in the gents'. It's odd, the three of us here in a line, pissing silently. I'm the suspect in the middle, protected and held captive by my pissing partners who are matter-of-fact as they unzip, direct, piss, shake, fold and tuck with the casually confident gestures of those who are not disturbed. My doctor and my lawyer even piss like professionals. But I'm finding it difficult. My prick is lifeless; it looks injured, a pinkish vole squashed on a road. I hold it gently trying to coax some warmth back into it, some life, even piss life, and feel the first stirrings of a new kind of panic (another layer: I'm panicking so much now that calm feelings are not to be trusted) as I wonder if shock has left me impotent for life. That last encounter with Wesley-Cope nearly felled me. I could barely stand, the shaking was so bad. It stunned me, the brutality of it, the way he tried to lead me; the forked paths, the traps, the labyrinths, not of truth

[197]

but professional deceit. And Claude. The shock of that, and the Australia trip. But where the hell is he now? Why isn't he here? Maybe he is – there's so much they keep from you here. Maybe they've got him in another room somewhere, keeping him waiting. Their ace. Their joker in the pack.

The jury. What did they think? The awful pathology photographs. Her skin. As I left the courtroom, I caught a glimpse of a tiny tawny fraction. The photograph was half covered by a scarf. A red scarf belonging to a woman juror, the youngest of the group, pale-haired, with translucent skin. I saw her veins, and her serious eyes which saw me looking, grey eyes, soft as a mountain animal's. I saw pity, then confused embarrassment as she picked up her scarf. Agony. As I passed the jury bench, another, older woman turned over the pathology photograph quickly but obtrusively and then laid her hand on it.

Dr Chase and Michael Laurence are waiting for me. They are getting impatient, glancing at their watches. Forget the jury, forget Claude, come on, piss, piss, piss on him. Now it comes out in short hot bursts on to the yellowing tiles of the urinal. My waste, the waste of my wasted wretched life. In my other life, pissing always used to calm me, not the act of pissing itself, but the moment of quiet reflection. Someone – perhaps it was Sergei – once said that when a man urinated he became closer to God.

I stop pissing, shake myself dry and pull up the slim zip of my best charcoal-grey trousers. I'm wearing a designer suit over a black cashmere poloneck. Natalie liked me to wear this sweater – she bought it for me from one of those London shops where the woollens are arranged like chinchillas in cages – but the soft wool is irritating me now and I see that it has given me a rash, a line of red welts around my neck. 'Petechiae', what sort of word is that? This suit is too big for me now, there are too many folds of expensive silk cloth for my diminished arms and legs, too many pockets and seams and an unfamiliar, soft, guilty newness about the material. I wash my hands. Dr Chase and Mr Laurence wait outside. I can see them talking through the frosted glass. Mr Laurence says something and Dr Chase nods his head very quickly. I dry my hands under the electric machine which allows me sixty seconds of warmth. I am on a countdown.

Back in the waiting cell and the guard has gone. The *Daily*

Mail is lying on the floor with the screwed-up chocolate-bar wrapper. Dr Chase comes in with a styrofoam cup of coffee for me and a cellophane-sealed egg and tomato sandwich. He is apologetic.

'I'm sorry, that's all they had. Michael and I are going out briefly; do you want anything, cigarettes?'

'Booze, bring me back a bottle of whisky.'

Dr Chase rests his hand on my shoulder. 'You stood up to him well. I'm proud of you.'

'Bring me some Silk Cut, sixty, a hundred, a fucking vanload.'

He pats my shoulder. 'Take it easy.'

He leaves and I pick up the newspaper. It smells old, as if it belongs to another century. I look at the dateline: 20 October 1994. Now I read the front page. I read this:

Winston Clark, the man held for the Hampstead Heath murder of two sisters, was found stabbed to death in his cell yesterday in what was believed to be a revenge killing by prison inmates. Clark was on remand and was due to make his first court appearance at the end of this week. It is claimed that he boasted about the killings to other inmates and had turned his cell into a macabre shrine. Newspaper clippings and photographs of the dead girls were pasted on the walls of Clark's cell where officers found his body in a pool of blood on the floor.

The paper has used the school picture of the girls on the front page and inside – I can't help it, I have to look – there is a school picture of Clark himself, about eight years old. The boy Clark is not smiling, but he is not sulky. He is very still, as if waiting for something to happen. A good-looking child. Dark-brown hair neatly brushed to one side, with the merest hint of greasiness, pale oval face emphasising his eyes, large, dark grey and luminous; they could be a model child's eyes, long lashes, each one separate and defined, a darkly beautiful web for compelling tears. Little bastard. But it's there. The killer in him is betrayed by a precision which could be mistaken for obedience. Look at him sitting there, hands neatly folded in his lap, his little-boy spine ramrod-straight against the photographer's sky-blue backdrop, his knees small and rigid under his grey school trousers. There is a remoteness about him, a sense of something being saved up. His precision demands that one day he will be known.

If I had any piss left in me I would direct it on to this image of half-formed evil, this beautiful still boy who grew into something diseased, who sought the dazzle of fame and found it in the glint of a knife. This boy I know so well because I am him. This could be my school photograph. The same stillness, the same quietness and precision. The same sense of waiting for something to happen. In this boy, I see my own terrible talent to disturb.

And now he's dead. They couldn't stand his mockery. They had to carve him up, cut him out of the order. That's justice. Blood on the heath exchanged for blood on the prison-cell floor. Tit for tat. Cell for cell. Blood the colour of geraniums. God, I'm crazy. The fucker's dead. It's over for both of you. But it's not. Look, the boy in him still mocks. The bastard never paid. Winston Clark died innocent.

— 26 —

'Andrew, it was yours.'

Mine. My little foetus fish. My baby. Oh, God. Was it a boy or a girl, I wanted to ask, but couldn't. I said nothing when Mr Laurence told me. He didn't even come in; he put his head round the door after lunch. He said the laboratory had sent a fax. A fax, for God's sake. A *fax* for my flesh and blood. Where was Dr Chase when I bloody needed him? Where was the bastard? Christ, my baby. Three weeks old. An embryo, maybe it was an embryo. What do they have at three weeks old? A tiny heart, lungs, eyes? What about fingers and toes? Could it feel anything? Would it . . . oh, Christ, would it have *known*? It never even had a name. Where is this fax? What did it say? Why haven't they given it to me, my fax, my foetus, and where is Dr Chase? Where is he?

He is here.

'All right?'

'Oh, my God.'

'I'm sorry I wasn't here. I wanted to tell you, but I had to meet with the police. Look, we can ask for an adjournment. You can take a few days off.'

'No.'

Hand on the shoulder. Hell in this cell. It was mine. Joy. But how can there be joy, euphoria, I'm crazy. But it was mine. It wasn't his. It wasn't that French bastard's. Claude Michel Fleur. What a stupid poncey name. I killed my child. I killed my wife and child ... in cold blood, Mr Schidmaizig, in cold fucking blood.

'I spoke with the police.'

'Oh.'

'They found Fleur.'

'Oh.'

'He was a friend, a photographer. He says there was no affair. The police wanted him here, but he can't come. He was in a motorbike accident a few weeks ago and fractured his pelvis.'

The pelvis. That's where it was cradled, in her bones, her lovely white bones. My bone and her bone. My child and her child. Ours. Something to strive for.

'Are you sure you don't want to ask for an adjournment?'

'No; I mean, I don't know about anything. Oh, Christ, why don't they just lock me up?'

'You're not guilty.'

'Oh.'

'I'll get you some coffee.'

He leaves. He leaves me here. Come back, bastard, don't leave me alone. The voices start then, the sick, murderous voices, the sound of evil. Long lashes, would it have had long lashes? Red hair, dark curls? Would it have been tall and thin like me or short and muscular like her? Would it – he, it was a boy, think of him, give him a name, make him real, a little boy. Winston. No, get away, stop thinking like that. A boy. A stocky little boy with green eyes, her eyes, I would have wanted him to have her eyes, moist little eyes, a certain innocent sadness, El Greco eyes, pure feeling and joy and delight. He would be a kind little boy, good-natured, one of those smiling, complacent kids that you feed and roll around, and feel dragging awe every time you look at them. A piece of your soul. A little piece of you that will go around the world being you, but not being you, a part of you set free. Smooth baby skin, smelling of apricots, you with all your experience and time and terrible history made smooth again. A child is a new start in life. A chance to make things better. A way of coming clean with the world. How can anyone hate when they see a child? Out in a field or a park, unsteady on nearly walking feet, flying a kite or a balloon. Or swimming free in water, laughing, kicking like a turtle. School days, grazed knees and curling pictures brought home for Dad to see. Might it . . . maybe . . . all right then, playing the piano haltingly, biting a lip. Then, later, finding things missing, gaps in the wallet, alien stubble in the razor and Dad, can I borrow the car? Girlfriends, pints in the pub, nights on the town, walks on the Heath. So, do you love her, son, do you really love her? Love, Dad, what do you know about love? You killed everything you love so how can you tell me about it? Love, son, keeps you sane. Love lightens your soul. Don't make me laugh, Dad. Look what love did to you.

'Mr Schidmaizig, did you ever stop to think that these strange dreams you claim you experienced might have been caused by alcohol?'

'No. I had the dreams whether I drank or not. Sometimes I drank to stop me dreaming. It helped me relax.'

'Miss Kesley has said that she smelled alcohol on you during the day when you were working. Did you need to drink to work?'

'Sometimes. When things were not going well.'

'"When things were not going well". Things were pretty terrible really, weren't they?'

'I was not having an easy time composing, if that's what you mean.'

'Without dazzling the jury too much with your musical, er, genius, can you describe what you were composing?'

'I was working on a piano concerto, influenced by Rachmaninov and also, well, also my own nightmares. I was trying to put them to music. I wanted to describe some of the emotions I was feeling, a sort of *Danse Macabre*. I wanted to make sense of the darkness. Rachmaninov composed his second piano concerto after a mental breakdown and I thought that maybe I could

[202]

channel my blackness into my work. It was a way of controlling it.'

'Would you say that you were experiencing a mental breakdown while you were composing?'

'Certainly not. I was a little mad at times, but I thought this was healthy.'

'Healthy, Mr Schidmaizig? How can madness possibly be healthy?'

'There's an intensity, a sort of falling away of the everyday, the mundane, when you're feeling mad – I mean tuned in a crazy way. All your senses are heightened. Colours seems brighter, skies wider, noises louder. I've found that even food tastes different when I'm composing.'

'And what happens when you're not working? When you – forgive my inelegance – pack up your piano at the end of the day? You must deal with the mundane then?'

'It's difficult. There is usually a transition period. A sort of coming back down to earth, I suppose you might say.'

'It all sounds a bit unsettling, Mr Schidmaizig. What I believe you're saying is that there are times when you are not quite all there. You are in another dimension.'

'Well, yes, but distractions can bring you back quite easily. I'm always aware of what I'm doing.'

'Except, Mr Schidmaizig, when you are killing. Thank you, I have no further questions.'

Every single member of the jury writes something down. The pale-haired girl spends longer writing than the others, curling her arm around the paper, shielding her words – her judgement – from the rest. She looks up, realises that I am staring at her and lowers her eyes, putting her hand to her face to cool a sudden rush of blood. The judge Wallace-Evans is also writing quickly, making little nods with his heavy thatched wig, which is too big for him and covers his eyes. He looks small up there on his green leather throne, an old aunt in an ermine-trimmed robe enjoying a rare night out at the opera. Wallace-Evans has small clawlike hands which fiddle with an assortment of courtroom accoutrements: pens, the fluorescent kind that professionals like to use nowadays to highlight a point, ring binders, a thick mound of

[203]

white paper, a fountain pen in a gilt holder (he never uses this: it's like a prop from a legal drama) and two glasses of water. He sips the water purposefully, as if he is tasting wine, alternating the glasses – one is always being taken away to be refilled by the clerk. He has not met my eyes.

Now the public gallery. Up there is the real jury, the morbidly curious, the professional observers, the arbiters who have come here to make up their own minds about justice. The benches are packed, the arbiters bunched up elbow to elbow like a crowd on a football terrace, thrilled at the spectacle but too tense to show it yet. A lot of older people have come, and some of them are even taking notes: my God, all this writing down, all this note-taking of one man's life. One miserable history. The lower benches are packed with younger spectators, some of whom I recognise. A violinist from the Philharmonic. A South Bank bar girl. The oboeist from Berlin, smiling secretly to himself. Oh, Christ, the sunburnt nurse, pale and unfamiliar in a black astrakhan coat, sitting next to another woman who seems . . . it is, it is Sara, plump in a bulky anorak, her dirty-straw hair razor-short, and she's still biting her nails. A woman who cannot take her eyes from Dr Chase. Thin, almond-eyed, darkish, Indian-looking. His wife? Perhaps a lover. It's funny, I can't think of Dr Chase with a lover. He's too careful for extramarital sex. A smitten student, then. She looks too young to be his wife and too attentive; a wife would be more casual, seen-it-all-before, not poised like this, fingers tapping the bronze bar which separates the players and the spectators. Timothy Phillips, wearing a sharp suit – Christ, he's probably a lawyer now; I bet he knows what's going on – still tanned and disgustingly healthy-looking, his hair blue-black under the fluorescent light. I don't believe it: they're all here. It's like a bad dream or death, all these people from my past, waiting to see how it will end. There is a strained silence, a sort of void waiting for a roar. But hold on, more spectators are arriving.

They are coming down the small flight of wooden stairs. The front-row arbiters are shuffling along for them, adjusting note-books, cardigans and bags to make room. My God, *them*. She is walking with tentative steps like someone very ill or very old, leaning on his blunt arm while he stares straight ahead, his jaw rigid. A spasm grips my gut, a wrenching pain as if a muscle has split. Now the courtroom is whirling in a storm of beige and green and red. I sit down in the dock, then I stand up again, then back down. I'm like an insane jack-in-a-box jerking up and down like this. There are murmurs as the spectators sense something exciting is about to happen. Maybe I'm going to faint. My name is called.

'Mr Schidmaizig, would you please return to the witness box? Mr Schidmaizig! Are you all right, Mr Schidmaizig? Perhaps the clerk would be so kind as to offer Mr Schidmaizig a glass of water.'

'Thank you, your honour.'

'Take your time, just make your way to the box when you're ready.'

'Thank you. I feel better now.'

'Please proceed, Mr Laurence.'

'Mr Schidmaizig, am I right in saying that you have been so traumatised by your wife's death and the manner in which she died that you have been undergoing psychiatric treatment?'

'Yes, that is correct. I was a patient, sorry, a client, at Highgrove Hospital.'

'And you had not received psychiatric therapy or psychoanalysis previously?'

'No.'

'The creative madness you spoke of earlier – has it ever affected your mental wellbeing to the point where you felt you needed medical help?'

'No.'

'Have you ever thought that you needed medical help in any way regarding your drinking?'

'No.'

'Has alcohol ever made you violent?'

'No.'

'Were you violently affected by alcohol on the day of your wife's death?'

'No.'

'Thank you, Mr Schidmaizig. I'd now like to call Dr Alan Chase, consultant psychiatrist at Highgrove Hospital and a leading authority on sleep disorders. My client Mr Schidmaizig was referred to you by the police doctor initially.'

'Yes. I am one of the few sleep specialists in Britain. Our

branch of psychiatry tends not to receive many clients as cases of automatism are quite rare.'

'Would you define automatism for the jury?'

'There has been some difficulty with this in the past as the medical and legal professions have not always been in agreement over what constitutes automatic behaviour but I will quote Dr Peter Fenwick, an eminent psychiatrist and sleep specialist who has been something of a mentor. His definition, I believe, is the most accurate. I quote from a paper of his:

'An automatism is an involuntary piece of behaviour over which an individual has no control. The behaviour itself is usually inappropriate to the circumstances, and may be out of character for the individual. It can be complex, coordinated, and apparently purposeful and directed, though lacking in judgement. Afterwards, the individual may have no recollection, or only partial and confused memory for his actions.'

'Thank you, Dr Chase. Sleepwalking falls into this category, I believe?'

'Yes. There is another somnambulistic activity called night terrors, which Mr Schidmaizig suffers.'

'Are they like nightmares?'

'No, they are different from classic nightmares. Night terrors occur in a different phase of sleep, in non-dreaming sleep. When the subject suffers a night terror he is partially awake. A feeling of intense fear usually jolts him awake, his heart rate accelerates rapidly and he sweats and often screams or cries out for help. Some people can become quite violent and lash out at their partners and attack objects. People have been known to slash pictures or smash windows.'

'Mr Schidmaizig has said that he was dreaming or having some sort of vision of an avalanche. Is this possible during a night terror?'

'Mr Schidmaizig's avalanche mitigates against him because it has elements of a narrative dream, which would seem to belong to a different phase of sleep. But – and this is very important – I have known cases of night terrors and sleepwalking where there has been dream content.'

[206]

'So, Dr Chase, you are saying that dreaming is unlikely, but not impossible?'

'Exactly. The dream theory cannot be applied absolutely because it doesn't follow a pattern. There are no patterns, in fact. Not every sleepwalker is the same.'

'Dr Chase, I understand that you carried out several tests on Mr Schidmaizig. Would you please explain these to the court?'

'The first test was a magnetic resonance imaging scan which shows the structure of the brain on film. I also carried out several EEG, or electroencephalogram, tests on Mr Schidmaizig, both while he was awake and asleep. All the tests showed normal brain functioning.'

'I'm sorry to interrupt your analysis, doctor, but we are to conclude from these tests that the defendant is not brain-damaged in any way?'

'Precisely, your honour.'

'Thank you, Dr Chase. Do please continue. I must say, I am finding this quite fascinating.'

'I also conducted an experiment in a sleep laboratory which produced a polysomnograph – your honour, this is like a map of the subject's brain waves during sleep – and a cardiotachometer graph of the subject's heart rate. Respiratory rates and sexual arousal were also monitored. The results of this test, your honour, were extremely fascinating. Mr Schidmaizig experienced a night terror while being monitored and again there was narrative dream content. Mr Schidmaizig's heart rate showed a dramatic increase from sixty-four beats per minute to one hundred and seventy-two beats per minute in just thirty seconds. I might point out that the highest recorded heart rate during a night terror is one hundred and seventy-six beats per minute.'

'I am wondering, doctor, I am a marathon runner, would my heart rate come anywhere near this?'

'No, your honour. You would have to be a sprinter, but even if you were an Olympic sprinter – '

'Linford Christie, say?'

'Yes, even if you were Linford Christie, your heart rate would not reach one hundred and seventy-two beats per minute. The only way most people can experience such an intense degree of heart activity is during orgasm.'

'Thank you, Dr Chase. I'm sorry for interrupting, Mr Laurence.'

'That is quite all right, my lord. I expect the members of the jury are finding your questions helpful. Dr Chase, please continue.'

'I should mention that during night terrors there is never sexual arousal. In dreaming sleep there is always arousal. Mr Schidmaizig showed no sexual arousal during the sleep laboratory tests.'

'So, let's be clear about this. The fact that there was no sexual arousal showed that Mr Schidmaizig was experiencing a night terror and not a dream?'

'That is correct. I carried out further examinations on Mr Schidmaizig and found his central nervous system to be in excellent working order, not surprising considering that his profession requires a high level of manual and intellectual dexterity. His anxiety level was quite high, but this could be considered normal in the circumstances. There were no signs of delusions or hallucinations. Mr Schidmaizig was extremely distressed, but there was nothing to indicate that he was in any way mentally ill. He was given a cognitive intelligence test which showed no abnormalities and neuropsychometry tests for verbal IQ and performance IQ. His verbal IQ was outstandingly high at 140 and his performance level was also susbstantially higher than average, at 126.'

'When did Mr. Schidmaizig's night terrors first occur?'

'He started sleepwalking from the age of about four. The sleepwalking and night terrors – the two are interchangeable being part of the same phenomenology, your honour – continued throughout his childhood and adolescence. He has described to me a series of vivid and terrifying visions which plagued his early years when he was brought up by his grandmother.'

'What of Mr Schidmaizig's parents, Dr Chase?'

'They died in Italy, your honour, when Mr Schidmaizig was two years old. He has no memory of his parents.'

'Mr Schidmaizig's grandmother witnessed the night terrors?'

'Yes.'

'And Mr Schidmaizig's wife?'

'Yes. He has told me that she often complained of him kicking her in his sleep. This is extremely common among those suffering from sleep disorders.'

'There are no living witnesses?'

'Unfortunately not. We have to take Mr Schidmaizig's word on his own history. He has described to me an incident which occurred when he was 14 years old. He needed hospital treatment for a cut on his hand received when he put his fist through a window during a night terror.'

'What caused him to act so violently?'

'He had a vision of an attacking tree, an experience not dissimilar to the avalanche dream in that he tried to ward off the tree to save his grandmother from harm. You will recall that he was trying to save his wife from being buried in the avalanche.'

'I'm interested. Dr Chase, do your sleepwalking patients or subjects – what do you call them?'

'Clients, my lord, the same as the legal term.'

'Do your clients often dream that they are trying to save someone from disaster?'

'Many clients describe sensations of falling or being crushed or struck by a terrific force. The documented cases include a woman who dreamed that her son was shouting that the house was on fire. She woke up and threw her child out of the window, killing him. Another man strangled his wife after dreaming that he was being chased through a forest by Japanese soldiers. I would say that Mr Schidmaizig's somnambulistic experiences are compatible with these cases. They all contain visions of a peculiarly vivid nature which appear to be dreamlike but belong to the delta non-dreaming state. It is unfortunate for this court of law, but we psychiatrists still do not know enough about Stage Four sleep to draw any conclusions about how a subject might behave.'

'So, Dr Chase, you are saying that anything is possible?'

'Yes, your honour. The phenomenon of sleep is still largely a mystery. When we study sleep, we are not concerned with the brain of man, but his mind. A simple way of looking at it is to imagine a map of the world with forests, lakes and mountain peaks. This is the map of the brain. It tells us where things are but it cannot reveal the history of the forests or convey the sensation of climbing a mountain or swimming in a lake. This belongs in the territory of the mind.'

'So the mind cannot be mapped, but surely it can be explained?'

'Not easily. The imagination is an elusive creature because it can endlessly reinvent itself. People can be anything they choose to be in their minds. I encountered a client who dreamed every night that he was a cat.'

'Dr Chase, forgive my ignorance, but that is madness, surely?'

'Perhaps, or it could simply be a more creative way of looking at things.'

'Thank you, Dr Chase. This has been most instructive.'

— 27 —

Lillian looks older. They both look older, less exotically expatriate despite their smart courtroom clothes. Peter is wearing a dark-blue suit with a peach-coloured tie, the same uniform he wore to our wedding, a tiny act of defiance which provokes in me a wave of admiration. I can barely look at Lillian for shame. She is reed-thin and her hair, although still immaculately groomed, has turned silver from shock. It covers one side of her face in a thick curtain which protects her from having to meet my murderous eyes. Her body is angled away from the pit where the men in black gowns are fighting for her daughter's life. This is her defiance. She does not want to be included, but her exclusion, her stillness and reserve have failed to make her invisible. The entire courtroom is watching her, irresistibly drawn to her silent pain. She bears the stares, the embarrassed curiosity, with dignity. There is nothing that Lillian cannot stand now. She fiddles with her wedding ring, straightens her shoulders and stares dry-eyed at the jury. The pale-haired girl flushes, perhaps remembering her own mother. Lillian could be everyone's mother, sitting here in her smart suit with her hands folded in her lap and her bag at her feet which pinch slightly in the navy blue court shoes she bought specially for the occasion. All the eyes on her in this courtroooom know that nothing can be done to help her. They almost hate her for being here, for reminding them of the pain they inflicted on mothers, lovers, sisters, women. Two male members of the jury are close to tears as they stare at her. Her mother's grief, her woman's pain is too much for them. A woman like this is too much for any man.

Peter most of all cannot bear it. He takes her hand and places it between both his meaty palms and holds it there. She does not look at him. There is a distance between them. He cannot comfort her. She has protected herself from all feeling. Impotent, Peter turns to the pit and anger boils in him as he watches the effete, overeducated lawyers pecking over their papers, all flapping black cloth and professional smiles. They get film-star salaries for poncing about like this. Peter leans forward, his bald head gleams; it looks obscene, raw and naked and red, almost an act of indecent exposure as it looms above the pit of fussy old wigs. Peter starts rocking on his feet, lightly like a boxer testing his weight. He wants to be included in the action, not stuck up here behind this bloody rail with all these long-haired music gits, friends of his, the bastard. Lillian pulls her hand away from her husband's grip. Now what? Peter begins punching the rail with his fist; the dull rhythmic thud sounds like a heartbeat, a rush of blood in the ears. The judge calls for silence and Peter stops rocking. He licks his lips as Wesley-Cope moves in to the centre of the ring.

'Dr Chase, a night terror is not a dream or a nightmare, but a disorder of sleep?'

'That is correct.'

'But not a medical or physical disorder. There is nothing in the defendant's brain functioning that makes him different from anyone else?'

'That is also correct. We all have the potential to suffer night terrors or sleepwalk, but most of us don't. Sleepwalking occurs in only about three to five per cent of the population.'

'Is it hereditary, is this a genetic disorder?'

'There is usually a history of sleepwalking in families, yes. Mr Schidmaizig's grandfather suffered from night terrors.'

'And you have no idea what causes this disorder? I believe you refer in one of your papers to a "physiological and psychological vacuum".'

'There is no explanation. We can only look at sleep itself and try to work out why some people's sleeping mechanisms are different from others.'

[211]

'How so?'

'Sleep has a very definite pattern. In the first ten minutes you fall into a light sleep which lasts for around ninety minutes before it becomes deep sleep. The heart rate slows. Then there is a sort of switch. The brain wakes up and the rhythms become faster and dreaming occurs. The body is paralysed at this point. If it were not, we would be able to act out our dreams, the consequences of which might be disastrous. After dreaming, the brain calms down and goes back to slow-wave sleep, but it is never as deep as before. The switch part of the procedure is worth studying and could perhaps hold the key to the disorder. I say perhaps because no one has yet been able to locate the switch. Brain surgery is still not that advanced. But it's a theory of mine, and only a theory, that in sleepwalkers the switch mechanism may be faulty.'

'Are you saying that this switch could turn on a night terror?'

'It is a possibility.'

'Excuse me, Mr Wesley-Cope, but I wish to ask Dr Chase if there is anything that can be done to stop this switching?'

'There is no cure for sleepwalking, your honour, but psycho-logical counselling can help lessen the trauma of its effects. Sleepwalking can have a very disturbing and damaging impact not only on individuals but also on their families. I have known cases where it has led to divorce.'

'But rarely killing?'

'As I said, extreme violence in sleep is rare.'

'Dr Chase, you are aware of course that sleepwalking is a disease of the mind in legal terms. It is a dangerous disorder that can occur again and again. How can you say that between three and five per cent of the population are pathological?'

'Sleepwalking can be a violent disorder, but no cases have come to court twice. No one has ever killed more than once in their sleep.'

'In Mr Schidmaizig's case, we have no witnesses of his alleged sleepwalking.'

'That is so in most cases of this kind. In the case of a killing, we often have only the sleepwalker's report of the events. I can only say that I have witnessed Mr Schidmaizig suffering a night terror under laboratory conditions. He most certainly suffers from a sleep disorder.'

'Mr Schidmaizig has admitted that his relationship with his

[212]

wife was going through a bad patch. How does this feature in the events?'

'There are two theories: the first is that aggressive people tend to carry out aggressive acts in their sleep. The second is that people tend to sleepwalk when they are under stress, which can lead to aggression.'

'We know Mr Schidmaizig was under a tremendous amount of stress: his work was not going well, he was drinking, he had been told by his wife that she was having an affair and then she became pregnant – a dangerous combination of events emotionally, wouldn't you say?'

'Mr Schidmaizig was under pressure, undeniably, but this did not *cause* his sleep problems. It exacerbated them.'

'The fact is, Mr Schidmaizig's life was getting out of control, a situation to which he might have reacted violently. Would his aggression not surface in his sleep? Come, Dr Chase, even sane men have been known to take out problems on their wives.'

'Mr Wesley-Cope, you should remember that Mr Schidmaizig *is* sane. He is also not alone or unusual in dreaming violently. A study of sleep in America found that fifty per cent of the population dream violently every night.'

'That is extraordinary, Dr Chase.'

'It is surprising, your honour. Fortunately the aggressive dreamers cannot act out their scenes of violence because they are paralysed.'

'That is indeed fortunate. If it were not so, our colleagues across the Atlantic might never be out of court.'

'Quite, my lord.'

'Please continue, Mr Wesley-Cope.'

'But Dr Chase, when we dream violently or aggressively, do we attack those we love or those we hate?'

'We are straying into psychoanalysis here. We attack both those we love and loathe in our dreams. Sleepwalkers may carry out mild acts of violence on those they love.'

'Is there any significance in the fact that Mr Schidmaizig and his wife were not on good terms?'

'It depends whether the act was out of character or not, on whether the client is normally violent or aggressive. I have found no evidence of a tendency towards violent behaviour in Mr Schidmaizig's personality.'

[213]

'However, Mr Schidmaizig is – let me put this delicately – a very volatile personality.'

'He is creative. One expects a certain amount of volatility with creative and artistic personalities.'

'He is creative. He has perhaps a more overdeveloped imagination than the rest of us mortals?'

'Mr Schidmaizig is very imaginative, yes, but this should not mitigate against him. I suspect your honour has a very active imagination.'

'I thank you for the compliment, Dr Chase, but my imagination remains, shall we say, somewhat restrained while I am in court.'

'What I am saying, Dr Chase, is that Mr Schidmaizig could have invented this explanation. He could have *dreamed* – forgive me – the avalanche to excuse the killing of his wife.'

'It is a possibility, but the avalanche is significant in another way. It is believed that Mr Schidmaizig's parents were killed in an avalanche in Italy. The avalanche is an image which belongs deep in his past.'

'You are saying that he is haunted by his past?'

'In a way, yes.'

'Was he acting out his parents' death by killing his wife and unborn child?'

'In the dream, Mr Schidmaizig was trying to save his wife from the avalanche. He was pulling her away from the snow with a rope. It was an act of compassion, not murder.'

'Forgive me, Dr Chase, but he was strangling her to death with her own dressing-gown cord. He killed her!'

'He did not intend to kill her. His actions were automatic and distorted by the dreaming vision. We must make a distinction between what he knows he is capable of and what he is actually doing. In sleep, we are not aware of our actions until we wake and remember them. We cannot be tried for murder for an act of the imagination. If that were so, we would all be criminals. I believe that in his imagined vision of the avalanche, Mr Schidmaizig was trying to save his wife from the past.'

'Forgive my ignorance, Dr Chase, but what's past is past. Why should Mr Schidmaizig want to save his wife, albeit in his imagination, from something that cannot affect her? From something that happened years ago?'

'Mr Wesley-Cope, this may be a difficult concept for you to

[214]

grasp, but the past is not just the past. Sometimes it becomes the present or even the future.'

'It is indeed a difficult concept – may I venture, a ridiculous concept. How can the past become the future?'

'We are straying into quantum physics here, but the new thinking is that all time phases occur simultaneously. The past, present and future do not travel in a line, they are part of a fourth dimension which is cyclical. Past time does not die. We may not be aware of it, but it remains with us, a silent echo which has been absorbed into the atmosphere. Past times are like old songs. The music fades but the sound waves remain. Most of us are familiar with the concept of *déjà vu*, when we believe we have been somewhere before, or the strange feeling of hearing someone call our name. We dismiss such feelings as superstition. We blame our imaginations for playing tricks on us. But it's possible that we *are* hearing something. We could be experiencing lost time. In a way, Mr Schidmaizig's avalanche was lost time, a time that haunted him throughout his life.'

'A time, Dr Chase, that killed his wife.'

'Sadly, yes.'

'Dr Chase, is Andrew Schidmaizig mad?'

'No, he most certainly is not.'

'You are sure?'

'Yes.'

'You would agree, would you not, that he is an extraordinary man?'

'I am not quite sure what you mean by extraordinary.'

'His night terrors – are they related to his imaginary powers?'

'Yes.'

'So, he could invent a terror just as he could invent a piece of music? A *Danse Macabre*, Dr Chase.'

'Yes, he could, he has the capacity, but I do not believe this is what happened. Throughout his life he knew that something was wrong. He thought he'd unleashed demons, dark forces over which he had no control and in a way he was right. But he was not possessed by demons. He had touched a deep part of his past.'

'Dr Chase, we all have pasts and ancestors and we all sleep.'

'Yes, and most of us experience violent dreams. However, the normal mechanics of sleep paralyse us, suppressing that violence. Andrew Schidmaizig was not paralysed, he was free to wander through his past. There were no boundaries in his sleeping experience.'

A commotion in the public gallery. The front-row arbiters are standing up and moving across to the steps. People are talking and Wallace-Evans has called for quiet, but no one takes any notice. I can see Peter now trying to squeeze his way through to the knot of people bunched on the steps. A security guard moves everyone out of the way and a space clears. Peter is down on his knees, attending to a collapsed navy-blue and silver bundle on the floor. Lillian is unconscious, her face sick white; her bony nylon-sheathed legs and thin hands trail from her body as if she is a bundle of thread come undone. Wallace-Evans calls for quiet again. The courtroom falls silent and everyone watches as Peter pulls Lillian's skirt down over her knees and scoops her up. He holds her across his chest like a sleeping child and carries her up the steps. Someone opens the door at the top for them. The last thing I see is Lillian's ghostly hair spilling over her husband's arm and her neck, her awful neck stretched smooth. The door bangs.

'Members of the jury, forget the fantastic elements of this case. Put them out of your mind, for they will only confuse you. Forget the avalanche from the past. Do not be swept up by it for it comes from nowhere. The avalanche is a theory concocted by Dr Chase, a dangerous theory because it is so seductive. Forget the mysteries of time and *déjà vu* and all the other voodoo mumbo-jumbo you have heard and think of this. A woman lying dead on her bed, strangled by her husband. A talented woman, a successful woman, a woman carrying her husband's child. A woman with everything to live for. Now consider this. A man who drinks to help him create madness. A man who enjoys playing with macabre and sinister imaginings. A man who has no time for his wife. A man obsessed with danger and success. A man whose work has been slated in the press. A man whose wife has found someone else. A man on the edge – perhaps the edge of madness. Do not consider why. Do not be swayed by science. Dr Chase as a man of science can only look for answers in science. His version of the events may seem attractive to you. Put them out of your mind. Andrew Schidmaizig killed his wife. This awful event was not a dream. It happened, members of the jury, it happened. But you have been told a colourful and outlandish story almost like a dream to explain it. Dismiss it, for dreams are unreliable. They belong in another dimension and that is not the dimension of this court of justice. Think only of the facts, make sure you consider how much force needs to be applied to a woman's neck to choke her to death. Make sure you consider that this happened in her own bedroom, a place where she might reasonably have expected to feel secure. But most of all, consider who killed her. Consider also that there were no witnesses. The idea of the perfect crime might spring to mind. If it does, it is worth considering. A crime with no witnesses and an explanation backed up by psychiatry. Very beguiling, members of the jury. Remember that we all have the potential to sleepwalk. We could all go home tonight and wander in our sleep, not knowing what we do. But how many of us would kill tonight? That is unknown and because it is unknown it does not concern you as a jury. You must consider only what is known. We are being asked to accept a fantastic dream to explain a death. Perhaps you might consider this to be an anomaly, a freak turn of events, or perhaps you might consider that creating anomalous situations comes easily to those granted the gift of inventiveness. Members of the jury, remember your role. You have no scientific instruments, no laboratory or electronic tests to help you make a decision on this case. You must rely on your good sense backed up by the facts. Some of you may feel sympathy for Mr Schidmaizig. His story is indeed a tragedy, but that is no excuse. Forget what is in your heart, the law is not emotional. The facts are simple. Andrew Schidmaizig strangled his wife while she lay sleeping and unable to defend herself.'

The jury leaves obediently like a herd of cattle, dazed after the summing-up. I return to the waiting room. Dr Chase tries to comfort me, but there is nothing he can do now. There is nothing to do except wait. I rest my head in my arms across the scarred table. I feel utterly alone. Caught in a void. I remain like this, half sleeping, half frozen, for three hours. Dr Chase brings me numerous cups of coffee, which I drink. I taste nothing, feel nothing, hear nothing, see nothing. It's as if all my senses have been stunned. All I have is echoes from the past, the voices

[217]

swirling round and round in my head, the endless terrible dialogue, the music of madness.

'Have you reached a unanimous decision?'

'Yes, your honour.'

I put any head down. I cannot bear to look at her. The pale-haired girl, she's the one, the foreman, the chosen one. I look down at my hands as she speaks. Her voice is clear and calm – the voice of an angel or a devil, I can't tell yet, my blood is making too much noise, rushing in my ears. She speaks ... I clench my fist, digging the nails in deep, wanting to break the skin. We are hand in hand, my killing palm pressed against her white judgemental one. She speaks.

'Not guilty,' she says.

But it is not over yet. She can send me away still. She can judge that I am insane.

She says nothing more. Her silence frees me.

'No!' The silence is shattered by this single exclamation, fired like a gunshot from the public gallery. The judge orders silence, but it is too late. Peter is up on his feet and shouting, leaning into the pit and banging his fist on the bronze rail.

'No. Bastards, bastards. He killed her. He killed my daughter.'

The courtroom erupts. Women on the jury start crying and someone bundles me out of the dock. The noise is terrible, the worst thing I've ever heard. Peter is sobbing now and still punching the rail while a police officer tries to prise him off. He kicks out at the officer, his face gorged with florid outrage. He shouts again. 'Bastards!' His voice is high with hysteria and then he begins to moan, a lone, low sound, a stag wounded in a forest. He goes down on his knees and bangs his head on the rail while the police officer stands over him, helpless, scared by the display. Lillian has not reappeared. She is not here to witness her husband's frenzy, his terrible clinging on to the rail, his flailing fists, his mad eyes, his agonised refusal to surrender. Peter fires a final condemning 'No,' looking me straight in the eyes, between the eyes, beyond the eyes, and lodges his hard bullet of hatred there in the soft blackness for ever.

Here I am on the floor and all my clothes are off. Did I pull them off? I remember nothing. I am simply here, lying naked on the hard wooden floor. My back is sore and there is an empty bottle next to me and something in my hand. A screwed-up photograph. I smooth it out and there I see a young man with cropped dark hair and laughing eyes, denim jacket open to reveal a tanned throat with a few twists of hair coming up like new shoots. Wide-open smile, relaxed, fresh, sexy. Also a scooter with a young woman astride it, an ice-cream cornet in her hand, her corkscrew curls casually ruffled over the collar of an unfamiliar leather jacket. Her face. So vivid, so perfect, so alive.

Leaving the photograph on the floor, I go to the bathroom where I wash quickly, standing over the bath, not wanting to immerse myself fully. I am aware that I am preparing for something as I wash my hair and my beard – I haven't shaved since I returned from the court – using her lemon shampoo. The smell makes me cry.

In the bedroom I dress carefully, selecting a blue cotton shirt, a pair of darker blue corduroys and heavy brown walking shoes. I notice everything as I dress, the eyelets in my shoes, the precise way they are spaced for the lacing, the dull sheen of the leather flecked with Somerset mud, the slight slippery pearliness of the shirt buttons, infuriatingly difficult to fix with shaking hands, the dust rising in the sunlight, a golden fountain containing the micro-particles of an old life. And the smell of charred paper.

I open a window to let in some air. The birdsong is so loud I close it again quickly, pick up my house keys and go to the front door. There's some post on the mat. A white envelope with disjointed, faintly disturbing handwriting. I open it. It's a note from Dr Chase. He wants me to call him. He says he's been ringing and receiving no answer. The handwriting on the second envelope is also familiar. It's from Linda. She has returned my cheque.

I leave the house and take a bus to Highgate. It feels strange to be on a bus. I never rode on buses before; I always took cabs in the city. But then I relied on other people to get me from place to place while I saved myself for work.

I sit at the back of the bus, right in the corner, and try to make myself as small as possible. This is difficult and my legs are cramped. I didn't know buses were so small inside. From the outside they look huge. And another thing, people smile more on buses. An old man has just got up to offer his seat to a woman with a young child. I never saw this happen on a tube. Two smartly dressed women are chatting, remarking on the weather. 'Still quite mild,' one says. 'But there will be rain later,' the other replies and then pats her hair, the colour of damson in the bright bus light. Ordinary things. Why is there so much pain in these ordinary things?

I miss my stop and have to walk along several streets lined with trees. I keep my head down and look at my shoes. I count the eyelets: six on each side. Six plus six equals twelve. Twelve multiplied by two is twenty-four. My feet are bound by twenty-four eyes. Twenty-four hours. A whole day. Is this significant?

I enter through the black iron gate and pass an angel, cracked across her face and smeared with leaf slime. Next to the angel is a black-boughed, stunted tree, clouded with unseasonal pink blossom. I hesitate. I already feel like a trespasser and there are too many people here, a pair of Japanese tourists snapping pictures of the vaults, a group of teenagers smoking behind a crumbling tomb, a tired-looking woman with a little boy who keeps picking up stones and throwing them at the angels, an old man carrying a bunch of roses. Now I remember that I've forgotten to bring flowers. I consider going back, but I can't face the thought of another bus ride. I reach into the pocket of my cords but there is nothing there except a few crumbs and Linda's returned cheque.

I walk slowly. The mud sticks to my shoes as I find the little holly bush, brilliant with berries – how can there be berries and blossom? It doesn't make sense. I snag my sweater on it. The grave is down a small path, in a hollow like the curve of an arm. I slow down; the mud is churned up here and I'm worried I might slip. I stop at the bottom of the path. A magpie screeches from a tree and a sudden gust of wind blows a strand of lemon-scented hair across my face.

[220]

I'm only a few paces away now. I can see the wooden marker, a simple cross, smaller than the others, and the new covering of grass rippling in the breeze. I can't go any further. The guardians are there on either side of the cross.

He looks up first, suspicious, then incredulous. She is looking down into a huge bunch of yellow chrysanthemums, inhaling their scent. He touches her arm and she looks up. She is not shocked to see me. Her eyes are perfectly still as they register who I am.

I take a step forward. She keeps her eyes on me and stares steadily. I try to hold her gaze but it is too much. I drop my head and watch the twenty-four eyelets shuffle one pace towards them. Now we are close enough to smell each other. Lillian is wearing a rose perfume and Peter smells of strong mannish soap and whisky. We remain like this for a long time, awkwardly poised in silence. Lillian exhales raggedly and brings the chrysanthemums up to her face, hiding her eyes. Then she drops down to her knees and places the flowers on the little green hillock, where she stays, crouched like a small hare, rocking backwards and forwards. Peter joins her and they rock together. They make no sound.

For a few seconds everything is perfectly still and then the wind rustles the holly bush with little cracks like spluttering flames. In the distance, a bus booms, echoing the roaring in my head as I watch my shoes move closer and closer. Now I'm standing behind them and I have an urge to take them both in my arms, they look so small and despairing crouched down there, but I know that to touch them would be an act of brutality. I walk round to the other side and go down on my knees, facing them. I look at the chrysanthemums and think of the last sunset on earth. Now I look at them. Not their eyes, I cannot do that, but their mouths, which are pulled tight. They are both breathing deeply and deliberately as if to ward off an oncoming spasm of pain.

A single tear falls from Lillian's silver hair and drops to the earth just as a chrysanthemum petal is torn from its yellow sunhead by the wind. For a moment, I sense I can smell spring. The earth feels damp beneath my corduroy knees and the cloying coldness brings on a memory of the first holes I dug in the sand as a child. I feel a shifting weakness and a slight softening in my bones and I'm that child again, kneeling in the mud of my first summer. The magpie screech becomes a gull scream, the roaring in the trees, a wave bouncing on a rock, hissing leaves, fizzing spray. I can taste salt in the wind.

We remain like this, with our silent rocking, our wrapped thoughts of life and death as we consider what to do, knowing that each possibility is charged with violence. We cannot stand up, brush the dirt from our knees, and link arms like other families here. Divided in death, we cannot even look at each other. We cannot explain what gaps in reason mean to reasoning human beings. We can only bow our heads in shame.

I stare at the wooden cross and feel pockets of grief explode in my head and chest. I start to cry, splitting the silence with my sobs, and then I'm reaching out towards them, grabbing at the space, the void between us. Lillian throws her head back and climbs to her feet. I know my remorse is out of place here, but I am out of control. My wild cries send Peter hurrying after his wife, who is now standing by one of the other graves, kneading her stomach with her fists. The sight of her stops my tears and I haul myself up and start running towards them, slipping and sliding on the mud. Now I'm holding my hand out to Lillian. Crazy thoughts are running through my head. I want them to take me with them, back to Australia. I want to live with them, eat silent meals with them, sleep my demon sleep with them. I want them to take me as their child, their unloved devil child, their captive. Their bastard son.

'Leave us alone, bastard!' Peter shouts as I reach them. 'Bastard! How can you show your face here? You're sick.'

'I want to come with you. Take me with you, please. I'll do anything you like.'

'You're mad. You're not right. They should have locked you up. They don't know what they've done. Go on.' He flaps his hand as if to ward off a vicious dog. 'Get out of here. Leave us alone. Leave us with something. You have no right to be here.'

Lillian cannot look at me. Her head is buried in Peter's shoulder as she clings to his body. The sight of her fingers plucking his coat suddenly brings back a memory of Natalie sitting on the floor picking holes in my sweater. The image jolts me out of my madness and I stumble back from them, almost losing my foothold in the mud. A sudden darkness rolls across the sky. The sun has gone down and I know the man with the keys will be coming round soon to tell us to leave. Lillian shudders at the cold and Peter tightens his grip around her. He looks at me once more, and then slowly leads her away.

I watch them go. They do not hurry; they seem like travellers nearing the end of a long journey. At the iron gate they pause. It is now too gloomy to see properly, but I think Lillian has something caught in the heel of her shoe. She bends down to fix it and I see the light silver of her hair flare like a match struck on a cold night. Then they are gone.

— 29 —

At Waterloo Station I am forced to buy a return ticket. The man in the booth thinks he's doing me a favour by not selling me the single I asked for.

'It's the same price.'

'But I might not be coming back.'

'It makes no difference. It's the same price.'

The voices in the station are amplified, a cacophonous shrieking like thousands of birds trapped in a cathedral. I hesitate. The man in the booth spins the ticket round with my change and I walk through the noise and on to the platform where I board the 4.15 to Penzance.

I choose a window seat with a table and put my bag on the seat next to me. I cannot bear the thought of someone sitting close to me. Things are so complicated now. Before I would have booked a first-class seat and not worried, because first-class travellers tend to be alone and not interested in talking. But this time I bought second class. I suppose it's obvious why.

Now I have to plan what to do if someone speaks to me. I could get round this by pretending to be asleep, but what if I really slept and woke up next to a woman and a child. I'm going to have to make up lies about who I am and where I'm going, because the truth cannot be spoken. Not here in this warm carriage filled with the faces of the innocent. People asleep, their heads tucked under their arms, vulnerable as sleeping ducks.

People on the move, self-absorbed, a sort of trusting calmness about them as they arrange sandwich boxes and small children. People eating and reading. People I could harm.

Someone is coming. He is walking up the aisle, he's spotted this space and wants to fill it with his bulk and plastic bags. He's sweating: he had to run for the train and now he's not choosy. I catch a whiff of country as he squeezes himself into the seat opposite. Warm straw and fermenting fruit, a slight mustiness about his clothes – smart going-up-to-town tweed jacket and heavy dun trousers. His big hands fumble with a plastic bag and draw out a magazine: the *Antique Collector*. He begins to read, making little puffing noises as he tries to catch his breath. I exhale a long breath of my own, glad that he has not acknowledged me.

Now I realise my mistake. I should have brought a magazine because there is nothing for me to look at except him. He feels my gaze and rustles his magazine crossly, his face flushing a deep red.

How would he react if I told him? Would his soft cheeks become rosier, or would they pale with shock? Would he get up and walk away or would he remain wedged in his seat with the *Antique Collector*, trying to forget what he's just heard?

Look, mister, I'm sorry for staring. I'm going to look out of the window now and leave you alone. Trees. Already. This surprises me and the speed of the train, savage as it slices through the fields. The trees look like athletes straining for the finish as they bend in the wind. And the colours: reds, greens, lavender and violet, all broken up, like smashed stained glass.

Now a tunnel. We plunge through the blackness. It's like diving into a city river, soft and choking warm. Voices babble nonsense on the surface and there's a charred fishy smell. The itching nylon of the seat feels like sandpaper against the back of my thighs. The tunnel swallows the train whole like a great snake feasting on a goat. The air is foul, suffocating, a mixture of sweat and ash. I've got to cool down, got to stay calm. I reach out and find the damp glass of the window and rest my shaking hands against it.

My ruddy travelling companion sees my hands against the window as we rip back into the light. He frowns into his magazine. I take my hands away and sit on them. I smile at him.

[224]

He does not smile back. He pulls another magazine out of his bag. This one is for connoisseurs of wine. He reads. I try to read the words upside down but he notices, picks up the magazine and holds it close to his chest. I close my eyes and leave him in peace. I listen to the noises around me, the rustling of papers, the pocking sound of styrofoam cups opening, releasing a sweet aroma of chocolate drink, a subdued laugh, stertorous grunts from someone asleep, a young man with a cold, a whistle-squeak whine from a yawning dog. This is how it must feel to travel blind.

I remember my first trip to London with Sergei and all the little signs, the knocking into the seats, the embarrassed apologies to the other passengers and to me. 'These trains go too fast for me, Andrei.' I had to hold his arm as we lurched down the aisle and mop up his spilled coffee with a page from my music magazine. I was a connoisseur of magazines then, Mr Rosy Cheeks. Stop looking at me like that, as if you've just recognised me. It's making me nervous.

I get up and leave my seat. I need a drink but I'm not sure which end has the buffet. Is it near the driver or right at the back? I can't remember. Why isn't there a sign? I could ask someone, but I don't want to draw attention to myself and if I ask someone now, Mr Rosy Cheeks will hear my voice and it will confirm what he's been thinking all along. *He's the one. I thought I recognised him from the newspaper photos.* My voice will give me away. He's a connoisseur. He listens to Radio Three. He'd be the sort to remember. *You know that talk you gave about Rachmaninov . . .*

I start walking up the train towards the driver. But moving is difficult, like trying to walk on a conveyor belt, one step forward, two steps back. I squeeze against a headrest to let a passenger pass. A fleshy woman, pungently alive, her salty breath warms my face as she eases her way past with an embarrassed laugh. I continue lumbering my way up, swinging from headrest to headrest, dragging my feet, which suddenly seem monstrously heavy and too large for my body. Everything about me is too big. Too loose and out of control.

I find the buffet and drink three paper cones of water. The waxy texture of the paper and the faint smell of disinfectant brings on a wave of nausea. I order a double whisky – Bell's, but never mind – down it in two gulps and begin my descent. All goes well until the train swings into a corner, catching me off balance. I land in a seat, crushing a young woman and a baby, which begins to cry. The sound ripples through the train, soft at first but becoming louder until it is an outraged scream. Now the other passengers are twisting round, annoyed at this shattering of the thrumming train peace. I'm half on top of the woman, paralysed with fear, not knowing what to do. She plucks at my arm and makes soothing noises, partly for the baby's benefit, partly for mine, and I lift myself off. The child stops crying and gives me a smile, all wet gums and bright eyes. I smile back, trying to appear normal, trying not to panic. I agologise to the woman and she laughs easily and bounces the baby up and down in her lap.

'No harm done, look at him!'

The baby blows a bubble from its raw-meat-coloured gums.

'He's a devil,' the mother says. 'Little devil!' Then: 'Do you have any children?'

Now I can't bear it, the tears are coming and I can't stop them. The mother turns and stares out of the window.

'I'm sorry,' she says. 'I shouldn't have asked.'

I return to my seat and Mr Rosy Cheeks gives me a searching look. I ignore him and close my eyes, trying not to think of the awful soft feel of the baby's skull under my hand. 'Poor little thing,' I hear a woman say.

The train thunders along, passing a row of pylons marching across the landscape like an advancing army of giant generals. The wheels beat a tattoo on the track. Gone, gone, gone. When I'm gone it will be the end. I'm the last of the line. The last Schidmaizig. Dr Chase was wrong. There is no future.

Now someone is speaking to me. It's Mr Rosy Cheeks. He is asking if I'm all right.

'Can I do anything? You seem very distressed.' The rosy face is paler now.

I shake my head. 'I'm sorry,' I say.

'Can I get you a drink or something?' He has a deep baritone voice.

'No, I'm fine. I don't need anything. Thank you, anyway.'

He returns to his wine magazine. I wipe my face on my sleeve. The train slows and pulls into a country station. In the gloom the hanging baskets look like shrunken heads swaying slowly in the night breeze. A small white dog runs up and down the platform yapping at the passengers getting off. The doors slam shut and we ease back into the night. We pass cider orchards, the trees all twisted and crusted with lichen, and long thin gardens straddled by deserted swings, before ducking under a small bridge. I am nearly there.

We stop and I haul myself out of my seat, painfully aware of my lack of luggage – other passengers around me are heaving bags, suitcases and coats down from the overhead racks – and my lack of purpose. I feel lost as I stand in the aisle and listen to the goodbyes and sighs from the departing throng. A small child pushes at my knees to get past me and I realise I'm holding everyone up. I put my small canvas bag on my shoulder and walk slowly down to the door.

The cold air snaps me out of my daze and I look around for a taxi. There is one parked nearby. The driver has the seat tilted right back and seems to be sleeping. I tap on the window and he sits up with a start. I get in. The driver is cheery and bombards me with questions about my trip. I reply calmly, grateful for the protection of mundane conversation and the warmth of the sheepskin-covered back seat. I watch the night trees flash past as he takes us along the lanes, driving fast, bumping over ruts and stones, wheels crackling as we flatten blown-down branches. He is an expert driver, fifteen years in the job, he tells me, squeezing into a gateway to let a Land-Rover pass. He pulls away with a screech of blackberry bush on glass and then roars up into second to reach another gateway, guided by the cat's eyes and pools of misty amber light from the oncoming cars. He catches my eye in the rear-view mirror and I smile, acknowledging his expertise at the wheel. Driving is important down here. I'd forgotten that.

He changes gear sharply and we begin our descent down through the longest village in England. He starts talking about the erosion. Several homes have been lost, he tells me. One villager woke to find his house teetering on the edge. I think of a lurching fairground ride, a pirate ship, I think it's called. The one where you rock backwards and forwards high in the sky and your guts start to liquidate.

'You know, he could have stepped straight out of the french windows and into the sea.'

[227]

I wind down the window a fraction and the driver launches into a conversation about rain. I can smell the sea now. I wind the window further and put out four fingers to test the air. There is no rain. The air is cool, soft and velvety, it's like running my fingers through cloth. A knot unfurls in my gut and I take a deep breath. It seems as if this is the first time I've breathed properly since it happened.

The knot in my gut tightens again as I pay the driver, giving him a large tip, and button up my overcoat and shift my shoulder bag around to make it look as if I'm preparing for something.

'Where are you staying?' the driver asks, squinting into the dark. He is confused. I have asked him to drop me in the middle of nowhere.

'With friends,' I lie. 'They live about a mile down there.' I wave my arm vaguely. 'I always like to walk a bit first. Take in the country air.'

The driver sniffs. 'There's no one down there. Not a mile away, not two miles away. You sure you got the right place?'

I feel caught out. 'Yes, I'm sure,' I lie again. 'It's not far. I recognise this.'

He looks at me closely, taking in my size, my small bag and my long hair, and decides or knows or feels that something is not quite right.

'What you doing here then?'

I've paid him so I could just walk away without answering, but I don't want to fuel his suspicion further. People down here like to know what's going on. I should have remembered. I should have known I wouldn't be left alone. You can't come down here and be nothing. Especially if you come from London.

'I'm a photographer.' My knees buckle slightly as I tell him this.

'Freelance?'

'Yes.' This seems to satisfy him. My freelance profession explains my strange behaviour and my unconventional dress.

'Should be a good day tomorrow, they reckon. Dry,' he says.

'Good,' I reply. 'Well, I'll be off then, thanks a lot.'

'Good luck with your pictures.'

'My *what*?

'Photographs, you did say you was a photographer?' He hands

[228]

me a small yellow card with a cartoon drawing of a smiling car on the front. 'Here's the number if you need me again. It's difficult to get around here without a car, but then I suppose you've got your friends to drive you. They wouldn't be living here without a car.'

'Yes, I've got my friends.'

My last lie.

— 30 —

The old woman waits for me now by the DANGER sign. We walk together most days and I've become quite fond of the dog. Sometimes I bring him scraps of bacon or cheese which he laps from my hand with his great, dripping, purple tongue. I like his black bulk and the way he sways between us, favouring neither me nor her, confident in our companionship.

At low tide we walk to the rocks where we watch the dog nosing about the bladderwrack-fringed pools. His body ripples with excitement when he disturbs something, a hermit crab or a shoal of tiny translucent shrimp, and he always looks back for our approval before lifting his head to bark. The sound muffled by the cliff is eerie, like the calling of a sea creature lost in fog.

One time he snatched a young rabbit and brought it to us, yelping with surprise. His mistress rewarded him by slapping him on the head before scooping up the tiny pouch of fawn fur.

'Don't do that again, mustn't go killing things.'

The rabbit twitched in her hand. Its fur was slick and dark from the dog's saliva and its heart was beating fast. The old woman gently stroked the narrow canal of its head before releasing it on the stones. 'Stupid animal! But I suppose you don't know any better,' she said.

The woman knows nothing of my past. She does not know my name and I have not asked for hers. Samuel is our link. We use the dog's name a lot. Speaking it somehow saves us from embarrassment.

We are strangers and yet her face is so familiar to me now.

Her pinched bird features, white feather eyebrows and her eyes, which always reflect the colour of the sea. On fine days they are aquamarine.

I believe she has seen many things in her life, but she has decided to forget them: all her sorrows and joys are secret, closed tight as the tiny white clams studding the rock pools. She still brings the metal detector, but most days forgets to turn it on. When I asked if she had given up her search she smiled and made her hissing noise. Tsssk, tsssk. 'I don't look, I find.'

She now collects shells, stones and polished sea glass. She likes the moonbeam swirl of mother of pearl inside mussel shells and every day I try to find better specimens for her. I must have given her hundreds of shells but she says each new one is more lovely than the last. She puts the shells in a tiny velvet bag and takes them home. I don't know where she lives. Another thing I haven't asked. I know only to wait for her every morning by the sign. Since we started walking together she has not missed a day.

She finds me stones. She knows I like the heavy warm weight of the flattish grey stones, scored with lines of white or pink. The clearer the line, the more the stone pleases me. I don't really know why. Maybe it's the comfort of handling something solid and primitive after spending so long slipping down the slopes of madness. I have arranged some of these stones in the hut in a large circle near my bed. Having them there makes me feel safe.

When we are not looking for stones or shells, we watch the sea birds. The old woman knows all the different types of gull. She knows how to tell a kittiwake from a Caspian tern or a fulmar from a Sabine's gull. She knows their habits, their breeding cycles and feeding patterns, their songs and cries. The geometry of their flying.

I lie on the beach and listen to her: 'There he goes. Ivory gull. You can tell by the little splash of yellow on the beak. Oooh, lovely, fulmar petrel, look at him. What a beauty.'

The woman also knows the secrets of the sea. She says the sea is a great garden containing millions of crystal treasure boxes. She knows because she has seen plankton under the microscope. When she told me this I was surprised. It seemed that she had given something away, a precious glimpse of her past, but she

[230]

had not elaborated. She had looked at me as if *I* were under a microscope, condensed into something tiny and interesting.

The hours, days, weeks – time is meaningless now – pass like this and our walks have become indistinguishable, part of a limpid loop of wandering along our circular bay. I am not even sure of the season, but not long ago when we were walking at low tide the woman bent down and pointed to a glittering spiral trail on a rock. She said it was the egg ribbon of a sea lemon and it meant spring was approaching.

Another time, she showed me something else. I was lying on the beach watching a fulmar petrel execute a perfect parallel turn in the sky and she was sitting next to me, one bony knee drawn up to her chin. Her hands were clasped around her knee. She always sits like this, like a ten-year-old girl. I thought she was watching the fulmar, but she moved her arm with a quick darting motion somewhere near her heart and then I saw it, a pale half-moon of skin. She had held her breast in one hand wonderingly as if it didn't belong to her, as if she'd just found it in a rock pool, and then slowly put it away. I found myself wondering if she'd ever worn silk. Ivory silk.

Today she tells me about the velvet swimming crab. She says it is the most ferocious of all the crabs.

'He's the best fighter. He won't give in. He'll just carry on snapping away with them claws. Even if he loses one, he just waits until he grows another and then takes his revenge.'

She throws a pebble into a pool and I watch Samuel dip his nose in after it and then pull back sneezing from the salt.

'Watch out for them crabs!' she says.

I move over to a rock where a single crab claw is lying like a casually discarded black evening slipper. The claw is light and cream-coloured inside like infant skin. I try to imagine how it would be if we could regenerate ourselves. Would there be more wars or less? I think of a battlefield with men slumped in trenches, rubbing their itching wounds, waiting for the first signs of new growth, and then another image drifts into my mind. A blue room, hazy and hot, a breeze from an open window fanning a slightly stirring body on a bed. I start to sway on the rock and to send the image away I pick up a stone and hurl it as hard as I can across the pools. It catches the dog on the ear and he yelps

[231]

in alarm. The old woman starts and turns, her feather eyebrows twitching with surprise. 'Mustn't go hurting things,' she says to the dog.

I return to my hiding place. There are butterflies on the cliff now. Clouded yellows, tortoiseshells and small coppers. I watch them flitting restlessly around the coconut-scented gorse, like children pretending to be busy. I always thought that butterflies lived for only a few hours or days, but the old woman has told me that some of them live for years.

It's warm enough to stay outside all day now and I have found a bed of sea plantain and grasswort on a ledge overlooking the sea which is just big enough for me to lie stretched out to my full length. I lie here with my toes pointing to the sea, my eyes to the serene blue sky, my ears to the cracking clouds, my fingers to the warm earth. Sometimes I feel a sensual tingling, a soft feeling of having warm water poured slowly over every bone, muscle and tendon, a sensation close to euphoria. When it first came I had to rush inside to the hut to shake off the feeling. But now I just let it happen. I am aware that my body can still feel joy without it touching my mind.

Soon everything will change. I used to wonder why the old woman did not tell me to eat, for she shows concern about my health in other ways, advising me on how to stop my cuts becoming infected and once bringing me a bottle of antiseptic for a painfully swollen toe. But then I still believed that I could live otherwise. That I could be saved. I thought I could make something of my life again; I even started writing another concerto. A few bars, they are still lying around somewhere. I wrote part of a sonata and stopped. Now I know that there are some experiences in this world that cannot be turned into music. That was when I gave up eating.

So now I'm drifting, waiting for things to end. I don't know how long it will take. When I first gave up eating I had vivid dreams. In one dream I was swimming in the sea near the great shelf of stones. Fronds of sea grass caressed my legs and soft creatures swam around me. The sea bed glittered with mirrored boxes through which I saw faces from the past. My grandmother, stitching a greeny-gold butterfly; Sergei, reading Bulgakov; and Natalie. She was asleep and looked utterly at peace. Her dark curls floated in the water, surrounded by a corona of tiny silver fish. I saw that I was on top of an underwater mountain. Thousands of feet below was a crystal glacier where two figures waited: a man and a woman holding each other.

I no longer dream but sometimes at night I hear a roaring like a distant tornado or the boom of a jet. I'm not sure if the sound is real or if it belongs in my mind. The less I eat, the harder it is to know what is real. Everything out there seems to be dancing around me, shifting and changing while I grow soft and still in my fugue. The threads of my past are becoming looser with time. Now I'm waiting for oblivion. For the links to break.

> I have cultivated, so far as I care to, my garden of
> dreams, and it scarcely seems to me that it is a large
> garden. Yet every path of it, I sometimes think, might
> lead at last to the heart of the universe.

Havelock Ellis, *The World of Dreams*

If dreaming is a universe, it is an uncertain one. An unpredictable state of mind that has in the past been likened to insanity. Now scientists are telling us that we live in an unpredictable world and that chaos is our state of being. We cannot make predictions about the universe because it is made up of particles which have every possible path or history in space-time.

For psychiatrists and all investigators of human behaviour these theories are as exciting as they are frightening. In my own work I have been concerned with how quantum theory applies to dream time. In sleep the concept of time, as we know it in our waking hours, melts away. We enter an abstract universe where each history appears like a stepping stone across our deep individual rivers. The stones may lead us to fantastic fields of colour and light populated by angels or wise creatures which whisper ancient stories in our ears. Or they may lead us to dark grottoes where diabolic forces and great beasts attack us. In this limitless arena we make the most amazing discoveries. We grow wings, build castles, communicate with animals and embrace dead souls. We perform extraordinary feats and yet nothing surprises us. In sleep we accept the no-boundary principle without question. Even reductionists with their disrespect for the human soul dream of the seemingly impossible time and time again.

Primitive man believed that he left his body in sleep. Now we know that the foreign sights and sounds of dreaming lie dormant within us. The parallel world of dreaming is a vital key to the mind and, as we try ever harder to determine our tiny role in the modern universe with its string theories, quarks and collapsing

[234]

stars, we should not forget that we have already found infinity. The astringent ocean of the imagination of which our dreams are only a part.

The notes above formed the basis of my lecture at a sleep conference in Washington which I invited Andrew Schidmaizig to attend. I had no intention of using him as an exhibit or living example of my 'uncertain imagination principle' – a criticism which was levelled at me after publication of my first paper on the case. But I believed the conference might have been valuable to Andrew in helping him understand his experience. He did not reply to my invitation.

I found myself missing him. I had of course tried to make contact after the trial and for many weeks afterwards I was still deeply involved both intellectually and emotionally. I wanted to reach him but at the same time I knew I had to respect his desire for privacy.

During his period at Highgrove I sometimes found Andrew Schidmaizig a difficult client. His mistrust of himself, fear and general unease with the world made me wonder how he would survive. His loss was profound. He had not only killed his wife, but also his unborn child and his music career. Essentially he killed himself and there were times when I felt helpless in my attempts to guide him.

But I still hoped that he would find the strength to rebuild himself and I waited for him to reappear in concert. It seemed a tragedy that a man of such talent should be silenced for ever. I talked to musicians who had known him, but they said he would probably never return. Andrew Schidmaizig had played out his life on the piano. He had never been interested in making music a professional career. He was, like his mentor Rachmaninov, a man who composed and played with the soul.

I was preparing to leave Andrew Schidmaizig alone in whatever new time phase he had made for himself when I received his manuscript in the post. It had been sent by a woman who lived in Devon. Many pages were torn and it was difficult to make sense of the writing, which was mixed up with musical notes and drawings of birds. The woman said she had found the manuscript on a beach. She gave no address, only her name, Elizabeth Bartlett.

I travelled down to Devon immediately, heading for the place indicated on the postmark. I discovered a fishing village with a long beach framed on one side by a red cliff which had severely eroded. There were great boulders on the beach and one or two fishing boats had been smashed in a fall. Signs had been put up warning walkers of the danger, and the erosion was the main talk in the village.

I visited all the shops and bars and showed the people there a photograph of Andrew. No one had seen him. They did not know who he was or what had happened. The case was unknown to them. It seemed that, here, Andrew Schidmaizig did not exist.

I booked myself into a bed-and-breakfast place near the sea and spent the evening reading. I woke at dawn and went straight to the beach, where I walked for a while and thought about the manuscript. It brought back the case vividly and I found myself becoming restless at the thought of seeing Andrew again. I was partly excited, partly curious and, I must admit, more than a little worried. My arrival here unannounced would possibly disturb him and bring back memories he had been trying to forget.

I walked along the beach until I came to a sign. There I lit a cigarette and waited. The sea was calm and a strange pink colour. Small gulls flapped around me, flying in quite close as if to inspect me, and I felt oddly guilty. I finished my cigarette and buried the butt in the stones. When I looked up, there she was, walking slowly, her head bent as if she were searching for something. She stopped a few feet away from me. I pretended to ignore her and lit another cigarette, which made me cough. I never normally smoke in the mornings. My coughing seemed to amuse her and she smiled and made a kind of hissing noise through her teeth. Then she started to walk up the beach.

I followed her, keeping my distance. The tide had gone out, revealing a great mass of black rocks at the far end. She stopped there and I drew level with her. I told her my name and said that I was looking for Andrew Schidmaizig. She frowned as if she didn't know what I was talking about. Then I remembered that she didn't know his name. I showed her the photograph and she took it from me and stared at it for a long time. There was a sadness about her, a sense of things ending. She handed back the photograph and without saying anything pointed up to an area of the cliff covered with trees and bushes.

The next day I returned with a police officer, who agreed to search the area. I stayed at the bed-and-breakfast place and spent the afternoon reading and waiting. Early in the evening the officer came to see me. He said they had found a chalet, but it was difficult to reach because the path had been blocked by fallen rocks. The officer said he would return the next day with more men and attempt to get through.

I spent a sleepless night. I knew this was the hut Andrew had written from, but I could not see how he could still be alive. The rock fall had happened several weeks ago and he would have been unable to get out. In the manuscript, he indicated that he was not eating and I was worried that trapped in this way he might have died from starvation.

Many people have since said that this is what he intended. He had already begun to deprive himself and had possibly died before the fall. Others have read into Andrew's last vision a desire to drown himself, but after reading the manuscript carefully many times I do not believe this was his intention. I believe Andrew had made some sort of peace with himself and that after swimming against the flow of his past for so long, he had finally appreciated its rhythms and succumbed to it. Not by taking his own life, but by realising that he was not a victim of history. I believe Andrew finally understood that the terrible events of the past were not the whole story. Once he accepted this he could reinvent himself.

I was eating my evening meal at the bed-and-breakfast place when the call came. The sergeant at Sidmouth told me there had been another rock fall. Two officers had been injured while trying to reach the hut. The cliff was too dangerous to climb and they were considering closing the beach permanently. He said the search would have to be put on hold for a while. He would let me know if they found anything. I thanked him for his time.

So now the case is closed. The police report arrived this morning after I had typed my letter of resignation as head of psychiatry at Highgrove Hospital. I have not been sacked, neither have I lost my faith in studying the intricacies of the human mind. If the events of the past have taught me anything it is that there is never enough time to think. The police report then:

18 June 1995: The body of Andrew Schidmaizig was found buried in a garden at a cottage owned by a Miss Elizabeth Bartlett. The grave also contained a metal detector, various items of jewellery and the remains of a dog. Miss Bartlett has not been charged with any offence. The body of Andrew Schidmaizig was taken to Exeter mortuary where a postmortem examination was carried out. The examination showed that he had died of a cerebral haemorrhage from a blow to the head, believed to have been caused by a falling rock. An inquest held on 15 June 1995 passed a verdict of misadventure.

Acknowledgements

I am indebted to Dr Peter Fenwick, of the Institute of Psychiatry, London, for taking time from his busy working life to discuss the phenomenon of sleep violence and the laws on automatism and for reading sections of the manuscript. The institute library was invaluable in leading me to psychiatric papers and case histories, including a reference to Bernard Schidmaizig who killed his wife in 1791, the first of twenty cases of murder during sleepwalking reviewed by Bonkalo (1974) in *Psychiatry Quarterly*. The *New Scientist* essay by Morton Schatzman, 'To sleep, perchance to kill', and *The Sleepwalk Killers* (Everest Books) by Leslie Watkins both helped to shed a clearer light on the subject. Illumination and inspiration also came from *The World of Dreams* by Havelock Ellis, *The Dreaming Brain* by J. Allan Hobson, *Creation Revisited* by Peter Atkins and *An Experiment With Time* by J. W. Dunne, published in 1927, which explores the theory that it is possible to dream of the future. Stephen Hawking's no-boundary proposal in *Black Holes and Baby Universes* and Richard Feynman's sum over histories theory excited the incarnation of Dr Chase, and any liberties taken with scientific work are entirely mine.

Thanks are due to my family and friends for their love and support and to Robin and Clemency Stanes for the use of 32 New Street, Appledore.